A Devil's Snare

Kit McKenna

McKenna Publishing, LLC

Other Books By Kit McKenna

THE BELLADONNA SOCIETY SERIES

A Pointed End

https://mybook.to/PointedKitMcKenna

A Murderous Intent

https://mybook.to/MurderousKitMcKenna

A Secret Revealed

https://mybook.to/RevealedKitMcKenna

A Devil's Snare

https://mybook.to/SnareKitMcKenna

A Predator's Threat

https://mybook.to/ThreatKitMcKenna

THE MORRIGAN MAFIA SERIES

Crossed

https://mybook.to/CrossedMcKenna

Coup

https://mybook.to/CoupKitMcKenna

Crashed

https://mybook.to/CrashedKitMcKenna

Trigger Warning

This book contains an instance of assault
which may be triggering for some readers.

Prologue

Alicia—Age Twelve

We're hiding from my parents even though I don't want to be. Tai doesn't know it, but they know where we are because I told. I wanted Daddy to be able to find me because we're leaving soon.

Tai is holding my hand so tightly that I think he might crush it. I tried to pull it away, but that only made him squeeze tighter.

"Tai, I need to go help my parents," I say, trying to escape.

"I don't want you to move."

"It's not up to me. Daddy is moving us to a house that's closer to the clinic and hospital where he works."

Daddy graduated from medical school and has been working hard to establish his practice. Now, he's moving us to a new neighborhood, which he says has better schools for me. He says that if I want to be a doctor like him, I'll need an excellent education.

I do want to be a doctor, but maybe not like him; I'm not sure yet. Until I started looking at some of his textbooks for school, I never realized how many kinds of doctors there are. I knew there were a few different kinds, but now I know there are tons of them.

Tai Dang and I are friends. He's been my best friend for most of my life. According to our parents, as soon as we met as little kids, barely even able to walk, we were best buddies.

A year older, Tai seemed to appoint himself as my big brother protector. The neighborhood we live in isn't exactly poor, it's mostly hard-working families, but it definitely isn't the best. Anytime anyone bothered me, Tai made them stop and eventually no one bothered me at all.

Unfortunately, that tough guy attitude put him in contact with a lot of other tough guys. Over the past year, he has changed and I don't like it. Some changes were the normal, growing up things, that had him looking more like a man than a boy.

He's taller, bigger, and broader. His baby face is becoming more angular. That stuff is fine.

The part I didn't like was how he and his new gang of tough guys did a lot of sketchy stuff, like shoplifting from the corner store. Lately they've been talking about bigger, riskier thefts. They are also always in trouble at school.

I tried to talk to Tai about it, but that only resulted in our first and last serious argument. Insults were flung at me, including telling me I was trắng bệch như ma, which meant I looked white enough to be a dead body. He meant I might as well be some random white girl who would never understand, rather than his Vietnamese friend who should.

A few days later, there was an apology, but things were never the same between us. A wedge of distance had been forced between us and our friendship never recovered, at least not for me. He was starting to scare me and that's why I was more than fine when Dad said we were moving at the end of the school year.

"What am I gonna do without you?" he asks.

I smile and pat his hand holding mine with my free hand. "You're going to be just fine."

"Not without you. It's supposed to be you and me forever."

My nice girl manners have me wanting to say something to comfort him, say we'll keep in touch or that I'll write, but I bite my tongue. It would be a lie because this new Tai isn't someone I want to be with for the next few years, much less for forever.

"When I'm older, I'll find you."

I smile again, but don't respond. He leans forward, and for a moment, I think he's going to kiss me. Thankfully, Bà's voice calls to me.

"Alicia! Đi thôi!"

"I've gotta go. Bye Tai."

Standing, I brush off my shorts and jog toward Bà's voice. "Coming!"

Without looking back, I climb into the backseat of the car, loaded down with our things that Mom didn't want to trust to the movers. Tai stands in his front yard, two doors down from our old house, watching as the car pulls away.

I lift a hand in a wave, and he waves back.

Fifteen Years Later

Although all I want is to go home and fall into bed, I promised Bà I'd stop by the grocery store on my way home tonight. She takes care of everything at home, so even though I work at the hospital all the time, I can't deny her when she asks me to do something.

I'm debating the differences between chunky salsa and picante sauce when someone says, "Monkey?"

Confused, I look around because the voice sounds close by. A handsome man who looks to be about my age is walking toward me, a glowing grin on his face. I recognize that grin.

"Tai?"

Of course, it has to be him. He's the only person who ever called me by that nickname. It's difficult to reconcile the gangly, knobby-kneed boy I last saw over a decade ago with the finely dressed and filled out man in front of me.

That boy is still lurking in the corners of his smile, though, and I see him peeking out at me. I'm stunned, and words fail me. However, just like when we were kids, he doesn't have a problem filling in the silence.

"It is you!" he exclaims and pulls me into a hug, seemingly oblivious of the baskets we both carry. I hope he hasn't broken my eggs. He tugs on the bottom of my scrub top. "I see you followed in your father's footsteps, after all. How's he doing?"

"He died eight years ago," I reply around the tightness in my chest that happens every time I think about my dad. Hopefully, my words come out steady.

His happy, smiling face falls with concern. "I'm so sorry to hear that. Is your mom?"

"She's still with us." Kind of, but he doesn't need to hear that story, so I change the subject. "It looks like you're doing well."

Based on his high end clothes and perfect stylishly messy hair, I'd say he's doing very well.

He grins again. "Yeah. I've got a few irons in the fire, but mostly real estate stuff."

"I'm glad for you, Tai."

Tai's family differed greatly from mine. Neither family had a lot of money, but in our case, it's because my father was in medical school. In Tai's case, it's because his father drank down every spare dollar they had while beating his wife and children along the way. I'm truly happy that he's risen so far above the circumstances of his upbringing.

"Thanks. Anyway, I won't keep you; you look like you're about to fall asleep on your feet. Here's one of my cards. Give me a call and we'll get together for lunch or dinner to catch up. It's great seeing you again, Monkey."

I finish gathering the items on my list and get in line to check out. As tired as I am, I don't trust myself to do self-checkout. Of course, there's only one checkout open, so there are four people ahead of me. Tai is just finishing his transaction at the head of the line where he's chatting with the cashier.

She's smiling at him and blushes at something he says. I wonder what he said. He seems so completely comfortable in his skin, charming and self-assured.

He puts his card away and takes his purchases, heading toward the entrance. Before he gets out the door, he pauses to look at something on the newsstand, then picks up a paper and goes back to the cashier.

Pulling out his wallet, he takes out a bill and hands it to her. She looks at it, then up at him and says something. He grins and nods and walks away with his paper.

Curious, when it's my turn at the cashier, I quickly grab the same paper and add it to my purchases. Once I'm in the car, I take the paper out. The headline reads *Masked Gang Strikes Again.* There's been another bank robbery.

This gang has been robbing banks all over the state and haven't been caught yet. This time, there is a photo of two of the members wearing the masks they're known for. They're Japanese kabuki masks. One of them is a snarling devil mask that makes me shudder.

I wonder why Tai was so interested in this. Maybe they robbed a bank he uses or something. Or perhaps he was interested in the sideline article about the Governor's latest tiff with the first nations tribes, but I doubt it.

Chapter 1

Alicia

I am so mentally exhausted that I don't want to think another thing today. However, I am so physically charged that I know there's no way I'll be able to sleep without burning off some of this energy.

One of my colleagues once said about this feeling that she either needed to fight or fuck. If Bà, my grandmother, heard me think such a thing, much less say it, she'd try to wash my brain out with soap.

I always feel like this after a successful surgery – fried and wired. Until Tai and I got together, most of the time I'd just go for a run. Sex is a much better alternative. Besides, it's almost January and way too cold to run outside.

I only started running to deal with the energy burn off I needed on days like this, not because I liked it. The health benefits from running are great, but I'm very much not one of those hardcore runners that is willing to brave the elements for the endorphins. I've been called a fair-weather runner like it's some kind of insult, but I will gladly live up to that accusation.

My job is why I was put here on this earth and I absolutely love it, which makes the stress of it extremely tolerable most of the time. It's only when I have these long days of having to be hyper focused for so many hours that my stress meter rises into uncomfortable levels and has me seeking release. A session of sex with Tai is always good for a release or three...sometimes four.

As a surgeon, I'd never risk my hands in a fight, but I might just be able to take care of the other. I pull out my phone and text my boyfriend. It's late by my standards, but not by his. He will be up wherever he is.

Me: *You home?*

Tai: *Yes. Coming over?*

Me: *Yes.*

With a smile, I tuck my phone back into my coat and head toward downtown. I want to say that my heart started going all pitter pat at the thought of seeing him, but that's never happened. However, I can feel myself getting very, very aroused.

It's been two years since we ran into each other at the grocery store and almost a year since we started dating. Our relationship is good overall, but mostly consists of a lot of great sex and accompanying him to fancy parties when I can. That doesn't bother me, though. Until I'm through with my residency and have established my practice, I don't have time for anything else.

Tai opens his door when I arrive wearing nothing but the lopsided grin I find so endearing and a pair of black silk pajama pants hanging low on his hips and showing off his washboard abs. He is looking so sexy that he barely gets the door shut before I've got my hands on him. A little above average height, his body is very muscular, verging toward bulky. Touching him is one of my favorite things.

His hair is slightly mussed, and he has the barest bit of stubble on his square jaw. If I didn't know better, I'd think I'd roused him from bed. The man is gorgeous. He knows it, too.

When we were budding teenagers, he was always a little cocky, but now he puts serious effort into his appearance and practically struts like a rooster. The claim is that it makes him more appealing to his clients.

As a minority, he says that people wouldn't take him as seriously if he didn't have the air of strength and control that he cultivates. The man honestly has a more stringent beauty routine than I ever thought about having.

At least that used to be the case. Before Tai, I couldn't afford to spend money on luxuries like regular facials, massages, and super expensive hair maintenance. As the woman on his arm, he says it is important for me to look my best as well. Plus, he says, he just enjoys spoiling me.

Spoil me, he does. Beyond the personal maintenance, he also supplies me with a closet full of high-end clothing, shoes, and accessories. I am thankful for it, because it allows me to take the money I would have spent on myself and use it to support my family.

My hands go to his shoulders as I stand on my toes to kiss him. It's a hungry kiss, needy and deep. He pulls me into his arms, and I melt against him.

I wriggle out of my coat and let it drop to the floor. My hands slide around his neck as I press against him, needing the contact. His hands cup my ass and pull me hard against him. His body is already roused, his erection pressing against my stomach. Knowing that he desires me so much makes my core go liquid.

I reach down and ruck up my skirt as he lifts me. My back hits the wall with a thud, my legs go around his waist, and he grinds his hips against my center. A desperate, moaning mewl escapes my mouth.

"Please," I breathe out.

That's all the encouragement he needs. With a sharp tug, the thin fabric of my panties gives way, and he tosses them aside. Another moment and his pants are undone, and he positions himself at my opening.

I'm so wet that he slides into me with one powerful thrust, burying himself to the hilt, making me cry out from the pleasure as he stretches me tight. He hisses out words in Vietnamese too low for me to understand.

The pace is blistering as he thrusts inside of me. I match him stroke for stroke. Just the thought of him had me so aroused by the time I walked through the door that I'm already feeling the climax building.

"Oh, God, yes!" I say as he fucks me against the wall, giving me exactly what I need.

My fingers fist in his hair and I find his lips again. The kiss is brutal, punishing in its intensity. I break it and put my mouth close to his ear.

"I've been thinking about having you inside me all day."

I pull his earlobe between my teeth and give it a nip, then kiss it gently. My journey continues as I lick and kiss my way down his neck until I reach my favorite part of his body, well, maybe second favorite after his cock.

You know that long muscle on the top of the shoulder, the trapezius? I have always found a well-defined trapezius to be so incredibly sexy. Tai's is beautiful and there's nothing I like better than...

"Don't do it," Tai growls, "or this will be over quick."

I smile against his skin and plant a gentle kiss there. Then, because I can feel an explosion building where the friction of our bodies has set fire to a fuse, I bare my teeth and bite him. His entire body flinches with the shock of it even though he knew it was coming.

His hands shift on my hips, dragging me hard against him, detonating the bomb. I cry out his name as the orgasm shatters me into a million tiny pieces of shrapnel. Tai curses under his breath and follows me into the chaos.

When I come back to myself, I'm still against the wall with Tai pressed against me. He's breathing hard, his forehead resting on my shoulder. My fingers stroke his head and neck, back and shoulders, feeling his muscles quiver as he lets the last vestiges of orgasm roll through him.

Tai straightens and looks down at me, his eyes dark and heated. "Well, hello to you, too."

"It's your fault," I retort, grinning wickedly at him. "Answering the door like that was sure to have me jumping your bones, stat."

He chuckles, then leans in to kiss my forehead. After a couple of strokes to empty his body completely, he lifts me up, then settles my feet on the floor. I push my skirt back down.

Once his pants are back in place, he leans down and retrieves my coat, hanging it in the hall closet. "I don't know why you're doing that," he says with a nod at my efforts to straighten my clothes. "I'm just going to be taking them off you when we get to the bedroom. Are you able to stay all night?"

He takes my hand and leads me through his condo to the bedroom. Tai's home is beautiful. As an investment, he bought a unit in the complex several years ago when the unit and entire facility, in fact, were in a state of decline. He refurbished that unit and bought another.

Rinse and repeat, several times and eventually he had updated all but a couple of the homes, eventually landing in the largest, most desirable unit where he now lives on the top floor. The entire facility has received a makeover and spaces now sell for over a million dollars each, more than double what he paid for that first one.

"I can, but I need to be up early. I have a parent-teacher meeting at school tomorrow with Kimmy's teacher."

"I have an early morning, as well. What's up with Kimmy now?"

"I'm not sure. I guess I'll find out in the morning."

Chapter 2

Alicia

I rush into the school, late for my meeting. It's my third meeting of the school year and we're only at Christmas break. I am officially my cousin Kimberly's guardian and therefore am obligated to show up when Kimmy's teachers want to discuss her behavior.

Kimmy is only thirteen and when it came to the lottery of life, she was dealt the harsh hand of parents that were losers and leavers. Her father was an alcoholic who followed his own father back to Vietnam soon after Kimberly was born. Her mother decided she didn't want to be tied down to a baby anymore, so she dropped her infant daughter off with my mom to watch for the day, supposedly so she could go to a job interview, and never came back.

Kimmy had the love of my parents for a few short years, but was only three when Dad died. When he succumbed to the cancer, Mom never recovered. She became a shadow of her former self, as if when we put Dad in the ground, everything inside of her went with him. That left me to assume guardianship just as I was graduating from college and about to start med school.

Mom's still alive, but she can't be relied upon for anything beyond the simplest of tasks. She sleeps, she eats, she floats around the house like a ghost. She can even drive Kimmy to and from school but ask her to go to the store to buy groceries and she has a panic attack.

Because she's developed such a phobia of strangers, we could never convince her to see a therapist. I even thought about admitting her somewhere, but with everything I was juggling, I didn't push too hard. If it weren't for Bà, I never would have been able to manage.

"I'm so sorry I'm late," I say as I rush into the room. I'm surprised that instead of one teacher, there are three of her teachers and the guidance counselor.

Kimmy is exhibiting some of the same behavior I saw in Tai when we were kids. She's angry and frustrated and lashing out. She is struggling and I know it, but I don't know what else I can do about it.

Her infraction this time is that she allegedly stole something yesterday. She was accused, but the item was never found on her person, in her things, or in her locker. However, the other student insists that Kimmy took her lip gloss.

The last time I was called in, Kimmy had been in a fight. It might have been the same girl that time as this time. There was no doubt there had been a fight last time, though. The evidence was plain on their faces in scratches and bruises, but it was never clear who threw the first punch.

I have the same discussion with the teachers that we have had before. They're concerned about her behavior. She has a poor attitude and is disruptive in class.

They want to suspend her, but I inform them that there is only an accusation and no evidence to support Kimmy stealing something. If they suspend her over an accusation, that could be grounds for litigation. I wax on about how terrible it would be if the school went to court just to discover that the other girl was simply trying to cause trouble for Kimmy over their past disagreements by making false and unsubstantiated accusations.

A therapist comes to the house once a week to talk to Kimmy. I know the girl got a crap hand in the parenthood sweepstakes and I know I'm not present as much as I'd like to be, but it's not like she's some latchkey kid stumbling through life with no guidance. Kimmy is loved, and she is shown that on a consistent and regular basis.

Perhaps I need to take her out of public school and put her in a private one. That seems like a good idea, but her poor grades would probably prevent it. I know Kimmy's smart, but she has no desire to do well in school.

I keep telling myself this is just a phase she's going through and that she'll grow out of it, but it has been going on long enough that I'm not sure that's true. I love Kimmy, but I am starting to feel like all my efforts to help her are futile. How do you stop someone who's hellbent on self-destruction?

How do you make someone believe they're worthy and valuable in the world if they just don't want to? Or if they're so blinded by their trauma that they are unable to see anything else? Kimmy hinges her entire worldview on the two parents who didn't want her instead of embracing the people around her who do. I have absolutely no idea how to change that.

She doesn't even remember her parents; she only knows that they weren't there. The most damning part is that they didn't leave through some act of God. They didn't get sick or suffer some horrific accident and die. They chose to leave of their own free will and left her behind.

I have no doubt Kimmy has had a better life than she would have had with her parents when it comes to physical things. She has had a roof over her head, clothes on her back, and has never missed a meal. However, the love of a parent is not a simple thing to replace. The love of a cousin and a grandmother simply don't measure up.

I leave the meeting and I'm sure the teachers feel as if nothing was resolved. However, when I asked them for input as to what else I could do beyond providing a stable home, regular doses of love, and ongoing therapy, they had nothing to offer.

Once I'm safely closed in my car, I slump in the seat, leaning my head on the steering wheel. Never in my life have I felt so inept, except when it comes to Kimmy. If my relationship with her is any indicator, I would be a horrible mom.

Tai and I have never talked about children. We've never really talked about anything beyond what we have now. That's fine by me, because I can't think about anything too seriously beyond finishing my residency, and there's almost a year left in the program.

Before I pull out of the parking lot, I make a note to visit with Kimmy's therapist about the meeting and the accusations to see what she suggests.

"How did it go?" Kimmy asks when I get home later that evening.

I don't tell her about them wanting to suspend her, although they'd probably told her that was their intention.

"Fine. They said you'd been accused of stealing something, but they found no evidence. My response was that it was all hearsay and empty accusations and could just be the other girl trying to stir up trouble for you. I don't know why they even bothered to call me in for a meeting for that."

I say it nonchalantly. I want her to know I'm on her side and won't let them try to push her around just because another girl made some accusations. If I weren't watching closely, I might have missed the small smile that crossed her face. I might be deluding myself, but I took that as recognition that she got my message that I'm in her corner.

Chapter 3

Carlos

My chair creaks when I lean back, rubbing my eyes. I've been going through the evidence from the bank robbery for hours. I know it's not my area. Not technically. But technically, I'm on my own time and although it's not my area right now, I know in my gut that it should be.

There have been four of these robberies over the past two years and the use of Kabuki masks by the suspects is telling. Although I can't prove it yet, I know it is gang related. I know that I know that it's also Tai Dang related, but again, I just can't prove it. Yet.

Everyone else in the gang unit thinks I've gone a little off kilter. They believe the hype surrounding Dang that says he's an upright citizen embroiled in nothing more scandalous than the occasional real estate deal that might be shady, but not illegal. I don't buy it.

Dang went from petty thug, running with a group of other Vietnamese boys to real estate investor, seemingly overnight. He 'inherited' a middling real estate company from a man who died under mysterious circumstances, but nothing could be tied to Dang. He had an unshakable alibi.

I met him once and I could practically smell the corruption on him. My gut tells me he's dirty and one of these days he's going to slip up. When he does, I'm going to be there to put the cuffs on him and put him away.

I start from the beginning with the photos. There has to be something here that can be used to identify the suspects. The hoodies are consistent with the kind you can get at any Walmart in the state. The pants are not unique. Hell, I've even tried identifying their shoes, only to find dead ends. They are covered from head to toe and the only things that are unique are the masks.

I can't find a single dealer in the entire state that sells those kinds of Kabuki masks. That means they were likely ordered out of state or online from somewhere overseas and there's no way to track that down.

I've done about a million searches for the exact kind of masks. I find dozens like most of the robbery team wears, but the leader's devil mask is the outlier. The only one I can't find a match for anywhere. That's my best lead, the only unique detail, and it's a dead end.

"Gutierrez, what're you still doing here?" Ford Pickering calls from across the room.

"Just finishing up some paperwork. I'm ready to leave, though, think I'll swing by for a quick beer and some stress relief on the way home."

"Paperwork. The bane of my existence."

"Ain't that the truth?" I reply as I close out of the file and shut down my computer. I'm going cross-eyed from staring at the screen, so I might as well call it a night.

I follow Ford out of the building. "Why are you here late?" I ask.

"Just bringing some evidence in. Now I'm headed home."

"Home to Cait. So when are you gonna put a ring on Cait's finger?"

Ford chuckles. "Probably never. I love that woman with all my heart, but the last thing I want for her is for anyone to ever think that I'm only after her money. The only way to do that is to be together but not marry. What we have is good, great even, and I don't want to mess it up."

Ford met Cait at the gym one day and that chance meeting turned into the kind of romance that's rare. They're crazy about each other; you only have to spend five minutes with them to realize it. No one would have put them together, the homicide cop and the socialite. Other than my parents, I've never seen a better match.

"No paperwork needed," I say.

"Precisely. You think you'll come to the open house? Cait's eager to show it off."

"If I'm not on a case, I'll be there. Catch ya later, Ford. Have a good night."

"Yeah, you, too, Carlos."

I stop off at one of the establishments frequented by cops that's between the station and home. Sidling up to the bar, the bartender sees me and slides over my usual brand. I take it in hand and turn my back to the bar, checking out the other people.

One beer is my limit in the bar because I'm not really here to drink. Penny, a pretty, curvy redhead, sees me and comes my way. She is one of several of the usual badge bunnies in the bar. Some of them will go home with anyone who has a badge, but Penny is slightly more discerning. But only slightly.

"Hi Carlos," she says when she draws near. "Long time no see."

I give her a grin before taking a swig from my bottle. "Yeah, work's kept me busy." The glass in her hand is empty, so I nod at it. "Do you need another one?"

"That would be great."

That's all it took, a smile, a drink, and a few minutes of conversation, and Penny was asking me back to her place. An hour and a half later, we've both found some release of pent-up stress and I roll off the bed, starting to pull my clothes on.

"You don't have to leave," she says, coyly. "You could stay the night and we could have some more fun."

She always pushes me to stay. I think she hopes that one of these days, one of the guys she brings home, will fall head over heels for her and put a ring on her finger. If that's what she wants, I hope it happens for her, but it's not going to happen with me. Temporary is all I'm looking for right now.

This whole one-night-stand thing is getting old, though. Mom has started hinting that because I'm over thirty, I should start looking to settle down. I've never thought about settling down, but random hook-ups have lost their appeal.

Maybe I should get one of those friends with benefits situations. Once I'm dressed, I give her a kiss and leave to head toward the house.

I pull into my driveway, glad to be home. Inside, Mom is asleep in her chair in the living room while the television casts a glow across the room. When I shake her shoulder gently, she snorts and sits up straight.

"Mom, you need to go to bed."

She reaches up and pats my hand. "I must have fallen asleep while watching HGTV."

"That happens to me every time," I tease.

She gathers her things and puts her glasses on before going down the hall. I follow her, just to make sure she doesn't trip since she is still half asleep. "How was your day? Did you arrest any hoodlums?"

"Not today, Mom."

"Oh well, maybe you'll arrest some tomorrow."

"I hope not. Tomorrow's my day off."

I wish Mom had something going on that would get her out of the house more. She goes to church but still spends way too much time sitting in front of the television. I keep thinking that one of these days she'll snap out of her grief, but so far, she seems just to be existing.

Maybe it would be different if she still lived on her own, but I have no way of knowing. When Dad was killed in the line of duty, she didn't get out of bed for almost a month. I couldn't stand it anymore, so I made her move in here with me. Although taking care of me hadn't been what I intended for her, having that little bit of purpose got her out of bed and occasionally out of the house.

My dad met Linh Le, the pretty young Vietnamese woman down the street, when I was only about three-years-old, and he needed a babysitter for me. My birth mom didn't like Dad being a cop. He loved the job and was well suited to it, so when she gave him an ultimatum, he kept the job and me. She didn't put up much of a fight over custody, so he got about the business of being a single dad.

Linh and her husband lived in our neighborhood. She loved kids but couldn't have any of her own, so she ran a small daycare out of their home. One day, when Dad came to pick me up after his shift, he noticed Linh had a black eye. She wouldn't talk about it, but took Dad's card.

A few nights later, he got a panicked call from her. Her husband was drunk, yelling and breaking things in the background. Dad raced down and arrested him, but not in time to prevent Linh's husband from slicing a gash in her pretty face so she wouldn't be flirting with the fathers of the kids she babysat anymore. The husband went to prison.

Dad says that he knew from the moment her husband was out of the picture that Linh was going to be his to protect. Dad helped Linh out from time to time around the house; not pushing, just being there when she needed him.

Over the next year, they fell in love, the same kind of crazy, all in, perfect match love like Ford and Cait have. I wonder if I'll ever find something like that. I doubt it, but a small part of me, deep down, holds out hope that I do.

Once Mom's safely in her room, I go to the kitchen and take a beer out of the fridge. I stand there in the kitchen drinking it, trying to let the day slide off my shoulders. I don't drink after every shift, just on days like today when the frustration gets to me. One beer at the bar and one at home. I never have more than that.

Maybe I need to take up yoga or something. It's too easy for one beer to turn into two and two to turn into six. Too many cops I've known have turned to booze to deal with the pressures and frustrations of the job. I pour the remaining half beer down the sink and put the bottle in the recycling, then head to bed.

Chapter 4

Alicia

It's New Year's Eve and I am waiting for Tai to arrive to pick me up. This morning was a flurry of shopping and a mani-pedi because my work schedule has been such that I hadn't had time to go before today.

Tai has a charge account set up for me at one of the most exclusive stores in the City. If it weren't for that, I'd be wearing whatever I could find at TJ Maxx for our dates and for him, that simply would not do.

I wouldn't mind, but he obviously does. My father never put much stock in material things, and I took after him in that, too. Expensive things are nice, but they're not a priority for me. As long as I am comfortable and happy, I'm good.

Most of the last several hours since I got home have been spent on hair, makeup, and choosing just the right dress out of the two options I picked up today. Tai and I have been dating for just over a year, so this is our anniversary celebration in addition to the holiday so I want to make him happy by looking like his version of perfect for him.

I look myself over in the mirror one last time. The first time I was all dolled up like this, all I could think was 'Holy crap.

I never knew I could look like this'. Now, I've seen it, but if it weren't for Tai, I'd probably go back to my less glamorous looking self. The effort it takes to look like this is exhausting.

I make an appearance in the kitchen where my family is eating supper. "Whoa," Kimmy says. "You look bee-you-ti-ful! Are you going out with the rich guy again?"

"He has a name other than rich guy," I say.

She lifts a shoulder and grins. "I know."

Bà makes a snorting sound and says in Vietnamese, "A duck cannot change its waddle." Bà understands and knows how to speak English, she just refuses to.

"What?" asks Kimmy, confused.

"She means that people don't change," I supply.

Kimmy frowns. "What's that supposed to mean?"

Thank goodness the doorbell rings and saves me from having to explain to her that Bà thinks Tai is a hoodlum. I open the door to, not Tai, but a mountain of a man in a non-descript black suit.

"Dr. Pham, Mr. Dang apologizes, but he has been unavoidably detained. He is going to meet you at the restaurant."

"Okay," I reply. This isn't the first time I've been picked up by a driver instead of by Tai. He's a busy man and I'm not one to complain, considering my schedule changes frequently, too.

I bid my family good night and follow the man out to the waiting car. He opens the back door of the sedan for me and offers a hand to help me in.

The driver takes me to Tai's favorite restaurant. I think he must be an investor from the way the staff treats him. Considering the place has excellent food and I'm the beneficiary of all that great service, I don't pry into the why's of it.

The driver escorts me across the street and rides up the elevator with me. His phone buzzes and he checks it. "Mr. Dang is right behind us," he tells me.

"Thank you."

I step out of the elevator and the driver follows me. We stand there in the entry. I know from experience that the driver will not leave until Tai arrives. The first couple of times it happened, I would tell them they could go, sure they had better things to be doing than babysitting me until my date arrived, but they never budged.

The elevator sounds and Tai steps off. "Sorry I'm late…" He pauses and looks me up and down with a look of approval. He leans in and kisses my cheek. "Monkey, you look beautiful."

Monkey is a nickname from childhood. We were seven and eight at the time and he was so frustrated that I could climb trees better than him, despite being younger and a girl, that he started saying I must be part monkey. Finally, he just started calling me Monkey all the time, and the nickname stuck.

"Thank you," I say, ducking my head, pleased I've chosen well and pleased him.

He turns to the mountain hovering nearby. "Thank you for keeping an eye on her for me. I'll let you know when we're about to come down."

The mountain nods. "Yes, sir."

We are led to a private room, as always. It is a small room with just one table, the chef's table. We're on the top floor of the tallest building in the City and the view is spectacular. The sun has set, so instead of cheery sunlight, there is an ambient glow from the city lights below. Blended with the low lights of the room, the atmosphere is very romantic.

A server arrives and shows Tai the label of the bottle he's carrying. Tai inspects it and nods, so our glasses are filled with the wine. I don't drink a lot, but with this being a special occasion, I indulge.

I also haven't made a food choice since the first couple of times we came here. Once the chef had a feel for my preferred proteins, I would receive something appropriate and have never been disappointed.

The server leaves and Tai gets out of his seat to come around to me. He leans down and cups my jaw with his hands, taking a moment to look deep into my eyes. "I love you, Monkey," he says before bending to kiss me.

I put my hand on his wrist in a makeshift embrace, returning the kiss. When he is satisfied that he has kissed me thoroughly, he returns to his seat. I look across the table at him.

"I love you, too, Tai," I say in response.

It's automatic. The first time he told me he loved me, I panicked, but I didn't want to start a fight, so I told him I loved him too. Now, when he says it, I say it back, but I'm not sure I am telling the truth.

I love being with him and enjoy how he treats me. The sex is amazing and we're compatible in a lot of ways. But love?

I pull my napkin onto my lap and situate it just as a different server brings in our first course. Taking the opportunity to taste the wine Tai chose, I let the flavor marinate my tastebuds before I swallow. It is excellent, as is everything Tai chooses.

"What kept you this evening?" I ask. "I hope you were able to get it settled before you had to rush off."

He takes a bite of his appetizer and chews for a moment. Once he swallows, he says, "I had a meeting with a competitor. We're both going after the same deal, and I was hoping to redirect him to a different project to avoid driving up the price."

"Oh? Were you successful?"

Tai nods. "Of course I was. He won't be bothering me on that front any longer."

No matter what it is, Tai always seems to get what he wants. I'd hate to be between him and something he wanted. Thankfully, we've been able to get along without much conflict thus far.

He likes to have his way and be in control. I recognize that, and so far we haven't come across anything where I wasn't perfectly fine with what he wanted. Someday we'll end up crossing swords, I'm sure. All relationships have their eventual disagreements, but I won't borrow trouble worrying about it.

The main course is done, and a trio of small desserts is placed between us with two spoons. Tai takes one spoon, and the other has a red ribbon tied around it. I frown at the spoon, wondering why on earth there would be a ribbon around it.

I pick it up and notice that in the center of the bow, there is something very sparkly. My eyes go wide when I realize what it is. That's a ring.

Holy shit.

That's a ring with a ginormous rock on top. A rock so big that if I didn't know Tai, I'd think it was fake, but it's not. Just like everything with him, he had to get something that was big and flashy and expensive. Even so, this thing is big enough to signal satellites in space.

Wide eyed and openmouthed, I look from the rock of Gibraltar that's supposed to go on my hand, to Tai's grinning face. "Whadda ya say, Monkey? Wanna get married?"

I'm speechless. Shocked. I never, ever expected this tonight. Sure, we've been seeing each other for a year and we've even said those three little words to each other, but somehow, I am completely blindsided. I thought we were nowhere close to this step.

I'm quiet for so long that he loses his grin and looks uncertain. Then uncertainty starts to slip toward anger. Tai Dang gets what he wants.

Although I'm not sure I'm doing the right thing, at this moment, I need to respond. I can't think of a single logical reason not to, so I quietly say, "Yes." Then my vocal cords gain some traction. I put my hand to my mouth, feeling my face go red. "Sorry! I'm just so surprised, but yes, Tai. Yes!"

His grin is back. Rounding the table, he unties the bow and slides the ring on my finger, then pulls me into a crushing hug and kiss. I do my best to match his enthusiasm with the kiss, but deep inside, I am stunned.

Maybe I just need to let the shock wear off. *Weren't you just thinking the other day about children? Yeah, but that was in terms of all the things that Tai and I haven't talked about,* I rejoinder to myself.

Yes, we've been back in touch for a couple of years and dating for a year, but despite all of that time, there is still a lot we don't know about each other. We've never even talked about living together, much less marriage or children. Tai doesn't seem to like to discuss things, so knowing I wasn't there yet, I just assumed he wasn't either.

Big mistake. Tai doesn't like to discuss things because he doesn't like to compromise. He makes up his mind about what he wants and just expects it to fall into place for him.

"You know what they say about assuming," my dad's voice says in the back of my brain.

I love you and miss you, but shut up, Dad.

Not content to sit across from me any longer, Tai pulls his chair next to mine as we eat the dessert. He's practically giddy with happiness. I smile and put on a cheerful face, hoping he doesn't read the thoughts rolling around in the back of my brain.

Chapter 5

Alicia

W e leave the restaurant and go to a hotel that has a piano bar and a small dance floor. It's crowded, but he has reserved a table for us away from the bulk of the crowd. We dance and drink and Tai even buys a round for everyone there.

I try to forget about Stonehenge weighing down my left hand and get into just having an enjoyable time. Dancing is a favorite of mine even though I'm not very good at it. We spend most of our time simply swaying to whatever song is playing, regardless of the beat.

Tai is all touchy and attentive. He is also drinking a lot. Before he gets too far gone, he takes me by the hand and leads me to the elevators.

"Where are we going?" I ask.

"You'll see," he replies, looking over his shoulder with a grin.

He opens the room's door with a flourish and motions for me to go inside. The room is enormous, and he has, once again, gone all out. There's what appears to be champagne chilling in a bucket and two glasses. I glance into the separate bedroom to see the bed is covered in rose petals.

Housekeeping is going to love that. I chide myself at the inane thought and watch Tai as he goes and pops the cork on the bottle, then pours us each a glass. He hands one to me and clinks them together.

"I can't wait to get married and start having babies with you," he says, his boyish grin firmly in place.

I don't even try to speak, but just grin back and take a sip of my glass. The champagne is excellent, as if it would be anything else. I drink down the whole glass but Tai doesn't pick up on anything, just pours me another.

Tai takes the bottle and goes into the bedroom. Also laid on the bed is a pearl-colored gift box and a small blue bag. Like Tiffany blue. As if having Kilimanjaro on my finger isn't enough, he's gone and spent more money.

"Tai," I say. "This is too much."

He slips out of his jacket and hangs it on the back of a chair before sitting on the bed, leaning against the pillows. "Nonsense. Besides, one of them is more a present for me."

I open the box to find lingerie in a deep blood-red color. Pulling it out of the box, I lay it on the bed. I have to admit, although it reminds me of blood and work, the color will look good on me.

I pull a small blue box out of the bag and my thoughts about the maker are proven true. Inside the box is a diamond pendant on a delicate chain. Fingering the stone, I'm fighting feelings of overwhelm.

Too much. My mind chants. This is all too much.

I look up at Tai. He mistakes the look on my face. "Oh Monkey, I know you're happy, but don't cry, baby. Don't cry."

I give him a weak smile. "Thank you, Tai. It's beautiful. I want to go shower before I change into your present."

He gives me a pleased look. "I'll join you."

We both undress and go into the bathroom. He opens a box on the counter and puts a plastic shower cap onto my head, which breaks the tension in me by making me chuckle. I tuck my hair in as he turns the water on to warm.

With the steam and water and slick soap being rubbed all over, it doesn't take long for things to heat up between us. He's hard and I'm wet in more ways than one. I start to kneel in front of him, but he stops me. I give him a confused look, but he just gives his head a little shake.

He boosts me up and slides me onto him, much like he did the other day, but this time, he's slow and purposeful with his strokes. There's no frenzied fucking; no animal drive for release. His kisses are tender; his touches are gentle and exploring.

He wraps me up and holds my body tight against his when I cry out with my climax, and he follows me soon after. Once I'm through shaking and back on my feet, he washes me thoroughly then himself. He turns off the water and steps out, wrapping a towel around his waist, then holding one spread for me to step into.

His care of me continues as he dries me from shoulders to toes, then lets my hair fall free of the cap. After drying himself, he leads me back to the bedroom.

Tai and I have been very sexually compatible falling some-where in the middle of the road between tender and tough. On a few occasions he's pushed the roughness edge with spanks of his hand and the like, but never has he been so tender, so gentle. I have to admit, it's kind of freaking me out.

Naked, he resumes his previous position, sitting on the bed propped up by pillows, while I put on the bra and the garter belt from the pearl colored box. I leave the panties off because I don't want him to rip them off me. They're too pretty to ruin.

Next are the stockings that are rolled up slowly with first one leg with my foot propped up on the bed so he can watch the show, then the other. Finally, I slip into the black stilettos that I'd been wearing with my dress at dinner.

I take the small blue box out of the bag again and round the bed. Standing in front of him, I take the necklace out and hand it to him. Then I perch on the side of the bed with my back to him and I gather my hair to lift it while he reaches around to fasten the necklace on my neck.

The stone falls perfectly into the divot at the base of my throat. I finger it and smile, then stand and let him get a look at me. He is already hard again and stroking himself. Just seeing the look in his eyes awakens my arousal again, too.

I round the bed and take the fresh glass of champagne he poured for me before we went into the shower and down it. My head swims a little, so that's my signal that I've had enough. When I set it down, I give him a broad grin and, on hands and knees, begin to crawl across the bed to him.

This time, he lets me take him in my mouth. With his hand fisted in my hair, he urges me on, pushing me faster and forcing his cock deeper until I'm gagging on the size of him. He's too big to take into my throat, but he seems to love it when I gag. My eyes are just starting to tear when he pulls my head away, his cock sliding out with a small pop from the suction.

"On your back," he says, his voice rough.

I guess it's my turn for oral as he moves to settle his shoulders between my legs. Tai is really, really good at oral. He approaches it with the same intensity as everything in his life. It is so good that in short order, my fingers are tangled in his hair and I'm bucking against his face when, with a hard suck on my clitoris, he sends me screaming over the edge into freefall.

He climbs up my body and settles his hips between my legs. His kiss is fire and force, claiming my mouth with his, letting me taste myself on his lips. With a powerful thrust, he buries himself in me in one sharp move.

All the tenderness of the shower is gone as he pounds into me, our bodies slapping together. The rhythm is fast; the strength is hard. Very hard and I love it.

My nerves from his tenderness fall away as I lose myself in the sensations. When he fucks me hard like this, my brain can stop thinking, overwhelmed with the blend of pleasure edged with pain melded with the sounds we make.

He started with his arms fully extended, hovering far above me, but lowers himself to his elbows, caging me between his arms. He is relentless, showing no signs of slowing and with little build-up, my already sensitive clitoris succumbs to the assault, and I cry out with another orgasm.

Tai stops for a moment and pulls out. "Turn over," he says, pushing my legs to the side.

I get onto all fours, and with another sharp thrust, he's inside me again. He grips my hips and resumes his tempo. My head is pulled back by his hand in my hair and it feels as if the roots of my hair are directly connected to my clitoris.

He's muttering something, but I can't make it out. When he leans down and kisses my shoulder blade, I can make out some of the words. Mine. Promised. Belong. I can't string enough together to make a complete sentence, though, because they're coming out between pants and growls.

Upright again, his hand smacks my butt. It startles me and is hard enough that I make a noise. He doesn't do this sort of thing often, but I love it when he does.

"That's it," he says, and spanks me again, even harder this time.

I cry out and squeeze him tight as yet another orgasm rockets through me when he groans and pounds into me one last time. He keeps a hold on my hips, grinding himself against me, then leans down and plants kisses on my back. After a few minutes, he strokes himself a few more times, milking out every drop of his seed into me.

Thank God I'm on birth control.

I'm shocked at the thought. I just said yes to marrying this man and my first thought after sex is that I'm glad I'm unlikely to get pregnant? What is wrong with me?

Tai loves me. I should be happy, right? What have I been doing for the last year if moving forward in our relationship isn't what I want?

He lets me go and collapses onto the bed. I go to the bathroom and clean myself up a bit. When I return to the bed, I crawl into his arms and rest my head on his chest.

We stay the night in the hotel. I don't have to be at work until the afternoon, so we get breakfast in the hotel restaurant before going upstairs to make love again before showering, dressing, and checking out.

As always, Tai has thought of everything and had a change of clothes there for both of us to wear the next day. Rather than a driver, his car was delivered sometime in the night and he drives me home. He keeps holding up my left hand, letting the sunlight spark off Mount St. Helens on my finger.

"I think we should get married in June," he says out of the blue.

"What? This June? As in six months away June?"

"Yeah, this June."

My brows furrow. How can he be serious about getting married that soon?

At my silence, he asks, "Why not?"

"Um, because I'll still have another six months left in my residency program. Being newly married is difficult enough without the added stress of the residency added into the mix."

"You could drop it."

I suck in a breath. Did he really just say that?

"Why on earth would I do that?"

"Well, you're already a doctor. This program is just to do surgery. You would still be able to have a practice, you just wouldn't spend so much time operating."

"So, you think I should drop out without completing a program I will have invested four and a half years of my life into?"

He's quiet for a moment. I can tell he thought this conversation would go very differently. The skin around his eyes and mouth tightens, and I can tell anger is simmering below the surface. That's just fine by me because I am pissed that he would even propose such a thing so flippantly, as if my entire career, everything I've worked for is of no importance.

"I mean, once you start having my babies, it will be too difficult for you to work, so you'll be staying at home in a few years, anyway."

I feel my skin flush. "What? I don't even know if I want to have children, Tai. I not exactly doing a bang-up job parenting Kimmy, so why would I want to bring more tiny humans into the world to fuck up?"

"That's different. Our kids will have both of us."

I don't reply, but hold my peace the rest of the way home. When he is pulling into the driveway, I say, "Maybe this whole proposal thing was a bit premature. I think there are a lot of things we need to discuss."

He puts the car in park and before I can blink, his hand is on my throat, pushing me back into the seat. "You listen to me; you're mine. I've waited a long time for this and you're not going to back out after saying yes. Your family made a promise, and it's time to pay up."

I claw at his hands, but I might as well be a flea hopping on his skin. Terror consumes me in that moment. Black spots start to dance in front of my eyes.

As if he was completely unaware of what he was doing, his eyes suddenly go wide, and he releases me. "Oh God, Monkey, I'm so sorry."

I open the door and make a stumbling leap out of the car, leaving everything but my purse and the clothes I have on behind. My legs pump as I race the rest of the way up the drive toward the front door. Digging my keys out, I have difficulty getting the door unlocked because of the tears blurring my eyes.

I hear him behind me, calling my name, but I keep fumbling with the goddamn keys. My fingers swipe at the tears, trying to clear them away and restore my vision. Just as the key slides home, he's there.

His hands cover mine and still them. My lips quiver at the caress of hot breath over my neck as he leans his body into mine. "Baby, I'm so sorry. I didn't mean it. Please, believe me."

I don't respond, my brain completely unable to form words in the aftermath of what just happened.

"You're right," he says, "we need to talk about some things." He turns the key in the lock but doesn't open the door. His arms wrap around me, and he pulls me close to his body, holding me tight.

I'm shaking so hard and can't make myself stop. Tai has never made me feel afraid, but now he does.

He presses his lips to the top of my head, then says low, "I love you Monkey. I've always loved you and I always will."

His hold loosens, and he pulls the door open for me to enter. I slip inside and close the door, turning the lock and the deadbolt to keep him outside.

Chapter 6

Alicia

Tai leaves me alone for the rest of the day. I go to work late that afternoon for evening rounds, all the while thinking about what happened between us. What is so shocking is how quickly a disagreement turned into a violent altercation.

I've never seen Tai get that angry and I never want to see it again. Was it there all along, lurking beneath the surface? He said he didn't mean it, but that kind of violence doesn't just come from nowhere.

I'm walking out to my car when my phone buzzes in my pocket. The caller ID shows that it's Tai. I start to ignore it, but I can't leave things unresolved.

"Hi," I say when I answer.

"Hey baby. I've missed you today. Are you still at work?"

"No, just got off and walking to my car."

"Do you want to come over?"

Normally, I'd jump at the chance to go to Tai's house, but the mere thought of it in the aftermath of him choking me makes me shudder and not in a good way.

"I can't. I have an early surgery in the morning and another in the afternoon, then evening rounds, so it's going to be a long day tomorrow and I need plenty of rest."

He pauses, as if making up his mind about what he wants to say. "Okay. I would tell you that I'd let you sleep, but I know I wouldn't be able to keep my hands off you."

He chuckles then.

I don't respond.

"Listen," he says, "I've got to go to Tulsa for a couple of days. If you're still available to go with me on Friday to the charity auction, we can have dinner before and talk. That will give us a few days to get our thoughts together and have a cogent conversation."

"Provided nothing comes up, I am still available. However, I don't want to go to the usual place. I'd prefer to be somewhere public, and I'd like us to either have a driver or I'll meet you there."

He's quiet for a long moment.

"Are you afraid of me, Monkey?"

Should I play it off? No, it's time to be truthful.

"Yes, Tai, I am. That you could go from zero to choking me in a rage until I was seeing black spots swim before my eyes was very scary for me."

"I told you I was sorry." His voice is clipped, as if he's speaking through gritted teeth.

I sigh. "I know, Tai. I want to work this out, but you have to understand that saying you're sorry is a good start, but it doesn't make it go away."

He goes quiet again.

"Do you really want to work this out?" he asks.

"I do. If we can work it out, I want to." I have been wondering about what he said all day, so I ask, "Tai, what did you mean when you said that my family made a promise that needed to be kept?"

"Ask your grandmother. I've gotta go; I'll see you Friday, Monkey. I love you."

Before I can reply, the phone goes quiet. I look at the screen to see that he's disconnected.

As much as I hate to, I have to get another new dress for Friday night. The reason I got two dresses for the New Year was to have one to wear to this event, but a plunging neckline would not work. Not with the bruises around my neck from Tai choking me.

Having to find another dress is the last thing I want to do. I hoped that something would happen, such as a schedule change or last-minute surgery for which I was needed, but no such luck so far.

Why is it when you want something to happen, it doesn't? My morning surgery went smoothly, and we closed the incision ahead of schedule. My rounds went smoothly as well, and I left the hospital early. Too much is falling into place for me to have a remotely plausible excuse for begging out of tonight.

I rush into the store, my last hope of an out, and keep checking my phone every few minutes, praying for something, anything that will make it so I am unable to go to the event with Tai tonight. Unfortunately, they have a dress that will work great for what I need, and it fits me well right off the rack.

I message Tai and let him know I'm able to go. He replies that a driver will pick me up at six and we'll have dinner in a public dining room before going to the event. At least he's trying to accommodate my requests.

Going through the motions of getting ready, I continue to check my phone. Still nothing. By five, I give up hoping and resign myself to going to the event with him. At least there will be people around.

A driver arrives alone right at six. He apologizes for Tai and says that he'll meet us at the restaurant. I wonder what is keeping him this time.

At the restaurant, we're in the regular dining room, but we're at a table in the back and no one is seated near us. I wonder if Tai paid to have those tables left empty. He arrives a few minutes later, carrying a dozen red roses.

I smile at the gesture and take them from him as he leans in and kisses my cheek.

"Thank you, Tai, they're beautiful."

"As are you," he replies.

He looks me up and down, and I know he doesn't like my dress. It's form fitting, like he prefers, but I'm covered up from neck to knees, which he does not prefer.

"Did you get another new dress?" he asks.

I am nonchalant when I reply. Keeping my voice casual and non-accusatory, I say, "I had to." Then I add quietly, without looking at him, "There are bruises."

He doesn't reply.

"So, what's good here?" I ask, trying to lighten the mood.

He tells me his preferred dishes and we order. We don't rush through the meal, but knowing we have somewhere to be, we don't linger. Unfortunately, we don't talk about anything of significance, either.

I ask him about his day and what kept him late, but he only gives a vague answer and deflects. Maybe it's because I'm so sensitive to him right now, but I realize he does that a lot. That probably explains, at least in part, why we don't seem to really know each other very well.

"Why do you do that?" I ask, since it's in my thoughts.

"Do what?"

"Whenever I ask you anything about your day or what you've done, you give a bare minimum answer and change the subject. Are you hiding something?"

"What?" He laughs when he says it as if I'm being completely ridiculous. "No, it's just that what I do is not nearly as interesting as what you do. If I told you about my day, you'd be asleep in no time."

I let it drop because I know it won't do any good to push the matter. Although I am irritated, I think that regardless of what his mouth is saying, he is hiding something and that his evasion is purposeful, so pushing wouldn't gain me anything new.

And he thinks what I do is interesting but wants me to walk away from it? That's rich. All Tai's flattery is starting to smell like he's shoveling bullshit on my shoes.

It's apparent after what happened that there is a lot going on in Tai that I know nothing about. The more telling thing for me is that I don't even know that I want to know what's going on in Tai. This last year has been great, but it was all surface.

What Tai feels for me may be deeper, but all he has shown me of himself is the veneer. Based upon what has happened during the past week tells me that there are monsters lurking in the depths. If he would let me in so I could get a good look at them, I might be able to love the beasts hiding in the shadows. Goodness knows I have some murky corners, too.

As long as he keeps me in the dark, it will hold only fear for me and I can't live with that. I can't put myself in a position of living with those kinds of unknowns in the short term, much less for the rest of my life.

"Ready?" Tai asks, pulling me out of my thoughts.

"Yes, let's go look at some art," I say with a smile.

I am actually very interested in this next part. One of the reasons I wanted to join the Belladonna Society was because there is such a powerful group of philanthropic women who belong to the club. Giving back to my community is important to me, and I'm eager to see how many ways I can take part in that.

I had visions of a stuffy gallery showing type atmosphere, but this is anything but. There is plenty of art on display, but it's very laid back despite all the very fancy clothes.

Tai takes his time, studying each piece of art, apparently seriously considering trying to acquire something. I look at everything, but I mostly study the people in the room instead of the artistic offerings.

I am surprised to see someone I know across the room. I lean over to Tai, "Hey, I see a friend. I'm going to go say hello."

I start to pull away from him, but he takes my hand and puts it into the crook of his arm. "I'll go with you."

Cait sees me as we approach and her face lights up even more than it had been as she laughed at something the man with her said. I'm not sure who he is, but I know it's not her partner, Ford. He's very handsome, though, and dressed better than even Tai, if that's possible.

"Hi Cait!" I say as we draw close.

"Alicia! It looks like you're making good use of a rare evening away from the hospital."

"I am. Cait, this is Tai Dang..."

Before I can finish, Tai leans forward and shakes Cait's hand as he interjects, "...her fiancé. It's a pleasure to meet you, Cait."

Cait gives me a sideways glance. They greet each other and shake hands, then Cait turns to the man next to her. "This is Beckett Masters. He and I are both board members for the charity that this auction will benefit."

There is another round of handshaking and nice to meet yous all around. I'm surprised when Tai tucks my hand back into his arm. I noticed that he and Mr. Masters took a beat to size each other up. Is he feeling territorial?

"Ford wasn't able to come tonight?" I ask.

"No, there was some big gang blow up that was discovered this afternoon. He was just about to get dressed to come when he got called out."

If my hand hadn't been in Tai's arm, I wouldn't have felt him stiffen at Cait's comment. I find that curious.

"Cait's Ford is a Homicide Detective with OKCPD," I explain to Tai.

"I'll bet that keeps him very busy," Tai says, his demeanor cool.

"Unfortunately, it does," Cait replies.

A young woman wearing a name badge puts a hand on Cait's shoulder and apologizes for the interruption. She leans in and says something low to Cait that I can't make out, but since it's probably none of my business anyway, I'm not concerned.

"I'm sorry," Cait apologizes. "I'm being summoned." She leaves with the young woman.

Beckett explains. Apparently, he had no trouble hearing what was said. "She's offered a Durand landscape as part of the auction and a private buyer wants to talk about purchasing it instead of letting it go through the bid process."

"I must not have gotten that far yet," Tai says. "I hadn't noticed anything from the Hudson River School. I would be interested to see it."

Tai has surprised me again. I have no idea who Durand is, but the Hudson River School sounds vaguely familiar from my humanities class in undergrad.

"Please, go peruse," Beckett says with a sweeping motion of his hands. "The auction will be starting soon, so you'll want to make sure you get a look at everything."

We return to the displayed art, but Tai is moving a bit more quickly through them now. I know I can't compete in a bidding war, so I go back to people watching.

"How do you know Cait?" Tai asks a while later.

"We met at the Society."

"The what?"

I tell him about being invited and joining the Belladonna Society a little over a year ago. He acts as if this is all fresh news, even though I have told him about it a few times. I tell him about my orientation group, Cait, Gabriella, Demi, and Serena, and how we have become friends.

Even once I talk about our standing Thursday night dinner date and admit how I miss more of them than I get to attend, he still doesn't tune into the fact that he's heard this before. I even divulge that I'm excited to be able to go more often once I'm in a regular surgical practice and have a more settled schedule.

"I never knew such a thing existed," he says.

His choice of phrasing is irritating to me, as if a club like the Belladonna Society for women is an outlandish thing. Men have had these kinds of clubs for centuries, so why not women?

At the end of the evening, we walk away without any art. Tai bid on a few things but didn't push too hard to win. After a couple of times, I started to get the feeling that he was just playing, bidding to drive the price up. I have no doubt that if he wanted something, he would have won it and happily paid out the money.

Once we're at my house, Tai walks me to the front door. "Thank you, Tai. I had a nice evening."

He looks down at me, his eyes intense. "I did, too. I'm glad you were able to go. I know we didn't get much talking done, but I wanted to keep things light tonight."

I nod. "I understand and I appreciate that."

I see it coming. I should stop it. I should, but I don't. Tai cups my jaw with one hand and leans down to kiss me. It's a delicate kiss, just a simple brushing of lips before he pulls away.

I manage a small smile as he tucks my hair behind one ear. There is no way to know if we can ever return to the point before he choked me in his car, but tonight makes me hope.

His mouth tucks up on one side. "Good night, Monkey. I love you."

"Good night. I love you, too."

Saying that in automatic response to him is something I need to stop doing, especially since I'm not sure I mean it. I go inside and close the door. Putting my back against it with a sigh, I close my eyes for a moment. When I open them, I notice the light on in the kitchen.

Pushing off the door, I head that way, hoping to find Bà there. My luck has turned because she's there, putting some dish or other into the refrigerator to marinate or some whatnot. She is a fantastic cook, and when I've asked her to teach me, she waves me off and tells me to focus on doctoring.

"You're home early," she observes, speaking Vietnamese, as always.

"We had a fight the other night, so he's being a good boy," I reply.

"Good, you're better off getting away from that du côn." A du côn is a thug or a hoodlum and she proceeds to tell me I should let him go and count my blessings to be rid of him.

"He said something about our family making a promise and that we need to pay up."

Her head snaps up, and she narrows her eyes at me.

"What does that mean, Bà?"

"It means nothing. He is referring to an old agreement between my father and that dog's great grandfather, but by the time I knew about it, it was too late."

"I don't understand."

I can tell she would like for me to drop it, but I can't. Whatever this agreement was is part of what is driving Tai so I need to know what it is. She sighs and sits on one of the chairs at the small kitchen table. I join her, taking a seat as well.

"My father was a powerful man in the military and had many influential friends, including Tai's great grandfather. They had spent their younger years in the same village and had been like brothers. My father went into the military, but the other boy went into the underworld."

I don't know what she means by that, but instead of asking questions, I let her talk.

"Tai's great grandfather joined up with the Bình Xuyên, a criminal gang that controlled the opium trade in Vietnam. He had a son a couple of years before I was born. At a meeting between the two old friends, in a state of drunkenness, they decided I would marry his son when we both came of age."

"What happened?" I ask.

"Many things, but mostly, war happened. Soon after that meeting, the Bình Xuyên became less about running opium and more about being revolutionaries, so the Dang boy, now a man, left and joined up with Đại Cathay's gang. During that time, my father could see that as bad as things were, they would only get worse, so when a friend of his said he was moving his family to Manila where he had business interests, my father sent me with them."

"Wait. I thought you left Vietnam through Operation New Life and went to Guam, but that didn't happen until the seventies."

Operation New Life was a program designed to relocate Vietnamese refugees around the time of the fall of Saigon during the Vietnam war. People were settled in many parts of the world, but a significant number were taken to the United States and a surprising number to Oklahoma. This contributed to Oklahoma City's thriving Asian District that we have today.

She gives me a small smile and pats my hand.

"We went to Manila when I was sixteen. Your grandfather was nineteen. It didn't take long for two hormonal teenagers to think they were in love and decide they were supposed to get married. My father and I stayed in touch as best we could, but as you can imagine, there wasn't exactly regular mail service in the middle of a war."

She stands and goes to the sink to fill a small glass with water, then returns to the table.

"By the time my father sent me a letter telling me of the agreement and that my promised husband would be coming for me, it was too late. I was already married, and your father had already been born. When my father caught wind of Operation New Life, he made arrangements for your grandfather and I to go to Guam and his contacts there put us onto the list for relocation to America."

"Were you able to let him know it was too late?"

"No," she says, shaking her head. "Tai's grandfather was not able to leave Vietnam to come to Manila, but he did show up here a few years after we arrived. By that time, I had both your father and your uncle."

"What happened?"

"Nothing. He came to the house, and we talked for a short time, and he left. Your grandfather was so angry, accusing me of cheating on him. Tai's grandfather was handsome, just like he is, but also just like him, his grandfather was a snake. A few years later, your grandfather went back to his beloved Vietnam, and I worked hard to raise my boys on my own."

It's my turn to pat her hand. I know how hard she worked for her children. Women didn't have it easy back then, but minority women, and an immigrant to boot, had an extremely difficult time.

She gives me a small smile. "I saw Tai's grandfather a few more times through the years when he would visit. The way he looked at you with Tai always made me uneasy, so I was very glad when we moved away from them."

"So, I guess Tai thinks that because you were promised to his grandfather, and no one bothered to tell you until you were already married with babies, that somehow translates into me being promised to him."

Bà flaps her hand in the air. "Not only a snake, but a stupid snake."

Chapter 7

Carlos

I finish my reports on the dead bodies of four men who, based on their tattoos, are part of one of the City's largest Mexican gangs. The secluded warehouse building is riddled with bullet holes and casings, making it look like a war zone. There's so much evidence that it's going to take forensics weeks to analyze everything.

It's amazing that this war zone happened in the late afternoon and the only reason we found out about it was because a couple of patrol officers were stopped talking to some kids playing basketball in the street two days later. The kids mentioned hearing shots, so the officers went to investigate.

Based on the medical examiner's preliminary estimate, the men were killed on Wednesday, which was New Year's Eve. Chicago has the St. Valentine's Day massacre, and we get one in honor of Father Time. Seems like that should be a metaphor for something.

The Mexican gang's biggest rival is the VCB, Tai Dang's crew. Maybe the evidence will bring a break that will finally put some cuffs on Dang or someone who might be convinced to flip. I start to do another search on Dang to see if I can find anything

I haven't already reviewed a thousand times, but I stop myself. I'm crossing the line from diligent to obsessed.

"We've gotta stop meeting like this," Ford Pickering says as he's passing through toward the exit.

"I know, right? You get your version of today submitted?"

"Yeah. Like you, I wanted to get it done tonight just in case I actually get a day off tomorrow. I want to spend as much time as possible with Cait."

"You guys are like a couple of love struck kids."

Ford's phone buzzes. He pulls it out and looks at the screen. "Speaking of my angel. Hang on a second."

Ford answers his phone, and it's like ten years disappears from his face. I guess that's what the love of a good woman can do for you. Then the ten years come right back a few moments into the conversation as he frowns. His words are light, but his cop face is back in place. I wonder what Cait's telling him.

I shut down my computer and stand to put my jacket on when Ford holds up a hand, signaling me to wait. Once I put the coat on, I lean against the edge of my desk while he finishes up, wondering what's so important. He drops the phone back into the inside pocket of his jacket, then levels a look at me.

"You're not going to believe who Cait met tonight."

"Who?"

"Tai Dang."

I blink, thinking I've misheard.

He tells me all about Cait's art auction and how he was going to go until the call came in about the murders we both got called out to.

"She felt obligated to go because she donated some of the art that was being auctioned. I knew a friend of ours would be there to watch out for her, so I was fine with it. Anyway, she ran into a friend of hers from the Society, one of her quint. That's what they call the five of them that went through orientation together."

"And Dang?"

"Sorry, I'm meandering. Anyway, this friend introduced Cait to her date, actually her fiancé, none other than Tai Dang. Cait said the name sounded familiar to her for some reason, but she couldn't place it."

"Probably because she heard it from you," I reply. "How is it that Dang has a fiancé and we don't know about it?"

Ford shakes his head in the negative. "Cait says it must be new because Alicia hasn't mentioned it before, but said the rock on her finger was significant and undeniable. She says she kept an eye on them throughout the night and it seemed that Dang was more into Alicia than she was into him, so I don't know what's going on with that."

"Alicia."

"Yes, her name is Alicia Pham. Dr. Alicia Pham. She's a fifth-year surgical resident over at OU."

I write the name down on a notepad. If I don't, I'll go to sleep tonight, and it will float away with my dreams. I can't imagine someone Cait calls friend being involved with a thug like Dang.

Ford's phone buzzes. He fiddles with it and turns it to me. "This is them. Beckett, Cait's friend, took a few photos of the not so happy looking couple. This is the best of the bunch."

I take the phone from him and look at the photo. The woman is beautiful. Petite with a sheet of long black hair hanging down her back almost to her nicely curved ass. Ford's right, she doesn't look happy.

She also doesn't look like the type of woman I've seen Dang with before. He usually goes for the scantily clad and slutty. This woman looks classy, and she's completely covered except for her legs. She has great legs.

I know I'm jaded because I know about how he really makes his money. Dang works hard to appear as a respectable entrepreneur and real estate investor with all that poor kid rags to riches bullshit. Words like slumlord and extortion don't look as good on a bio.

"Do you think Cait would introduce me to her?" I ask, hopeful. I know I can't exactly bring her in and interrogate her, but I'd like to talk to her and find out how she knows Dang.

"Why don't you wait a few days and see what Cait turns up? She's curious about their relationship and if I know her, which I do, she's going to be asking a lot of questions. She's better at ferreting out information than anyone I've ever met, and she does it without you even knowing it. Even once you realize you've laid out your life story to her, you aren't bothered at all."

I nod. "All right. I think I'd still like an introduction, eventually."

Ford looks at me, his face serious. "You know I'm as serious about upholding the law as anyone around here. However, if you're thinking of trying to turn Alicia into some kind of CI and push her to cough up information on Dang, you'd better squash that idea right now. Cait would kill you, and I'd have to help hide the body, and I'm too old for that shit."

"Understood," I say as we both head toward the exit.

It was like he read my mind because that's exactly what I'd been thinking. Not that I'd try to force Dr. Alicia Pham to do something she didn't want, but if she was friends with Dang, maybe I could get to be her friend, too, and maybe something might slip.

Or maybe I could flex a little machismo and be really good friends, exploit whatever is making her unhappy...I stop that thought.

Wow...I really am getting obsessed because that is definitely crossing a line. That's a level of sleazeball that I never thought I'd stoop to. I'm glad I have a day off tomorrow and now I see I need to spend it doing absolutely nothing related to work.

As soon as I get up the next morning, Mom announces that she's going to the Asian market, so I decide to go with her. It will be a great opportunity for us to spend some time together instead of just seeing each other in passing when I'm either leaving in the morning or waking her up to go to bed when I get in late.

Mom has mastered a sort of Asian-Latin fusion way of cooking that blends both sides of my heritage, and it's phenomenal. I keep telling her she should open a restaurant so we can get rich and I can retire. I tell her that again when I remind her to get the peppers I like, and she just laughs. It's good to hear her laugh.

When a conversation in rapid-fire Vietnamese breaks out between Mom and one of the ladies who works there, I start to wander. I'm meandering down an aisle when I hear voices up ahead.

A young girl's voice says, "I really think you should get me a cream bun for breakfast. After all, I didn't get a chance to eat anything before we left."

An older woman replies in Vietnamese, "You shouldn't eat so many sweets, it's not good for you."

"Yeah, but it tastes delicious," the girl says.

A third voice says, "The reason you didn't get breakfast is because you wouldn't get out of bed until we were leaving. You could have stayed home with Mom and had breakfast."

"But then I wouldn't get a cream bun, would I?" the girl says, clearly teasing.

"You're killing me smalls," the third person says, and it brings a smile to my face. I loved that movie when I was a kid.

I round the corner and see three women. A girl who looks to be twelve or thirteen, a petite woman who looks to be about my age, and an older woman who is probably their grandmother.

The grandmother and the kid eye me speculatively as the other woman gives me a small smile and turns away because the salesperson is ready to take her order.

She orders a few things, including a cream bun in Vietnamese, then says in English, "We should move down so this man can see the case."

"Thanks," I say with a smile. "I was just looking for something to hold me over until I can get some breakfast. My mom informed me she needed me to bring her shopping the minute I got up this morning."

The woman is very petite and pretty. Not in a made-up kind of way. She doesn't have on a drop of make-up and has her long black hair pulled back into a simple ponytail. Even so, there's something about her.

Something about her catches my attention, and not just the yoga pants that are tight enough to show me she's in great shape, either. I can't put my finger on it; maybe it was just the movie reference, maybe something else. She looks familiar, but I can't place her.

"See, I'm not the only one," the girl says with a grin.

I grin back at her.

She puts out her hand, "Hi! I'm Kimmy. This is my grandmother and my cousin Alicia."

I shake her hand. She's way too young to be this forward with strange men.

I bow slightly to the older woman and say, in my best Vietnamese, "It is a pleasure to meet you, grandmother."

She nods back with a small smile.

"And you, Alicia. I'm Carlos."

"You, as well," she replies formally.

With damnable timing, the clerk hands over Alicia's order and interrupts the conversation I had hoped was just about to get started. He then turns to me.

"Have a good day, Carlos," Kimmy says as they start to walk away.

"You, too," I call after them.

Then I hear Kimmy stage whisper to her cousin. "He's hot."

"Kimmy!" she hisses in reply.

She starts to look over her shoulder to see if I heard, but I turn to the clerk with a grin on my face to save her the embarrassment of knowing I did. I place my order and proceed to wait.

Once I have my order, I go in search of Mom. She has a basket brimming with items, so I catch up and take it from her. We gather a few more things before making our way to the check-out lines.

Mom and I are just about to walk out when I hear Kimmy call, "Bye, Carlos!" Only a teenager would yell out across a stream of people in line to say goodbye to someone with no reservations whatsoever.

I turn and grin at her. "Hang on a sec, Mom. I'll be right back."

I head back to where the three women are standing in line. With a grin, I hand Alicia the card I'd taken out of my wallet and put in my pocket in case an opportunity presented itself.

"Have a good day, ladies," I say before going back to my mother, hearing Kimmy squeal with delight behind me.

Chapter 8

Alicia

It has been the longest of long days. My feet hurt, my eyes are bleary, and even though I'm really, really hungry, I don't have the energy to chew. I toe off my shoes and strip out of my scrubs, but that's all I can manage before I flop onto the bed and pass out from exhaustion.

"Leave me alone, I need to sleep," I groan as Kimmy tries to shake me awake in what must be just a few minutes later.

"You need to go to the hospital and get your rounds done so we can go shopping," she says in a voice way too chipper for this early in the morning. "Plus, you need a shower; you stink."

In my weariness, I forgot I'm supposed to take Kimmy shoe shopping today. She's had a growth spurt, mainly in her feet, it seems, and what she has no longer fits. After a couple of ingrown toenails, we discovered her shoes were the culprit, and I promised her I'd take her shopping on my next day off.

Hello day off.

"Okay," I say, trying to keep the grumble at bay.

It's not her fault that she doesn't know how late my night was. She only knows that it is almost eight in the morning, and I am usually long gone by this time, so to her, I have already slept in late. Maybe if I get my rounds done quickly and we can get her shopping done without having to visit every shoe store in the City, I can come home and take a long nap this afternoon.

When we return, my lust for a long nap is shot, but we're arriving back home in time for me to take a short one. Kimmy and I had a good day shopping. I didn't rush her in any way, but when I couldn't keep from yawning frequently at the last store we visited, she was the one telling me I need a nap. She's happy with her three new pairs of shoes, so she doesn't grumble when I point the car toward home.

Today was great with Kimmy. She seemed like a happy teenager; something she's never been before. Not once did she give me attitude or start an argument just for the sake of arguing. Maybe we've turned a corner.

"You got a delivery, Alicia," Mom says as soon as we walk through the front door.

On the table where we normally put the mail is a small box. It has my name and address on it, but there is no return address and no postage. I frown, trying to puzzle out who could be sending me something.

"There's no postage," I say.

"It didn't come in the mail," Mom says. "It was delivered."

Kimmy comes to look over my shoulder. "Open it! See what it is!"

I go to the kitchen and get the utility scissors we keep in the junk drawer to cut the tape on the box. Kimmy follows me and watches. Inside is a smaller box with a notecard in an envelope on top. The smaller box is blue. Another Tiffany blue box.

Surely not.

I open the note card to read a message written in neat block letters with a firm hand.

Happy early birthday, Monkey. I was going to save this, but thought you deserved to go ahead and have it.

It's unsigned, but it doesn't need a signature. It's clear who it's from. I haven't seen Tai for almost a week since the art auction. He has texted, but that's all. Not even a phone call.

I figure he's lying low, hoping that with time, my concerns will blow over. However, his lack of contact isn't having the impact he's hoping for. If anything, I'm more convinced than ever that it's time to end things.

"Monkey?" Kimmy asks.

"It's a nickname that Tai gave me."

I flip open the top of the small blue box. Inside is a pair of earrings to match the necklace he gave me at New Year's. The man seems to think that money will fix anything.

"Ooo," Kimmy says. "Those are pretty! You should put them on!"

"No, I shouldn't." I snap the box shut, putting the blue box back into the shipping box along with the note card.

"What? Why?"

I ignore her questions. "I'm going to go take a nap. If I'm not up by suppertime, please come wake me."

"Okay," she says in a tone that makes it seem as if she is really saying 'whatever' as she rolls her eyes at me.

I take everything to my room and place it on my dresser. I'll need to call Tai, but first, my brain needs some sleep.

Dreams of dragons infiltrate my sleep. I dream of a tattooed man who has a serpentine dragon on his chest. Tai is there and we're talking casually.

The dragon comes to life and slithers off his skin. It twines around my ankles like a cat and slowly grows in size. Before I realize it, the snake-like dragon is wrapped around me as if it is a boa constrictor and begins to squeeze.

I look to the man for help. His face has been replaced by a kabuki mask in the visage of a scowling man. I turn to Tai, but his face has been replaced with a snarling devil kabuki mask.

I'm suffocating as the tight embrace of the dragon pushes all the air from my lungs. *But you're not even Japanese...* is my last thought before everything fades.

I lurch awake and sit up straight, gasping for breath. I roll out of bed and go to the bathroom to throw some water on my face before going to the kitchen where Bà and Mom are fixing supper. The dream has shaken me, and it takes me a few minutes to brush it off.

Why on earth would I have such a dream and put Tai in a devil mask? I pause at that thought as a memory floats up. It's been a while, so I can see why I didn't remember.

Soon after Tai and I started dating, the first time I spent the night at his house, I woke in the middle of the night to find him gone from the bed. Padding down the hall on bare feet, I was almost silent and when I saw light coming from under the door to his office, I thought that's where he must be.

When I cracked the door and peeked inside, he barked at me to get out. He later apologized and said that his office is private and that I shouldn't go in there because there is often sensitive information on his desk, including non-disclosure agreements and the like. Having lived the last several years of my life being ruled by laws such as HIPPA in relation to my patients, I understood the need for privacy and let it go.

However, now, I remember the item sitting prominently displayed on the shelf behind him. It was a red-faced horned devil kabuki mask, just like the one in my dream. Just remembering it makes me shiver.

Kimmy's laughter ringing down the hall pulls me out of my thoughts. She sounds like a normal, carefree kid at that moment, and I'm glad to hear it. More than anything, I wish that for her. I wish she could find her happiness and her path in life.

She looks up when I step into the kitchen. "Where are your earrings?" she asks. "I really think you should put them on; they're so pretty!"

"What earrings?" Mom asks.

I tell her about the gift in the box that was delivered today and who it's from. Bà says I should throw it in the trash and proceeds to call Tai a du côn, again and tells me, yet again, that I need to stay far away from him.

I ignore the last part of her comment when I reply. "It is too expensive to throw in the trash, but I will be sending it back."

"Why would you do that?" Kimmy asks. "It's a super nice gift."

I let the conversation drop as I start putting the bowls of food onto the small kitchen table, where we eat most of our meals. After supper is done and the dishes are washed and put away, I go to my room. I dial Tai's number, feeling butterflies flittering around in my stomach for some reason.

"A lô, baby" he says when he answers the phone.

"Hi."

"I'm glad you called, Monkey," he replies, and I can hear the smile in his voice.

"I received the delivery with the gift. Thank you, but my birthday isn't for months."

He is quiet for a moment and the smile gone from his voice when he says, "So? They match the necklace. What's wrong with me giving my fiancé gifts?"

My voice is soft and conciliatory when I respond. "There's nothing wrong with it. I'm just surprised considering we're not on the best of terms right now and haven't had a chance to talk."

"As far as I'm concerned, all of that is behind us and instead of focusing on the past, we need to focus on moving forward."

"Tai, I can't just forget what happened."

"I'm not asking you to forget it, but you need to get over it. It happened, but it's over and done with."

Anger sparks. "Do you seriously think I can just get over you nearly choking me out in a fit of rage? What happened showed me that there is a lot I don't know about you. You keep a lot of things hidden from me and blow me off whenever I try to dig deeper. What happened let me know that I really don't know you at all."

"So, what are you saying?"

"I'm saying that I'm not sure I can be engaged to a man who is a mystery to me."

I rub at my forehead, feeling the beginnings of a headache coming on.

"I thought you said you love me."

"And I thought I did, too. But that was before I realized that the only part of you I know is an illusion."

"What does that mean?"

I sigh. "When I was a kid, my dad bought me a toy that I'd been wanting. All I'd ever seen was the picture on the box, but I just had to have it. He brought it home one day and when I opened it up, what was inside was nothing like the picture. That's how it feels with you. You keep this wall up, this hard plastic shell that makes everything look one way, but underneath, there's something different."

I pause and wait for him to reply, but he doesn't.

"I've asked you questions to help me get below the surface, but you have a tendency to blow me off or redirect the conversation. I'm not saying I couldn't love what's under there; I'm saying I have no clue what's under there, so I haven't even had a chance to find out, even though we've been together for over a year. If I don't know you any better than I do after a year, that's a sure sign that we're not supposed to be together."

He remains quiet for a long time. When he finally speaks, his voice is low and menacing.

"You belong to me. A promise was made, and you need to keep it."

I bark out a harsh laugh. Is he for real? It's as if he's heard nothing I've said.

"Two old drunk men made an agreement over sixty years ago in Vietnam for Bà to marry your grandfather, but no one bothered to tell her about it until she was already married and had babies. It's not her fault that she didn't know, and I don't see how you or anyone else could possibly extrapolate that to mean that I am somehow promised to you."

"Be careful how you speak to me."

"Why? Are you going to choke me into submission again?"

"Stop throwing that in my face!"

"You had your chance with me, Tai, but you chose to hide yourself from me. I love the surface you, but now that I know without a doubt that it's only the surface. It makes me sad that you never gave me a chance to...that you didn't trust me enough to let me try to love the whole of you."

"You don't understand."

"Then help me understand."

Silence.

I wait, not wanting to give him an out. It goes on long enough that I know he's not going to say anything. This has to end. I can't go on like this.

Suddenly exhausted, I say, "Your silence lets me know that deep in my heart, there will be no working things out for us. I'll send the necklace, earrings, and ring to your condo. If you want me to send the clothes and shoes and everything else back, let me know and I will, or I can just donate them to charity."

Silence.

I look at the face of my phone and see that it's still connected. I'm just about to put it back to my ear when I notice that Tai disconnects.

So, there's my answer; a big fat nothing.

Chapter 9

Alicia

Having a rare Thursday evening off, I go to the Belladonna Society for dinner. The Society is an exclusive, invitation only women's club like the old school gentlemen's clubs frequented by wealthy men.

I joined over a year ago and can count on one hand the number of times I have been able to go for dinner with my original orientation group. Sometimes I think I should have disregarded the invitation, especially considering the extreme hit to my savings the membership fee caused.

However, I doubted second invitations were ever granted, and I knew that a membership in this group of women would benefit me in my career. Although I wasn't always able to make it to dinner, I came to use the fitness facilities occasionally, so it's not like it has been a complete waste. Ten more months and my residency will be complete, my schedule will settle down, and I will have more freedom to start building a life.

Part of me has hated the infernal countdown that had lodged itself into my psyche when I was just a girl and decided to follow in my father's medical footsteps. Until Tai was able to distract me, I had put life on hold, wholly focused on my education and career. My life has been in a holding pattern for almost the entirety of my soon-to-be thirty years, waiting to begin.

"Alicia! I'm so glad you're here," Caitlyn Foster says when I approach their table.

"I'm glad to be here," I reply with a smile. "I've missed seeing everyone. Look at you!" I say to Gabriella Masters, who is newly married and heavy with child. "You're positively glowing!"

"Girl, that's all sweat. It's thirty-four degrees outside and I'm sweating like a piglet," Gabriella replies with a laugh. "I am so ready for this boy to be birthed."

"How much longer?" I ask.

"Any day now, I hope. His original due date was Valentine's Day and I swear they must have gotten the date of conception wrong because there's no way I'm going to last another four or five weeks."

That makes us all laugh.

"Hi Serena. I'm glad you're here."

"I'm glad I could make it, too. I swear I need to put a reminder in my phone because I can't tell you how many times I've been sitting in my office grading papers only to look up and realize it's nine o'clock on Thursday and I've missed dinner again," Serena replies.

Serena Chilton is a professor at OU's law school and fairly new to the position and the area, from what I know about her. It seems she and I are the worst ones about making it to these dinners. I want to change that for me because I'm finding that even when I feel like going home and going straight to bed because I'm so tired, if I make myself come to dinner on these nights, it re-energizes me.

"I see you've gained a new appendage, Demi." I say, pointing at the giant ring on her finger.

She blushes. "Yes, Kellen and I are engaged. Do you remember me talking about him? I think you were here for dinner once soon after we started dating."

I nod. "Yes, I remember. He's Ella's husband's brother, right?"

"Yes, he is."

"What happened to your new appendage?" Cait asks, pointedly looking at my naked left hand.

I shake my head. "Well, it might not have been the shortest engagement in the history of the world, but I'm thinking it's over and done."

"What happened?" Ella asks, clearly concerned.

I tell them the story of my wonderful New Year's Eve, sullied by the light of New Year's Day. It makes me sad recounting it, but even so, I'm surprised that I'm just a little sad, not completely heartbroken like I'd think I should be after breaking it off with the love of my life.

"I realized I don't know him at all beyond the surface. Here I thought we were having fun and had no idea we were on the marriage track, but as much as I thought I loved him, I discovered I loved the façade of him because the man behind the façade is a complete stranger."

"Big red flags, for sure," Demi says. "It's better that you found out now than after the wedding."

"Yeah, you're right. Anyway, back to lighter topics. Demi, when are you two planning to have your wedding?"

We chat about weddings and babies for a bit with Ella telling me all about her wedding that was just a few weeks ago and showing me a ton of pictures on her phone. I was invited and hated to miss it but had an emergency surgery pop up that day. I update them on the non-Tai goings on in my life, mostly how pleased I am about the residency being almost complete.

It feels good just to be in the company of women with whom I have no ties with beyond friendship. When my father died, I felt like I had to step into his shoes and take the leadership role in the family in many ways while still balancing respecting Bà as the matriarch. I had to become a parent to Kimmy, dutiful granddaughter to Bà, caretaker to Mom, and breadwinner for the whole family. It was, and still is, exhausting sometimes.

We're winding down when Cait says, "Oh! Alicia, I almost forgot, Ford and I are having a housewarming this weekend so that people can come see the finished remodel. Ford wanted to wait and have a barbeque when the weather is warmer and we will, but I can't wait to show it off. Ella's designs turned out so beautifully. I know your schedule can change at a moment's notice, but we'd love to have you, if you can come. Here's the address and particulars. No need to let us know ahead of time. If you can make it, just show up."

She hands me a postcard with the information printed on it and I tuck it into my purse.

"Yes! You should come if you can!" Demi says. "I'll be there, so there will be at least a few familiar faces."

"Me, too," Gabriella says, rubbing her belly. "Unless I'm in labor, that is, fingers crossed."

I smile and nod. "I'll try."

"Excellent," Cait says.

When I walk out into the frigid evening after dinner, I feel lighter and happier than I have for a while. I look forward to spending more time with these women in the coming months and getting to know them better. I can't even be jealous of their well-established lives compared to my return to a holding pattern. I'm happy for them.

The lights from the building cast a warm glow onto the sidewalk, making the otherwise deserted area less intimidating. The Society building is a three-story squat brick turn of the century building set on the edge of Automobile Alley among a row of buildings that are primarily office space and, therefore, empty at this time of night. I walk down the block to my car, pulling my scarf up to cover my nose to block out the wind's bite.

As much as I hate the thought of going back to waiting for some finish line to start trying to live a fuller life again, I think it's for the best. Tai had me thinking it was possible to have a life despite the demands of the residency program, but instead I allowed it to keep me from fully engaging in the relationship. I blame myself for not taking the time to see what was really going on.

He should have gotten the box of expensive jewelry back by now. Although I tried to set a time over the past few days to meet face to face to give it to him, I think he knew what I wanted to see him for and decided to be unavailable. However, I didn't want to put it off, so I had the box couriered to his condo. I thought I might hear from him, but part of me just wants him to go away and is glad I haven't.

I have a feeling that won't last, though. Tai is very persistent when he wants something. Or someone.

Chapter 10

Alicia

F riday has felt like a Monday all day. I am walking up my driveway, glad to be home after a fourteen-hour shift, which included three surgeries, two of them back-to-back. I only had two scheduled when the day started, but got assigned to an emergency case just as I was getting ready to leave for the day, a little girl injured in a car accident.

Working on children seems to take twice as much energy as working with adults. It's difficult to see a small body broken and damaged and not want to fix every little thing to make it all right, even knowing that most of the time, that's impossible. You can only fix what you can fix and hope it's enough.

I am all kinds of exhausted but am looking forward to almost an entire day off tomorrow once I check in on my patients in the morning. The housewarming at Cait's tomorrow evening should be a much-needed bit of fun.

I hear car doors, but ignore them until I hear someone say, "Monkey, I need your help."

It's Tai's voice. I want to run into the house and lock the door behind me. In my current state, I don't know that I'd be able to help anyone with anything.

But I don't run away. I turn around and see Tai, along with two other men. One of them is shirtless, with a bloody towel pressed to his side. I already know where this is going.

"You need to take him to a hospital," I say.

"We can't," he replies. I start to respond, but he holds up his hand. A hand covered with the blood of his friend...employee...victim, I'm not sure.

"Just hear me out," he says. "You said you wanted to know more about my world, well, this is part of it. Not all of my properties are in the best of locations."

He pauses and I nod for him to go on.

"He was working and came across a homeless kid in an empty warehouse just looking for a place to keep warm and maybe sleep a few nights. The kid panicked and pulled out a gun, shaking so bad with fear that the gun went off. We don't want to get him in trouble, he's just a kid, and if we go to a hospital, they'll be obligated to report it and some kid who was just trying to stay warm will go to prison for something that was an accident. It looks like it's a through and through and didn't hit anything important. I just need you to verify that I'm right and stitch him up. Please, Monkey."

I should have turned around and made that dash into the house. I should send them back to their car and tell them they're on their own. I should tell them again to go to the hospital.

Instead of any of those logical and reasonable options, my mouth opens and "Okay, just this once and you've got to be quiet, everyone is in bed," comes out.

I am officially an idiot.

We go into the house, and I point them into the kitchen, which is on the opposite side of the house from Kimmy's bedroom. However, it is near the master bedroom which Mom and Bà share. Mom couldn't stand sleeping alone in a room after Dad died, so we pulled the king bed out and put two doubles in there so that Bà could share the room with her.

I know Mom won't wake up, though. Bà is another story, but I put it out of my mind, figuring we'll cross that bridge if needed.

I have the man sit on the small dinette table in the kitchen. It's sturdy enough that it can hold him just fine. He's not a big man. He looks to be in his twenties and is slightly built. His torso is covered in tattoos, the most prominent a snake-like dragon. It makes me pause when I realize it looks exactly like the dragon in the dream I had.

On his left breast are the initials VCB. I wonder for a moment if those are the initials of a girlfriend or some long-lost relation. Something about it is familiar, but I can't place it.

When I pull the bloody towel away, I'm relieved that the bleeding is a slow ooze. I pull a clean towel from a drawer and put it over the wound, telling them to keep pressure on it while I go get my first aid kit. As I pass Tai, he puts a hand on my arm to stop me.

"Thanks, Monkey."

I nod and pull away.

Tai's assessment is accurate. The bullet went all the way through and seems to mostly have passed through the fatty tissue of the man's side. I clean the area thoroughly, which has the man hissing through his teeth.

Although my first aid kit is extensive, I don't keep any painkillers other than over-the-counter meds in it, so he cries out a little when I first start stitching. Tai tells him harshly in Vietnamese to put his teeth together, in other words, shut up, and the man goes back to hissing.

I have washed up and am putting my things away when Tai tells the others to go to the car. "I can't tell you how much I appreciate this, Monkey."

I don't look up at him, just nod and say, "You're welcome. I understand this was a unique situation, but I have to ask you to please not put me in this position again. Treating patients with non-emergency issues outside the hospital without their knowledge can end my career before it even starts."

"I know."

That's all he says before he follows his friends, employees, whoever they really are, out to the car, taking the bloody towels with him. He said he'd take them to avoid having them discovered by my family, for which I am grateful. I am zipping up the kit when Bà comes into the room.

Tai didn't mention getting the box of rocks back. I wonder if he hasn't gotten them yet. Perhaps he just hasn't been back to his condo. I'm sure I'll hear from him when he sees I've followed through on my promise to return them.

"What did that snake want with you?" she asks in Vietnamese.

"One of his employees was hurt, so he asked me to take a look," I reply in English.

"I thought you were done with him."

"I thought I was, too."

"That snake is going to bite you and poison everything you've worked for if you aren't careful."

I know she's right. It won't happen again. No, it *can't* happen again. If the hospital found out, they could kick me out of the residency program for unethical behavior and my chances of recovering from that would be slim.

When I first started the program, one of the fourth-year residents was caught regularly practicing medicine on his own and he was sacked from the program. I heard he's a doctor on a cruise ship now because he'd been unable to get into any other surgical programs.

I have worked too hard and am too close to the finish line or starting line, depending upon how you want to view it, to be knocked out by ignoring the hospital's policies. I work for them, so I have to follow their rules.

However, remembering Tai's words the day of our fight, he doesn't really care if I'm a doctor or not. He thinks I'll be content to spend my time at home caring for his children. Motherhood is a noble calling, but while I know I may want to be a mother someday, I know my calling is elsewhere.

He said this was a peek into his world. As much as I want to believe his story, it simply doesn't ring true. It's too clean, too innocent. If it were truly an accident, they would have gone to the hospital.

In Oklahoma, there's nothing in the law that says a gunshot wound is automatically reported to the police unless it's obviously a case of domestic violence which this was not. My hospital has the policy that gunshot wounds are reported, but there are several emergency clinics that do not have the same requirements.

Besides, some homeless kid in a warehouse wouldn't be likely to stick around for the police to come to arrest him. The chances of him being found are almost nil, so the probability of him going to jail is also highly unlikely.

Too many things don't add up with Tai's story. Could he have manipulated the situation to make me believe it was something accidental to see if I would help? An even worse thought pops into my mind. Could he have manufactured the whole thing to gauge my reaction?

"He's going to hurt you one way or another if you don't cut ties with him once and for all," Bà says into the silence.

I look over at her and see her face soften, and her eyes are bright with tears. "Oh, Bà..." I say, and go to her, wrapping her thin frame in my arms. I put my head on her shoulder as she pats my back.

"I know you're probably lonely after working so hard and spending all this time living your life for a girl who doesn't appreciate you and two old women, but that boy is poison," she says into my hair. "He always has been. Maybe if he had been born to different parents, he might not have turned out the way he did, but you cannot let him drag you down."

I'm not sure she's right about Tai being poison, but he has proved that he has no respect for me or my profession. He doesn't care if he causes my entire career, everything I've worked so hard for, to come crashing down around my ears.

Bà is right about one thing, though, it's time to cut ties completely with Tai Dang.

Chapter 11

Carlos

I walk into Ford and Cait's house, surprised at the number of people here. A couple of other cops I know greet me. "Ford?" I ask.

"Kitchen," one of them tells me with a point of his finger.

I make my way through the room, pausing to talk to a few people I know along the way. When I make it to the kitchen that looks like something out of a magazine, I find Ford and Cait. Kissing. Kissing like a couple of teenagers in a backseat on a Saturday night at Lover's Lane.

Cait must catch the movement because she looks up and says, "Oh!"

"Sorry," I say, "I didn't mean to interrupt."

"No, you didn't." She's blushing.

"Yeah, he did," Ford says deadpan.

Cait laughs and swats at his arm. "No, he didn't. We have a house full of people and we definitely shouldn't be here in the kitchen making out."

He steps behind her and nuzzles her neck. "Sure we should. Maybe if we do, they'll all leave," Ford says.

She trembles. Visibly trembles. God, I hope I'm lucky enough to find a relationship like theirs someday.

"Carlos," she says, looking at me and ignoring Ford. "Welcome. Ford is teasing."

She sees the bag in my hand. "You didn't have to bring anything."

"I know," I tell her and hand her the bag, "but my mom taught me it's just good manners to take a gift the first time you visit someone's home."

She looks inside and pulls out the first item. Ford looks over her shoulder, his hands on her hips. She looks at the item and up at me.

"I wasn't sure what to get a couple who probably has everything, so I went with something from my culture. That is pink chalk, and it represents Vietnam, where my mother is from. It's usually given from a mother-in-law to her soon to be daughter-in-law to signify that she sees a rosy future for them. You're not getting married, but from the way Ford can't stop talking about you, I think your future is very rosy."

She smiles and touches the chalk with a tip of one finger. "That's so sweet."

She reaches in and pulls out the other item, a bottle of rum.

"Excellent," Ford says, taking it from her.

"That was my father's favorite brand of rum. It's produced in the Dominican Republic, where my father's father is from."

"Thank you, Carlos! The gifts are so thoughtful." Cait says, coming around the kitchen island to hug me.

"I'm surprised you remember me," I tell her. "We only met the one time."

"It is one of her many superpowers," Ford says with great affection. "Thanks Carlos."

Cait shoos me out of the kitchen and points me in the direction of the bar and the food. I go to the bar and get beer from the selection of very good, locally produced beers, then move around the room, talking mostly with other cops. There seems to be a cop side of the room and what I can only guess is the Cait side of the room.

I look over and see an African American woman and a tall, dark-haired, possibly Latina, woman, heavily pregnant, talking to a petite blond. The blond and the pregnant woman are book ended by men who look like they're probably brothers. The dark-haired woman is laughing as her man pulls her to his side. When she shifts, I see her.

I see the woman I gave my card to in the grocery store. The petite Asian woman I haven't been able to get out of my mind since that day. She's standing there smiling broadly up at whatever it was that made the other women laugh.

Kimmy had said her cousin's name was Alicia. Ford had said Cait's friend's name was Alicia Pham. Pham is a fairly common Vietnamese surname. Some detective I am to not even consider a connection.

I had done an internet search for Alicia Pham on Monday and found nothing. The woman does not do social media. We got called out before I could start running driver's licenses and the week had been so busy, I hadn't picked it up again.

I can't be blamed completely for not making the connection. Her all dressed up compared to her casual look that day in the grocery store are light years apart. All dressed up, she looks to be in her late twenties, but clean faced and casual, I would have put her at barely out of her teens.

If she had looked the way she looks tonight, I wouldn't have overlooked it. I can clearly recognize the delicate jawline. The graceful curve of her neck was obscured by the neckline of her dress in the photo Ford showed me, but even in another turtleneck, I can recognize it being this close to her.

Her lips looked different with the dark lipstick she'd been wearing in the photo, too. She's not all glamorous, like she was at the party, but she has on makeup and her long hair is down. She's dressed casually, but it's somewhere in between the fancy dress and the yoga pants she had on in the store.

I kind of miss the yoga pants.

The giant ring on her left hand that showed clearly in the picture is gone, too. I wonder if something has happened to break the engagement. For her sake, I hope so, but maybe she's one of those women who likes to take her ring off when it suits her.

I had been formulating a plan about how exactly I would guide the conversation with her. How I would couch every question to her to draw out as much information about Tai Dang as possible.

I had plans within plans for when I met her. As I cross the room, drawn to her like a magnet, all those plans evaporate from my mind.

She looks up and sees me coming, a look of surprise crossing her face. I wondered if maybe she'd been put off by me being a cop and thought that's why she hadn't called me. Now I know it was probably because of Dang. Then her look of surprise is replaced with a smile and I find myself grinning back.

"It's good to see you again, Carlos," she says and holds out her hand. "I'm Alicia. Alicia Pham."

"Likewise." I guess I made at least a little bit of an impression since she remembers my name.

"Carlos, these are my friends," she nods to the African American woman first. "Serena Chilton." Then the blond and book end number one. "Demeter Lawson and Kellen Masters and Gabriella and Morgan Masters," she says, nodding to the tall dark-haired Latina woman and book end number two last.

I greet everyone and shake hands all around. The blonde tells me to call her Demi with an engaging smile. Then I realize the names Alicia has said. "Morgan Masters," I say. "Morgan Masters of Masters Construction?"

There had been a serial killer operating in the City last year and Ford was working the case. The guy was finally arrested because his intended eighth victim's boyfriend showed up and detained the man. His name had been Morgan Masters.

"The very same," bookend number two says.

"So how do you to know each other?" the blond asks. Demi, I remind myself. Her name is Demi.

"We kind of met at the grocery store, but I never got her name," I tell her, and go on to relay the entire story to the group. Alicia's cheeks go pink when I confirm I heard Kimmy's declaration.

She blushes again when I tell them about my grand exit. She is so damn cute. In the store she seemed almost shy or maybe cold, but here with her friends, she's much more animated. I don't know how I could have ever thought she'd be cold.

I grin at her. "Here I thought I played it so cool, and I was sure you'd call me, but nope, total radio silence."

Both of the other men groan. Morgan whistles as his hand arcs downward, then makes an explosion noise.

"Stop!" she says, laughing, and bumps my shoulder with hers.

We talk for a while longer until Morgan takes his wife to go in search of their belongings so he can take an obviously tiring Gabriella home. The other Masters couple leaves soon after, saying they are expected to pick their son up from his grandparent's house early the next morning. Serena also excuses herself with a claim about needing to get home, too.

My beer is gone. I've been talking so much I didn't notice.

"I'm headed to the bar. Can I get you something?" I ask Alicia.

"Yes, thank you, but I'll just come with you if that's okay."

"Absolutely."

I get a water figuring the party's starting to wind down, so I don't need another beer. She asks for water, as well. I motion to a loveseat over in the corner. "Would you like to sit?"

"Sure."

I let her choose her spot and sit down once she's settled. "So tell me all about you."

She barks out a laugh and shrugs. "There's not much to tell."

Oh, I beg to differ, Dr. Pham, but I'm fine coaxing it out of you.

"What do you do for a living?"

"I'm in my last year of an orthopedic surgical residency at OU. I'll be finished at the end of this year."

"Congratulations," I tell her, impressed. "That must have taken a lot of hard work."

She smiles shyly. Damn. Did I say cute earlier? More like fucking adorable.

"It has been," she replies, "but I love it. Even when I am exhausted and my brain is so overworked I can't see straight, I still have such a feeling of fulfillment that I've been instrumental in helping someone regain use of a part of their body they might otherwise have lost."

"How did you decide to go into medicine?"

"My father was a pediatrician. When I was eleven or twelve, I found some of his textbooks from medical school and found them fascinating. I decided right then that I wanted to be a doctor, too."

"Does he still have a practice?"

Sadness crosses her face as she shakes her head. "No. He passed away almost ten years ago."

I put a hand on her arm, wanting to comfort her. "I'm sorry to hear that."

She shrugs. "He was a wonderful father, and I was very lucky to have him as long as I did. Now it's just Mom, Bà, Kimmy, and me."

"And Kimmy's your cousin, right?"

"Yes."

She tells me the unfortunate story of Kimmy's parents. I can relate to Kimmy regarding her mom. I was very lucky with my dad, though. He stuck like glue. It hurt enough to know my mom didn't want me; I can't imagine what it would be like to know both your parents were alive in the world and just didn't want you.

"She's lucky she had your family to take her in."

"I know she was better off with us than she would have been in foster care, but Dad got sick when she was barely a toddler, and he was gone before she turned four. When he died, he took most of Mom with him, so that left Bà and me. We've tried our best, but despite it all, Kimmy has some issues. When I took over as her guardian, I was just about to start medical school and once that was done, I started a residency program, so I haven't been around nearly as much as I probably should have been."

She pauses, takes a deep breath, and gives me an embarrassed smile.

"Sorry, I don't know where all that came from."

"It's okay."

"No, it's not. I'll blame it on a very stressful week. So anyway, that's probably way more about me than you bargained for. Tell me about you. Do you still have your parents? Any brothers and sisters?"

It's my turn to tell the story of a great man gone too soon as her hand goes to my arm this time to comfort me.

"I'm sorry about your father. So, the woman I saw you with in the grocery store is your stepmother."

"Yeah, but she's the only mother I've ever known."

"It's good you have each other," she says.

"I can't argue with that."

"Your card said you're a detective with OKCPD. Are you also in homicide like Ford?"

"No. I'm in the gangs unit."

She looks surprised by that.

"I thought about going into homicide, but the gangs unit is a really good fit for me. There is often overlap with other departments, so I get a lot of variety in the kinds of cases I pursue."

I tell her about the case Ford and I are currently working on without going into all the gory details of the massacre or divulging anything that could compromise the case.

"Because there are murders involved, and it seems to be gang related, our departments are working together."

"Do we have a lot of gangs in the City or is it still mostly the Bloods and Crips I heard so much about when I was a kid?"

"Those gangs are still around, but the larger gangs are Mexican and Asian. That's one reason I'm well suited, because I'm fluent in both Spanish and Vietnamese. The largest and most violent gang in town is Asian, but most of the members are Vietnamese. They call themselves the Viet Cong Boyz or VCB."

Her hand snaps out and grabs my arm in a claw-like grip. I look at it, then up and down her and see she's gone paper pale.

"What did you say?" she asks in a choked voice.

"Are you okay?" I ask.

She doesn't answer, so I ask again. "Are you okay?"

She lets go of my arm and chokes out, "Excuse me," before she clamps her hand over her mouth and springs up off the couch. Although she doesn't run, she rushes out of the room and down the hall.

Chapter 12

Alicia

I ask Carlos about the gang presence in the City and he replies, "Those gangs are still around, but the larger gangs are Mexican and Asian. That's one reason I'm well suited, because I'm fluent in both Spanish and Vietnamese. The largest and most violent gang in town is Asian, but most of the members are Vietnamese. They call themselves the Viet Cong Boyz or VCB."

What did he say? Did he say what I think he did?

Of its own accord, my hand grips Carlos' arm.

"What did you say?" I ask in a choked voice.

"Are you okay?"

Am I okay? No, I'm not okay! Ohmygod. Ohmygod. Ohmygod. VCB, the letters tattooed on that guy's chest. The guy with a gunshot wound that I treated on my kitchen table against my hospital's policy less than twenty-four hours ago.

Not only am I in danger of losing my entire future career, but I'm in danger of also losing my freedom. For all I know, I'm now an accessory to a violent, gang-related crime. What did Tai get me into?

I'm starting to hyperventilate, but I don't know how to stop. My calm, clinical doctor's brain has left the building and I'm panicking.

"Are you okay?" Carlos asks again.

My stomach starts to roil as blood pounds in my ears. I'm going to throw up.

I manage to choke out, "Excuse me."

I put my hand over my mouth and get up, moving as quickly as I can without running to where Cait pointed out the bathroom when she was showing us the remodeled areas of the house earlier.

I crouch over the toilet for what feels like an eternity as my stomach turns inside out. Heat waves rise and fall through my body, leaving beads of sweat on my forehead. When my shaking legs give out, I sink down to my knees trying to hold my hair out of the mess, a mess of tears and snot and vomit as I try to come to grips with the fact that I have most likely ruined my life.

My family's lives, too, my brain dredges up. What will they do without me there to support them, to keep a roof over their head and food on the table? I am indeed an idiot. A stupid, stupid girl whose years spent working hard and planning carefully are about to go up in flames.

When the nausea finally subsides, I stand, testing the strength of my legs. They hold me up, so I move to the sink, turning on the water. I palm water from the tap to rinse my mouth, then I find a washcloth in the vanity and wet it. Trying to return my face to some semblance of order as I clean away the sweat, and other things I don't want to think too hard about, I start to calm.

My clinical brain is coming back online as the initial shock passes. My fear is mostly, not completely, but mostly turning to anger, and I'm pissed off at Tai. I'm even more pissed off at myself.

I should have sent them away last night. Bad idea was flashing like a neon sing as soon as I saw them walking up the driveway, but it was dimmed by him saying he was letting me see under the veneer.

I can handle a lot of things, but violent gang related activity is not one of them. Fucking Tai. How deep is he in with the gang? I wonder how much of that money he flashes around is gained through illegal activity.

My thoughts are interrupted when there's a quiet knock at the door. "Alicia, are you all right?"

It's Cait. I give myself a once over in the mirror and figure I'm as good as I'm going to get and open the door. She looks me over.

"Oh, honey, what's wrong? Did you have a reaction to something in the food?"

I shake my head. "No. The food was delicious."

"Carlos said you two were talking, and you suddenly went pale, then got up and left the room. Was it what you were talking about that upset you?"

I nod.

"He said you had asked about what part of the department he worked in and when he said he was in the gangs unit, you asked about gang presence in the City. Is that what bothered you?"

I nod.

"Can you tell me exactly what bothered you?"

Unsure how to answer, I pause then settle on, "I don't want them to have to arrest me."

Her eyebrows raise. "Did you kill someone? Because unless you tell me right now that you willfully killed someone in cold blood, I give you my word that I won't let them arrest you for whatever it is you think you might have done. If they try to, I'll tell Ford he's cut off from sex and that will pretty much guarantee he'll leave you alone."

That makes me chuckle.

"But if you didn't murder someone, I think you should talk to Ford and Carlos and see what they say. Do you think you can do that? If you can't, I understand and will make your excuses, but I know Carlos is very concerned about you."

Carlos is very concerned about me. Why? He doesn't even know me. It doesn't really matter why, once he hears what I've done, he won't be concerned anymore.

"Yes, I think I can."

She pulls me into a hug. "Good. You carry so much responsibility on your shoulders with your family and your work, but it's okay to lean on other people every once in a while."

I just nod against her shoulder, hugging her back. Accepting her comfort, I set aside the hard shell for a brief moment. We stand there for a few minutes, and it feels so good to be hugged like this.

I know Bà and Mom love me. I know that in my bones, but Bà is not a touchy-feely person. She's a stand on your own two feet and stand strong regardless of the circumstances kind of person. Mom was always the one with the hugs and kisses, but she hasn't been capable of being maternal or nurturing since Dad died.

Before Tai came back into my life, there were times when I ached to be held. Even with Tai, it was a rarity that he would just hold me without it being a precursor to sex. It feels good to have someone's arms around me like this in a gesture of comfort. I didn't realize how much I missed it.

"Ready?" Cait asks.

I nod against her shoulder again. She lets me go, but takes my hand in hers and leads me back into the room where Carlos and I had been talking. Everyone is gone except for Ford and Carlos.

"It was getting late anyway, so I shooed them out." Cait whispers to me.

Carlos looks up and sees me, his face etched with worry. He crosses the room in long strides and stops in front of me to cup my jaw in his hands. His thumbs stroke across my cheeks, wiping away a few tears that had managed to sneak out without me realizing.

"Hey," he says, his voice gone gentle. "What's going on here? Did I cause this? Did I do or say something wrong?"

He's so worried and that touches me to my core. I put my hands on his wrists, enjoying the feel of his hands, but his tenderness almost undoes me. I take a deep breath as Dr. Pham enters the building and stuffs little girl Alicia into her locker.

I nod and look down, then say, "Yes, but not in the way that you mean."

"Can you talk about it?"

The way he asks, I know in my heart that if I were to say no, he'd let it go. But I don't want to say no. I nod.

"Alicia needs to talk to you both, but she's afraid that she may be in some trouble, so I gave her my word that unless she confesses to committing a murder that neither of you will be arresting her tonight. If you break my word, Ford will pay the price with his celibacy."

That makes everyone, including me, laugh...well, maybe not Ford so much, but it breaks the tension I'm feeling.

Carlos moves his hands away from my face, leaving my skin tingling in their wake. He takes my hand and leads me back to the loveseat where we'd been sitting. He releases me and leans back, his arm across the back of the seat in a very non-aggressive posture.

Ford sits in a wing chair across from us and pulls Cait down onto his lap. They're both doing all they can to signal casualness and it helps.

Feeling the steel in my spine that comes from years of prac- ticed detachment, I start. "I did something last night that I'm afraid might turn out to be illegal."

"I think you need to start at the beginning," Cait says, having divined that it relates possibly involves Tai's involvement with gangs.

I nod. "I think you're right. I have a...friend." I stop and shake my head. "Well, we were friends as children, but the last time I saw him, I was twelve until a couple of years ago. A little over a year ago, we started dating and became engaged on New Year's. However, some things happened, and the engagement was off before another week had gone by."

I pause to take a drink from the glass of water I'd left on the table. For a moment, I almost tell them about the choking incident with Tai. Unsure why, I want to tell Carlos everything, but I don't.

"We got into an argument the very next day after he'd proposed. I shouldn't have said yes when he asked, but in the heat of the moment, I didn't feel like I could say no. A lot of things were said when we argued, and I began to realize that I really didn't know him beyond the surface persona he presents to the world. He had ideas of what our life would be like after we married that were so out of left field I was shocked."

"What kind of ideas?" Cait asks.

"Well, things like getting married in June and me dropping out of the residency with only six months to go. Then there was the fact that I would give up being a doctor because I'd be busy raising our children as if all these years of study and practice were just a whim that I should be fine walking away from."

Just thinking about it sharpens the anger I was already feeling from being slapped in the face with the implications of last night that Tai is likely balls deep with a criminal gang.

"So that's why you broke off the engagement?" Ford asks.

I shrug. "Yes. It took the argument for me to fully understand what I had subconsciously discerned. I think that's why I was so shocked when he proposed, because deep down, I didn't feel truly connected with him because I didn't know him. Looking back, I feel stupid for not seeing it clearly. He was very withholding with personal information. Not even like super personal information. For instance, for New Year's; he had a driver retrieve me and take me to the restaurant because he was going to be late. When he arrived, I asked him what had kept him. He said..."

I pause for a moment, frowning as I try to remember his exact words.

"He said he had a meeting with a competitor. They were both going after the same deal, and he was hoping to redirect him to a different project to avoid driving up the price. I asked him if he was successful, and he just said, 'Of course, I was. He won't be bothering me on that front any longer'."

Ford and Carlos look at each other, but they don't say anything. I go on to tell them about me confronting Tai about his secretiveness. I describe how he just blew that off, too, saying that my career was so much more interesting than his.

"Anytime I asked him questions, he did that. Gave me a vague answer, then deflected. When we argued, I asked him what else he was hiding, kept pushing and something flipped in him. He was suddenly filled with rage."

"Did he hurt you?" Carlos asks.

I don't want to answer.

"It's okay," Cait says. "You can trust Ford."

I pull down the turtleneck sweater that has become a staple of my wardrobe over the past week. The bruises are fading, but they're still tinged with that sickly greenish yellow color of healing contusions. I hadn't wanted to tell them, to tell Carlos, but for whatever reason, I feel like he needs to know.

"He choked me," I say. "I was just about to pass out when he finally let go. Until that point, I had never once been afraid of him, but when he did this, I became terrified. I put some distance between us for a couple of days and when he wouldn't see me in person, I told him over the phone that I felt like the engagement was a mistake. Then last night, he showed up on my doorstep."

Now that I'm at the big reveal, my heart starts to pound, and my hands start to shake. I grip my knees, but I feel Carlos shift on the seat next to me and he takes my shaking hand into his much larger one and laces our fingers together. Our commingled hands draw my eyes and I just stare at them for a moment.

"It's okay," he says. "Go on."

His voice is so gentle, grip firm, but not crushing. His presence next to me is so solid that I just want to lean into him.

"I could blame it on being exhausted after a fourteen-hour day," I say. "I could blame it on feeling some obligation to the money he had spent on me, but in the end, those are just excuses."

Instead of leaning into Carlos, I sit straight because I couldn't bear it if I leaned into all his comfort, only to have him pull away. I tell them about last night. When I get to the end, I turn to look at Carlos. Up to this point, I'd mostly been looking at the floor or Cait, afraid to see the reactions of the men.

"When you said VCB, I thought of that tattoo on the man's chest and the realization that because I had stitched him up, I might have not only violated my hospital's policy but been made an accessory to something that could land me in prison. I apologize for my reaction."

He gives me a sweet smile and smooths my hair back from my face. "Your reaction is understandable. We're not aware of anything that went on last night, so it might be just what he told you it was. I think you need to hear about some of the things we know about Mr. Dang."

"Okay," I say, and brace myself to hear the truth.

"We know that Tai Dang has been a long-time member of the VCB, if not one of the founding members, and we believe he is the leader of the gang. We have been trying to nail him for years, but so far, we can't get anything concrete on him."

"It's like he's made of Teflon," Ford agrees.

Carlos tells me that Tai does, indeed, have some legitimate businesses in real estate and otherwise, but that most of them exist for the purposes of laundering money. Much of Tai and the gang's money comes from illegal activities like drugs and guns, but most of it comes from human trafficking. Carlos also believes that Tai and a few select members of his gang are the masked bank robbers that have been in the papers, but that it is pure supposition on his part and many on the force don't support the idea.

I take in everything he's told me, and I feel numb, as if I'm swaddled in cotton. The clothes, jewelry, dinners, fancy hotels, and that giant ring he put on my finger, all that money came from drugs and human trafficking. How many women, or God forbid, children, did he have to sell to buy that ring?

I start to feel sick again, but Carlos wraps his other big hand around the back of mine, caging it in strength and warmth. That simple motion grounds me and the nausea subsides.

"I think your decision to stay away from him is an excellent one," Cait says.

"Yes," I agree.

I suddenly feel completely spent, physically, mentally, emotionally, and spiritually.

"I need to go home," I announce, then look at Cait. "I'm sorry I ruined your party."

"Oh honey, you didn't ruin anything. It was all but over anyway, and you needed us."

"I was glad to have a reason to run 'em all off," Ford grumbles.

I guess he's teasing; I can't tell, but Cait just grins at him and kisses him on the cheek. She stands and holds out her hands to me. Releasing Carlos' hands, I take hers and she pulls me up and into a hug.

"You call me if you need to talk more about anything, okay?"

"I will," I promise.

She releases me. "Carlos, would you mind following Alicia home to make sure she gets there all right?"

"Sure," he replies. "I'd be happy to."

We say our goodbyes to Cait and Ford, then Carlos walks me to my car. I pause with the door open before I get in.

"You really don't have to follow me home. I'm fine now," I tell him.

A grin spreads across his face. "But I do," he says. "If I say I'm going to do something, I do it."

He cups my jaw with one hand, and I look up at him. His gaze is serious.

"If you ever want to talk about anything, even if it's just about the weather, you can call me. Okay? I'd really like it if you did."

I nod, leaning into his touch and closing my eyes. "Thank you," I say, then pull away and slide behind the wheel of my car.

He does as he said he would and follows me home. He even waits for me to park and get the front door open before he puts his car in drive and returns my wave as he starts to pull away.

Chapter 13

Carlos

I follow Alicia to a house in the Belle Isle neighborhood and watch until she has the door open and is ready to go in. She turns with a smile and gives me a little wave. I wave back and put my car into drive.

This night did not go at all how I expected it to. I thought I'd go to Ford and Cait's house, see a nice, remodeled home, drink some beers, and shoot the shit with some guys from work for a few hours. Nothing special.

If it weren't Ford, I probably would have skipped it, but I like the guy. He's a good cop, but seems like he'd be a good friend, too.

So many other guys in the gangs unit are jockeying for position, trying to move somewhere else that they think is more prestigious, like homicide. It makes it difficult to just hang out with someone when they're always looking for some way to outdo you.

I like the gangs unit. It suits me and being trilingual has served me well when I've gone undercover on a case. I also like that we get to see a lot of different kinds of cases when there's overlap with homicide. I'm looking forward to being proven right on the bank robberies and working on that.

Alicia's story about Tai is very interesting. It's not solid evidence of anything, but it is interesting. Thoughts of Tai and what he did to her pisses me off.

I wonder if he was or is hoping to pull her in deeper. Possibly turn her into his very own doctor on call, who can dig out bullets and stitch his guys up whenever needed. Hopefully, she follows through and stays far, far away from Dang.

She's smart and doesn't seem to be swayed by the money he has already tried to throw at her. However, she has a family for which she is the sole source of support. Someone like Dang could be ruthless about trying to leverage that.

If I can find a way to stick close to her, maybe he'll back off. I wouldn't mind sticking close to her at all. Not only is she smart and beautiful, but from what Cait says, she's just an all-around good person, too.

Cait said she's friends with the Director of Alicia's residency program. It seems like Cait is friends with a lot of people in interesting places.

The Director said that Alicia is a very talented surgeon and was being pushed to go into more prestigious and lucrative fields like neurological or cardiac surgery, but she chose to specialize in orthopedics because she liked it best. In addition, he says he's already gotten calls from orthopedic hospitals all over the US asking about her.

Alicia has done more rotations in under-served rural areas than her peers in the same program. She has talked about getting involved with Operation Rainbow, an organization that organizes missions to underserved countries to provide ortho services and surgeries, once her residency is complete. A big brain and a big heart to boot; definitely the kind of woman I could spend some time with.

Of course, for Tai Dang, a potential rival might cause him to redouble his efforts and lean on Alicia harder. I would be happy to have a reason to convince him otherwise. It's all in the hands of Alicia, though.

I'll just have to wait and see if she calls. I hope she does. Really, really hope she does.

When I get home, Mom's asleep in her chair as usual, so I shake her awake.

"Time for bed," I tell her.

She pats my hand and asks in Vietnamese, "How was your party?"

"It was very good. Do you remember the woman I gave my card to at the market? She was there. Her name is Alicia Pham."

"Ah, a nice Vietnamese name. You need a good Vietnamese girl to take care of you," she tells me as she shuffles down the hall to her bedroom.

"She's a doctor, Mom, a surgeon. I don't see her being a stay-at-home wife for anyone, not even me."

"A doctor, huh? Maybe you can take care of her and stay at home where you'll be safe and not doing that dangerous job anymore."

"That's not going to happen, Mom. I love my job."

She clicks her tongue at me and goes into her room.

"Good night, Mom," I say as she closes the door.

I'm in the middle of changing the oil in Mom's car the next day when my phone rings. I don't recognize the number, so I start to ignore it. However, it's local, so it might be important.

"Gutierrez," I answer.

"Carlos, hi, it's Alicia."

Just like that, my whole day is brighter.

"Alicia, I'm glad you called."

"Well, I wanted to apologize for how I acted last night. I'm sure you must think I'm a nut."

How on earth could she think that? If anything, I admire her courage in talking to Ford and me. It took guts to admit to two cops that she thought she might have committed a crime.

"Not at all. I think your reaction to discovering you were being manipulated by someone you thought cared about you was normal. Then you were brave enough to tell your story to two cops, despite thinking you might have done something illegal. Not nuts at all."

"You're very gracious."

I grin. "That's me, gracious Gutierrez. What are you up to today?"

She doesn't laugh, but I can hear the smile in her voice when she replies. "I have evening rounds tonight and I'll probably go in a little early to do some paperwork."

"Ah, paperwork. If I had realized how much paperwork was involved with being a cop, I might have considered a different career."

"Really?"

"Nah, I love being a cop."

"What do you love about it?"

I pause for a beat, trying to think of how to put into words how I feel about being a cop.

"That motto of protect and serve was painted on the side of my dad's cruiser, and I always liked that idea. I think I'm pretty good at it, but honestly, I feel like I was put on this earth to stand between the people who want to do bad things and the regular folks who just want to live their lives to the best of their ability. Helping people and keeping them safe makes it all worthwhile."

She's quiet for a moment and I start to wonder if I've said something wrong. I'm just about to say something into the silence when she finally speaks.

"That's nice. I like that."

"You said you like being a surgeon?" I ask, even though I already know the answer.

"I love it," she says. I can tell she's smiling again. She steals my words and goes on. "I think I'm pretty good at it, but honestly, I really like helping people, restoring their mobility and improving their quality of life. One of my first orthopedic surgeries was assisting with reattaching a man's hand after it was almost completely severed in a construction accident. He was able to regain significant use of the appendage with only slight diminishment from his previous range of motion. After that surgery, I was hooked."

"Wow, that's incredible."

"What are you up to today?" she asks.

I look down at my greasy hands and grease-stained clothes. I wonder what she'll think of a man who looks like this on his day off.

"I'm just about through changing the oil in my mom's car. She doesn't drive much, but I like to keep it maintained in case she needs to go somewhere and I'm not around."

"It's nice that you can do that for her. I'm hopeless with anything mechanical."

I'm struck with an idea and start talking before I can talk myself out of it.

"What time were you planning on going in?"

"I have to be ready to start rounds at four-thirty and I was hoping to have a couple of hours for paperwork. Why do you ask?"

"Want to grab some lunch before you go in? I'm almost done here and would just need to take a shower, then I'd be ready to go. We could do something casual, something quick, near the hospital, if you like."

She goes quiet again, but I let it stay quiet. If she doesn't want to go, she can say so and I'll try again another day. I can be persistent when I see something or someone I want, and I definitely want to get to know the good doctor better.

I hear her take a breath before she says, "Sure, okay. Do you like soul food? There's a great place not far from the hospital campus."

Yes! I am pumped that she said she'd meet me. I was all prepared for her to turn me down because I can see where she might not be so keen on going out with someone after that asshole Dang tried to do a number on her.

She gives me the location of the restaurant and we agree on a time to meet. Now to get finished and cleaned up. I have a stop to make before I meet Alicia.

Chapter 14

Alicia

I can't believe I agreed to have lunch with Carlos after breaking off my engagement only a few days ago. Maybe I'm feeling a little stung by my stupidity and want to bolster my confidence with another man who seems to like me. I just hope I'm not proven to be the worst judge of character ever.

I was touched by Carlos' kindness and tenderness last night. He is handsome, but he seems to have a big heart, too. I like what he said about being a police officer and keeping people safe.

When he was holding my hand, I certainly felt safe. It felt like I could tell him anything and I wanted to tell him everything. If he was at my back, I could face anything. At least that's the way it felt when I was with him.

Goodness knows I could use somebody at my back. What Cait said is true. I'm so tired of trying to carry everything on my own and I've been doing it since I was nineteen.

I love my family and am happy I am able to take care of them, but sometimes I am simply exhausted by it all. However, it's either keep moving forward or let it all crash and burn, so I just keep putting one foot in front of the other.

I shower and take a little more care with my appearance than I normally do when I go in on Saturdays. Although I know I'll still be dressed in scrubs and sneakers, at least my hair will be blown out and I'll have on some blush and mascara. I debate about putting my hair up or leaving it down so much that I'm giving myself whiplash. Finally, I decide to leave it down because I can always pull it into my usual ponytail when I get to the hospital.

I go into the kitchen where Bà and Mom are fixing lunch while Kimmy looks on. Hanging out with my family when it's like this is one of my favorite things. It's almost tempting enough to make me want to cancel lunch with Carlos.

Almost.

I remember when Kimmy was very young, we'd have the radio on, and she and I would dance around the kitchen dodging the other women as they cooked. Those times were the best.

Over the past few weeks, Kimmy has been doing really well. She's been going to school and her grades have improved. They still aren't great, but they are getting better.

She's actually been pleasant and helpful around the house, which is amazing. Maybe she's finally turned the corner for the better. Now if we can just keep her pointed in this more positive direction.

"I'm headed out," I tell the room at large.

"What are you going to do for lunch?" Bà asks.

"I'm going to grab something on the way to the hospital," I reply.

To Bà, eating out is tantamount to a mortal sin. Her opinion is - why on earth would anyone eat subpar food from a restaurant when there was excellent food at home? Her food is excellent, to be sure, but there wouldn't be a handsome man sitting across the table here.

Kimmy must have seen something in my face. "Ooo...are you meeting that rich boyfriend of yours?"

"No," I tell her. "I won't be seeing him anymore."

"What? Why? He spent so much money on you! What did you do to make him break up with you?"

Bà passes by me to put a dish on the table and pats my arm with a nod. She's glad to hear about this recent development in my relationship with Tai.

"Money isn't the only reason to be with someone."

"So, who are you having lunch with?" Kimmy presses.

"Who says I'm having lunch with anyone?"

"You've got makeup on, and your hair is down. You're meeting someone," she retorts, waggling a finger at me. "Is it a woman? Are you gay? I mean, that guy has so much money and he is really good looking, so maybe you don't like him cuz you're gay."

I frown at her, wondering what makes her think Tai is handsome. He is, but how would she know? There's not a single instance I can think of where she would have seen him, despite our being together for over a year.

He never came into the house and, more often than not, a driver picked me up. I shake my head; I don't have time to get into that with her or I'll be late.

"I'm not gay and I have to go. I love you all."

Once kisses on the cheek are given to Bà and Mom, I grab Kimmy to kiss her, too. She starts howling about how gross and gay I am and squirming to get away. Finally, I manage to plant one on her cheek before letting her go, and rushing out the door.

I park at the restaurant and swipe on some lip gloss. Last night, I didn't really pay attention to Carlos' car, only noted it as a dark sedan. There are three of them in the parking lot, so I'm not sure if he's here yet or not.

I'm always so nervous about interacting with people I don't know very well. Last night was comfortable with him, but that was because we weren't flying solo and talking one on one until after the warmup session with my friends.

I'm not really shy. There's no fear of talking with people, but until I get to know them, I tend to be more of an observer. Even as a girl, I was more quiet than talkative. In school, being a minority can be a minefield of social situations and you never know which one will blow up in your face, so I always took the observation before interaction approach.

I step inside the restaurant and start taking my coat off. It's warm and filled with the smells of yeasty bread and rich foods. Whenever I want something comforting, Francine's is my go-to place.

Carlos stands up at a table across the room as soon as he sees me. He smiles broadly, and I notice he has dimples. Oh my God, I think as my heart does a stutter step, he's not just handsome, he's beautiful.

His dark brown, almost black, hair is short, but long enough on top that it has a little curl. There's a bit of scruff on his face, but it is well-trimmed, which lets me know it's intentional. His face is so sweet that without it, he would probably look much younger, like a college student.

When I get close, he puts his hand on my arm and draws me close to kiss me on the cheek. I think of my tussle with Kimmy before I left the house, and it makes me grin. He notices.

"What's that for?"

I tell him about what happened, and he's grinning now, too, his deep brown eyes dancing with mirth.

"So, hi!" I say.

"Hi. I'm glad you came."

"Me, too."

He puts a little bag on the table. "I brought you something."

I look at the bag and up at him, having flashbacks of Tai and how he seemed to think he could buy my affections. "Carlos, you didn't have to..."

He lifts his chin at the bag. "It's just something I thought you'd like."

I reach into the bag and pull out a tiny planter that is shaped to look like a person laying on their stomach, head propped up on their hands and feet kicked up behind. It's almost like someone daydreaming. The head is a bowl that holds a tiny succulent.

I laugh and put it on the table. "Oh, my goodness, it's adorable!" I look up at him. "Thank you!"

"You're welcome. My Tia Mari makes them."

"Tia means Aunt, right?"

"Si, yes," he replies.

"You're fluent in Spanish, Vietnamese, and English. Are there any other languages you speak?"

"A little bit of Cantonese, but not enough to even be considered a novice. Other than that, I speak body language, but that's it."

I know he's teasing, but I also know that body language and being able to read it is a legitimate skill.

"You'll have to teach me Spanish. It would come in handy at work."

"I will be happy to teach you Spanish. If you ask nicely, I'll even teach you all the curse words."

I laugh. "I might need to know them so I can tell when my patients aren't happy with me."

I shouldn't have been nervous about talking with Carlos; he is quite adept at keeping the conversation going. He's also kind of funny and likes to tease. We delve into family and work more and he has me laughing like a loon, with some stories from when he was a rookie patrol officer.

My sides are starting to hurt from laughing so much. I can't remember the last time I had so much fun and laughed like this.

After my experience with Tai, I really like that Carlos gives as much information as he gets. It's a bit of a surprise since I was engaged to be married just a couple of weeks ago that I'm enjoying the company of another man. Does that make me a bad person?

Or is it just a sign of how oblivious I was to my own feelings about Tai? That thought makes me feel stupid. Stupid and guilty because Tai had no idea that I wasn't right there with him on the love you forever boat. The idea that I have hurt him fills me with guilt. I never meant to lead him on.

Carlos and Tai are night and day in so many ways. I like Carlos. He's so easygoing and down to earth and the fact that I'm sitting here in scrubs and ratty tennis shoes doesn't seem to bother him at all.

Tai always acted like my appearance was a reflection of him and hated it when I was dressed for work in my scrubs. He especially hated it if he found me with no makeup on and my hair pulled up in a less than perfect bun or ponytail. He was always dressed to impress and even when he was casual, his jeans were designer, and his shirts were tailored.

Carlos has on an old pair of faded Levi's and a t-shirt with a pair of work boots that look like they've seen plenty of work. Not that I'm complaining, though. The tee is just tight enough to show off some serious time spent in the gym. And his trapezius...oh my God.

I wonder if his jeans fit his butt as well as the tee fits his pecs. Realizing Carlos isn't speaking any longer, I look up. He's grinning at me with his dimples on full display and eyes full of laughter.

My face flames with heat. "I'm sorry. What was that?"

"I'd like to know what you were thinking just now. The look on your face was...intriguing."

I didn't think I could get anymore embarrassed, but the heat crawls up to my hairline and down my neck. "Nothing. Absolutely nothing."

"Liar," he teases.

I check my watch. "Oh, my! Look at the time."

He narrows his eyes at me, not losing his wicked grin. I like that grin. It makes me want to lean in and bite his lip as I kiss him.

What the actual crap? Why am I having thoughts about kissing this man, much less biting him on his lip or his shoulder or anywhere else, for that matter? What is wrong with me?

I hear Carlos chuckle through the sound of my heart pounding. It is getting late, and I need to get to the hospital before I tackle him to the ground, so I look around for our server.

"I need to get my check," I say, trying to get back to some semblance of normal.

"I took care of it."

"What?" My eyes snap to him. He's still grinning that evil, wicked, sexy grin at me.

"While you were...um...lost in thought, I took care of it."

Now I really am embarrassed. "I'm so sorry. You didn't have to do that. I'll be happy to pay for mine."

"Nope," he says. The grin is more relaxed now, but still there.

"Well, thank you, then. I wasn't intending to get a free lunch when I agreed to meet you today."

He leans in, putting an elbow on the table and resting his chin on his hand. "You're welcome. So, are you going to tell me what you were thinking so hard about?"

I meet his eyes hold his gaze as I reply with a voice gone husky, "No, I'm not, but maybe one of these days I'll show you."

Chapter 15

Carlos

She looks me in the eye and says, "No, I'm not, but maybe one of these days I'll show you."

Her voice is low and sounds so fucking sexy that my dick decides he wants to explore every inch of the insides of this woman. I quirk an eyebrow, and reply, "I hope that day comes soon."

She grips her bottom lip between white teeth and tilts her head down so she's looking up at me through her lashes. Holy fuck. This woman comes off all sweet and nice, but it would appear that underneath, she's got a naughty side, too. Getting to know her is going to be all kinds of fun.

When Ford first told me about her, all I could see was a potential connection to Dang. However, the instant I saw her at Ford and Cait's, I was drawn to her. After hearing her story, everything but wanting to be close to her went out the window. Then, when she showed us the bruises around her neck, I wanted nothing more than to hunt Tai Dang down and put him six feet under so he could never hurt her again.

Her eyes flick to her watch again. "Oh my gosh, I've really got to go."

She stands up and reaches for her coat, but I already have it in hand, holding it out for her to slip into. Once she's gathered up her things, I have my own coat on and follow her out the door. I open her car door and she sets the bag with her plant on the seat and turns to me.

"Carlos, thank you so much. I love my plant and it was so nice of you to buy. It was fun spending some time with you."

"We'll have to do it again soon," I say.

I'm pleased when she nods emphatically and says, "Yes, I'd like that."

Leaning in, I kiss her on the cheek and say, "Have a good night at work, Alicia."

I watch her car until she pulls out of the parking lot in the direction of the hospital several blocks away. Her car is an older Toyota sedan, the same one she was driving last night. I don't know what I was expecting, but somehow, I was thinking that she'd be driving something fancy that Dang bought for her.

Just the thought of him starts to piss me off again. I can't believe that asshole had his hands on her. They were together for over a year, and it seems clear she's no virgin, so he touched her body all over. How could he do that, then put his hands on her in violence?

She said she didn't love him. I'm glad about that. He doesn't deserve someone like her. Hell, I don't deserve someone like her.

The surgeon and the cop. That sounds like a disaster waiting to happen. An image of Ford and Cait in the kitchen last night comes to mind. The socialite and the cop would have seemed like just as unlikely a match, but matched they are.

They're great together. It's undeniable. I'm drawn to Alicia; that's also undeniable, so I'm just going to keep moving forward, taking my time, and getting to know her.

She's definitely not like the other women I've dated. If you can call it dating. Anything that lasted more than just one night was still driven mostly by satisfying carnal needs.

I have no doubt that Alicia could satisfy those needs, but she deserves someone who can take care of her, too. She's been carrying a heavy weight on her shoulders since her father passed away, and it's a testament to her fortitude that she didn't crack under the pressure.

Her car disappears around the corner a couple of blocks away and I'm pulled out of my thoughts. I'm on my way back home when my phone rings. I check the display and see that it's Ford, so I answer the call. "Hey, I'm driving."

Ford's voice comes through the car's speakers. "Just wanted to let you know that I checked my email and some of the forensics came through late yesterday. I'm headed into the office to take a look."

"I'm on my way; I'll meet you there."

"See you there," he says, and the call disconnects.

By the time I get to the office, Ford is already there. He's looking at something on his computer screen.

"Whadda we got?" I ask as I walk in.

"We've got IDs on two of the four." He turns and looks at me. "One of them is Julio Cardena."

My steps falter for a moment. Julio Cardena is the leader of the Grande Barrio Centrale, or GBC.

"And the other?"

"Ramon Esquivel," Ford says. "The remaining two have GBC tats but aren't in the system."

I whistle. Ramon Esquivel was believed to be Cardena's second in command here in the City. "So, GBC's two top dogs are knocked off at once. I can't believe they both showed up at the same meeting."

"Me either."

"There's going to be an uptick in violence in their turf as they try to fill the vacuum. No priors on the others doesn't mean anything, though. They could have just come up from Mexico the day before."

Ford nods and sighs. "Yeah. It's gonna be a mess."

"Did you get anything else from forensics?"

"All four men were strapped with nine mils that they never pulled. All the casings that were found on site were likely from ARs."

"What if Dang set up a meeting with the GBC? He brings three guys and tells the GBC to bring four guys. They talk about whatever deal they're both going after and when the GBC refuse to back down, Dang has extra men who came after everyone had arrived and they step in and gun down the GBC crew with ARs. There was nowhere to hide and a whole lot of guns between them and the exit, so the GBCs went down in a hail of bullets before they could even draw their own weapons."

Ford sits for a few minutes staring into space. "So, you're wrapping in what Alicia told you that Dang told her. It's plausible, but don't let it stick in your head. We have to follow the evidence to let us know what happened. If you get a story too settled in your head, you'll start looking for evidence that supports the story and possibly ignoring something important just because it doesn't support the narrative."

"I know, I know. It works, though."

"It does. Ballistics is still going through the bullets pulled from the scene and so far there are at least four different shooters. Based upon the trajectories, the shooters were spread out in front of the victims in an arc as they fired."

"Execution by firing squad," I breathe.

"Seems like. Anyway, that's it so far. It's going to take them a while to get through everything, but they wanted to send me what they had so far."

Ford shuts down his computer and pushes up out of his chair.

"You headed back home?"

"Yeah. I've got some hot tub time scheduled with my lady, then two massage therapists are coming over to do a couple's massage."

"Nice." I wait as he puts his coat on. "If you don't mind me asking, how did you two meet?"

Ford chuckles. "At the gym."

"Really?"

"Yeah. She is the whole reason I joined. She was there when they were giving me the tour and I was instantly infatuated. I'd catch sight of her from time to time, but I never approached her because she had a very prominent diamond on her left hand. Although I didn't understand it, despite the diamond, I felt drawn to her."

I hold the door open for him to pass through.

"Then one day, we ended up working out very close to each other and said a few words. Her ring was gone. I was on my way out after the workout, and she literally ran into me. I walked her to her car."

"Let me guess, you ran her plate."

He chuckles. "Yeah, I sure did and saw that her address was in Gaillardia. I convinced myself that she was way out of my league, then the next morning, the desk Sergeant tells me there was a 415 call out to the same address. So, I went to check on her and as soon as I saw the blossoming black eye, something in me clicked and I desperately needed to protect her. Then she fed me breakfast, and I decided I would keep her forever for just her food."

"Sounds like love at first sight."

"Nah, I wouldn't say that, but it was fast, for sure." He pauses for a few minutes as we make our way downstairs. "You know, I married my college sweetheart. She hated the City and hated me being a cop, so we split after a few years. We were just kids, but I thought she was the love of my life. What I felt for Cait after just a couple of weeks was light years beyond anything I'd ever felt for my wife."

We stop in front of his car.

"And it's good?"

"It is beyond good, more like fucking fantastic. She's incredible and I have no idea what I did to deserve her, but I thank God every day for her. Anyone on the outside would say we're completely mismatched, but we're so well suited that I can't imagine my life without her."

"Well, I'll let you get home to her," I say.

I think about what Ford said about having a need to protect Cait. It's very much like what my dad said about Mom. Also, very much like what I felt when Alicia showed us her neck last night.

Whatever the universe is up to with all this, I'm intrigued to see where it goes. If I end up in something even half as great as what my mom and dad had or what Ford and Cait have, I'd be a fortunate man. Mismatched or not, the surgeon and the cop is starting to have a nice ring to it.

My plan for the next encounter with Dr. Pham is already coming together.

Chapter 16

Alicia

I drive away from the restaurant and don't even try to wipe the goofy grin off my face. Carlos had me laughing so hard at lunch. I never laughed with Tai. There were plenty of smiles, a few chuckles here and there, but he never made me laugh.

The thought of smiles makes me picture Carlos grinning at me with those dimples. Just that tiny bit of remembrance makes my skin prickle with heat and my nipples tighten. I swear I think those dimples put a spell on my ovaries.

I park and step out of the car, thankful for the crisp air of the day that cools my skin. A gust of chilly wind tips the balance the other way and I'm rushing toward the entrance to the hospital when I'm stopped by someone grabbing my arm. I'm spun around to face the person.

To face Tai.

His face is a hard mask. "Do you really think you can break up with me over the phone and just send the ring back in a box? You said you wanted me to show you who I am, so I let you have a peek into my world and the next day you're off whoring around with another man."

"I tried to talk to you face to face, but you blew me off. You didn't let me peek into your world…" I look around to make sure no one is close. "You involved me in something that could torpedo the career I've spent over a decade working for."

"And I told you that you don't need a career."

"That right there shows you don't know me at all. You don't know me. I don't know you. We had fun for a year, but it's over now. There, I've told you face to face. We're through, Tai. I'm glad you got the jewelry, but like I said, if you want me to return the other stuff, I'll be happy to. Otherwise, I'll donate it."

I turn to walk away, but he grabs my arm again.

"Dr. Pham. Are you all right?"

I look up to see Chester, one of our security team, pointedly looking at Tai's hand on my arm.

"Yes, Chester, I'm fine. Thank you." I jerk my arm away from Tai and go inside.

"This isn't over," Tai says to my retreating back.

"Yes, it is!" I call back without turning around.

I make my way upstairs wondering how Tai knew when I was due at work and how on earth he knew I'd been with another man. His use of the term 'whore' is more insight into his personality. His true personality. The fact that he said it isn't over after I've told him repeatedly that I don't want to see him anymore worries me.

I wonder what it takes to get a protective order. Although I don't have any idea, I know a couple of someones who probably do.

My paperwork is done, and I have a little bit of time before I need to start rounds, so I take my phone and close myself into one of the storage closets so my conversation can be private. Hospitals have way too many big ears with big mouths lurking around.

"Miss me already?" Carlos asks by way of answering his phone.

"Did you leave?" I tease right back.

"Ouch. I guess I'll have to work harder to make an impression."

Daaaanng. Any more of an impression and he's going to have me biting that shoulder of his.

Not trusting my mouth to say something non-sexual, I chuckle.

"I thought you were going to work," he says.

"I am at work but had a few minutes before I need to start rounds and needed to ask you a question."

"What's up?"

"How hard is it to get a protective order?"

"Did something happen?" His voice has gone sharp.

I tell him about Tai stopping me as I was on my way into work and his parting remark. Although I hesitate for the briefest of moments to tell him about the whore comment, I go ahead and tell him. He says something in Spanish that I don't understand.

"You really need to teach me Spanish," I say.

"You don't want to know what I said."

"Hmm…it seems to me that earlier today you promised to teach me all the bad words."

He chuckles. "You've got me there."

It only takes a minute for him to walk me through the process of getting an order in place. I'm not sure I want to do it yet; I think it might piss Tai off, but the threat of filing one might be more effective. He's so appearance focused that the thought of having something filed in the court system would be a stronger deterrent than actually filing it.

"So, what are you doing now?" I ask.

"Heading to the gym."

"What are you wearing?"

He chuckles again. "Pervert. I'm wearing jeans and a tee. It's too cold for my workout clothes, so I'll change at the gym."

"It's all your fault…well, the fault of your trapezius, anyway."

"My what?"

"Never mind. Unfortunately, I have to go start my rounds. Have fun working out, Carlos."

"Text me when you get home, so I know you made it safely. Have a good night, Alicia."

The goofy grin returns.

I walk out of the storage closet and almost plow into someone coming down the hall. "Oh, I'm so sorry!"

"For someone so small, you're quite the steamroller," the woman laughs.

"Nicole? What are you doing here? I thought you moved to Tulsa."

"I did. I'm just here today for some meetings. Are you on rounds tonight? If so, when's your break? We need to catch up."

"I usually break around seven. It makes the end of the night go more quickly and when I return, half the people are asleep, anyway."

She chuckles. "So true. I'll come back at seven and bring some Thai. You still like Penang curry?"

"I do, but you don't need to do that."

"I know, but I want to. I'll see you at seven."

Gee, I'm getting two free meals in one day. First from a handsome man and now from an old friend. It will be good to catch up with Nicole.

Nicole Webb was also an orthopedic surgical resident and completed the program last spring. She moved to Tulsa after being offered a position at an orthopedic hospital there, so I hadn't seen her in a while. As I make my way to check in with the nurse's station to let them know I am on the floor, I try to remember the last time I'd seen her.

I think the last time I saw her was over the summer. Yes, I was out with Tai at some charity function or another. It seemed like we went to one just about every month. She was also attending with a date and the four of us ended up sitting at a table and visiting for a while.

Tai and her date didn't talk much, but she and I did most of it. I can remember Tai making some excuse about needing to go, so I said my goodbyes to Nicole and her date, and we left. It seems so obvious in my memory now, but Tai seemed almost irritated that I'd spent so much time talking with a friend instead of keeping him at the center of my attention.

A little before seven, my phone buzzes and I see a text message from Nicole letting me know she's downstairs. I'm at a good stopping point, so I let the nurses know I'm going on break and head down to the dining area.

Finding Nicole is easy. There aren't many other Nordic goddesses hanging around down here at this time of night. That's how I always thought of her. Nicole reminds me of that model, Claudia Schiffer, tall, blond, and robust. She waves when she sees me coming.

She looks great, so I tell her. "You look great! The new gig must really agree with you."

"It does," she replies. "It also helps when you can go from working eighty or ninety hours a week to just working sixty or seventy. You know, being able to get fresh air and sunshine, exercise and eat regularly, those kinds of things."

"Yeah. Sometimes I feel like a vampire because I rarely see the sun."

She laughs and starts pulling out food. We sit down and start opening containers.

"Tell me all about the new job," I say.

She shrugs. "It's a lot like the program was, just heavier on the surgeries and lighter on the rounds."

"You still happy you focused on hands?"

"Absolutely. I like the challenge of the intricacy of hands."

I nod. "I couldn't decide on one thing, so I've stuck to general ortho and get to see a little bit of everything. The variety is wonderful for me, but I get what you're saying about hands. I've done a few, and it is very detailed work. It requires a very intense level of focus."

"Yes, it does."

We eat for a bit. She knows from experience that I don't get a long break, so there's not much time to dawdle.

"I heard you got engaged," she says.

"Yes," I say with a sigh.

"That doesn't sound good."

"I'm always amazed at how quickly news spreads. I was only engaged for about a little over a week before I decided it was a bad idea."

"What happened?""When he asked, it was that whole pressure of the moment thing, so I said yes, but honestly, I was completely surprised. It never occurred to me that we were even close to that point. Once I had a minute to think, I realized it was a bad idea."

"It's probably a good thing, then." She takes a few more bites, then continues. "There's something I need to tell you."

I look up at her to see she's eyeing me cautiously.

"What's that?"

"My brother was in from Chicago the week before Christmas. He was staying at a hotel because, well, he's a weirdo and has a thing about staying in other people's homes. Anyway, we were having dinner at his hotel the night before he was due to fly out."

She pauses as if she's considering how much to tell me about whatever it is.

"It's okay, whatever it is, just tell me."

She nods. "I saw your boyfriend. What's his name, Tai?"

"Yes. He went to Tulsa the week before Christmas for a few days on business."

"Well, he might have been there for business, but he was having some playtime, too."

I tilt my head, not sure what she means.

She goes on. "He was in the restaurant with a woman and they were quite...friendly." She pulls out her phone and fiddles with it for a moment. "At first I wasn't sure it was him, so I took some pictures."

She places her phone on the table and on it is what she said it would be: a photo of Tai with a woman in a restaurant. "There are several, so keep scrolling."

I do. There are several of them in the restaurant, holding hands, sharing intimate looks, leaning in close. Then they get up from the table and walk out, Tai's hand on the small of her back.

The woman is of medium height with red hair and curvy all over, including extremely generous breasts. She's the complete opposite of me. Well, except for the hair, makeup, and dress that are presented exactly to Tai's liking.

The next picture is of them in a hallway.

"It was completely unplanned, but somehow, we got onto the same elevator. I'm not sure if they stopped at the bar for one more drink before going up to the room or what because we lingered at our meal for a bit before leaving the restaurant."

I scroll to the next photo. It shows Tai with the woman pushed up against the door, his hand gripping her breast. Her head is tilted back, exposing her neck as if his other hand is pulling her hair. It probably is. He used to do that to me.

A few more photos and they disappear into the room.

"I'm sorry," Nicole says.

"You know, I'm not even hurt," I reply with a shrug. "A little pissed that he would cheat on me, but based on what I've found out the past few weeks, it's not surprising."

"I was going to tell you right after Christmas, but things got busy and then, it was after New Year's and I heard you were engaged, so I kept it to myself."

"It's really okay. I understand it's hard to think you might be the person to throw a monkey wrench into someone else's life, but I promise, I'm fine. Really glad you told me, too. Would you mind sending those to my phone?"

"I don't mind at all and will send them right away. As for now, I know your break's about over, so let me clean up."

"Thanks. It was so good seeing you; we'll have to get together sometime. If not soon, once I'm done with the program, we'll make a point to."

"It's a deal," she replies. We both stand and I give her a hug.

"Thanks again for dinner, Nicole. I'm really glad to see you doing so well."

"You're welcome."

I give her a little wave and race back up the stairs to my floor.

Chapter 17

Carlos

The house is quiet and mostly dark as I'm sitting in the living room with the television on, reading a book. My phone pings with an incoming text. It's odd to be home alone, but Mom decided she wanted to go to church this morning and back again tonight. I'm glad to see her getting out more.

She used to be very involved in her church even though Dad and I didn't often go with her, but after Dad died, she stayed shut in so much that I worried about her. I worried so much that I pretty much just showed up on her doorstep and started packing her things.

Once I moved her in with me, I'd make a point to get her out when I could. When I accidentally on purpose messed up her grocery list, she insisted on going to the store with me. On a few occasions, she would let me coax her into going to the park for a walk. She didn't return to church, though.

About six months ago, she started going once a month or so, but never for more than the morning service. I know grief takes time to heal and maybe she's starting to come out of hers. At least I can hope.

I check my phone to see it's about nine o'clock and the text is from Alicia telling me she's home with an emoji blowing a raspberry. That makes me laugh. I send her one back, seeing if she wants to talk. My phone rings almost immediately.

"Hi," I say.

"Hi."

"How was work?"

"Good. It was a calm night tonight. Right after I hung up with you, I was coming out of the closet I'd gone into for privacy and literally ran into a friend of mine."

"That's cool."

"Yeah. I got a free dinner out of it, too," she says, sounding proud.

"Two free meals in a matter of hours. It must be your lucky day."

She hesitates for a moment. "Well, the free food was lucky, but she gave me some news that was, well, not necessarily bad, but not good either. It just confirmed that I've made the right decision."

She goes on to tell me about her friend seeing Tai and the woman in the hotel. Not only did she see them, but she had the photographic evidence to support her story.

"I'm sorry Alicia."

"Like I said. Good decision." She pauses for a moment. "I guess I should probably get some bloodwork done."

"Are you concerned?"

"Only slightly. We were usually very careful, but weren't perfect, so there's a chance. Better to know for sure and be safe rather than assume. We're tested fairly frequently anyway because of work and I'm about due, anyway. So how was your workout?"

"Good. Tiring. I had a lot of energy to burn off today."

"Is that so?"

It may be a total fabrication of my mind, but I picture her biting her bottom lip again.

"It is."

"What are you doing now?"

"Reading."

"What are you reading?"

"It's a story about a girl who has vowed to avenge her murdered parents and brother."

"Real world or fabricated?"

She seems completely unsurprised that I would crack a book to read for pleasure. A lot of women I've dated are, as if the fact that I'm a cop didn't take a lot of brain power, much less the college degree I earned.

"Fabricated. I get enough of real-world murder and mayhem at work."

"I can see how that would be." She sighs. "I miss reading for pleasure."

We spend several minutes talking about books and favorite authors, and I'm surprised by some of her choices.

"What are you doing right now?"

"Lying in bed talking to you."

"What are you wearing?"

She laughs. "Pervert."

"Absolutely, especially when it comes to you."

"This is kind of weird, isn't it?"

I frown, not sure what she means.

"What's weird?"

"I mean, not counting our brief first meeting at the grocery store, I've only known you for a little over twenty-four hours, but I feel strangely connected to you."

"Oh that. That's just my natural machismo luring you in."

She laughs. "Is that so?"

"Yep. Give me another week and you'll be swooning for me."

"Swooning?" She's laughing in earnest now.

"That's right. Fainting at my feet from overwhelming attraction."

Her laugh turns to a giggle that makes something deep inside of me turn loose. Something that was wound a little too tightly. That I didn't even realize was there.

My voice is less playful when I reply. "I feel it, too."

Her laughter trails off. When she speaks, it's so quiet I can barely hear her. "I like it, though."

"Yeah, me, too." The admission surprises me. I'm usually one that keeps his cards close to his chest. "What's your schedule like this week?"

"Monday and Tuesday are long days. Wednesday, I have a morning surgery and afternoon rounds. Thursday is another long day. As of right now, I'm done at four-thirty on Friday. Saturday is like today, paperwork and evening rounds. Sunday, as of right now, is supposed to be a day off."

"What does long day mean?"

"Two or three surgeries during the day, usually starting early and evening rounds. Fourteen- or fifteen-hour days."

"Wow, those are long. I'm thinking that with our schedules, we take it a couple of days at a time."

She sucks in a breath. "Are you saying you want to see me again?"

"How else am I going to have you swooning?"

"True. Extended machismo exposure is probably integral to your effectiveness."

"Exactly. As of right now, I'm off Wednesday evening, too. How about you come over here for pizza and a movie? You can even be comfortable and wear those cute little yoga pants you had on in the grocery store."

"Pervert," she says again, and I can hear the smile back in her voice.

I repeat myself, too. "Especially when it comes to you."

Chapter 18

Alicia

I take a deep breath before I knock on Carlos' door. He opens it a minute later, and it's all I can do to keep my mouth from dropping open because he's pulling on a shirt giving me a quick glimpse of a great expanse of sculpted man flesh including the hard v of muscle from his transversus abdominis disappearing into the waistband of his jeans hanging low on his hips.

Tai had a sculpted body, too. He was focused on bulk and breadth while Carlos is leaner, but no less ripped. While Tai was pretty to look at, he'd never affected me like this. This is something visceral.

"Sorry. I just got back from the gym and grabbed a quick shower, Carlos says, pulling his shirt into place. " Please, come in."

Act cool and keep that mouth closed so you don't drool.

"No worries," I reply with a shrug, doing my best to appear unaffected.

I step inside, looking around at the room as I toe my shoes off and leave them by the door. Carlos takes my coat and hangs it in the closet nearby. Carlos' house is a brick Tudor in a trendy area near Edgemere Park. For some reason, I expected him to live in some ultra-modern ranch. That's the kind of thing a lot of men seem to like.

Now that I see it, this actually suits him. Someone updated it with modern finishes while retaining the character of the original architecture. It's nice.

"What do you have there?" He asks, motioning to the dish in my hand.

"Oh! Brownies. I made brownies. You know, for after the pizza."

"Excellent. I have a weakness for chocolate."

He takes the dish from me, and I follow him to the kitchen. It has been updated with sleek modern appliances, new cabinets and some kind of composite countertops.

"Your house is nice."

"Thanks. I still have a little work to do, but since Mom moved in, I can't work on it like I used to. Having a saw or nail gun going after nine tends to make her a little cranky."

"You did the remodel?"

He sets the dish on the counter and looks at me.

"Yeah. One of my uncles does remodeling and maintenance work around the City. I worked for him throughout high school and summers during college, so I learned a little bit of everything. For a while after I graduated, I was buying a house every year. I'd get a property with good bones and do the remodel myself and flip it for a healthy profit. I've been in this one for a few years now. It's the longest I've ever stayed in one house since I moved out on my own."

"Wow. I'm impressed."

He shrugs, almost embarrassed, it seems. "Thanks. Come on, I'll show you around."

The more he shows me, the more impressed I am. Carlos is definitely a man of many facets and talents.

"Where's your mom?"

"Church, so she'll be home in a few hours."

"Are you religious, too?"

"Kinda."

"How are you kind of religious?"

He gives me another one of those shy shrugs.

"Mom and Dad went to a Catholic church. I went to Catholic school for grade school but transitioned to public school in Junior High. I've grown up with God, but I can't say I buy in whole-heartedly with organized religion. There are too many abuses and I have always had a problem with using God as an excuse for bigotry."

I nod. "I understand. My dad didn't do the whole church thing for a lot of the same reasons. My grandmother's father was an atheist, but from the time she was a pre-teen, she lived with sort of a foster family that was Buddhist."

"How did she end up with sort of a foster family?"

I tell him the story of how Bà came to America.

"Mom's family also came here through Operation New Life. It's amazing to think how many of the Vietnamese population here in the City did," he says. "Okay. Down to business. What kind of pizza do you like?"

A half hour later, we're sitting on his sofa watching a movie, eating pizza, and drinking beer. We chose a movie that's a kind of a dramedy with a tiny bit of action mixed in. We're sitting at opposite ends of the sofa, but once I'm finished eating, I sit back and sneak glances over at him.

His face is very animated as he watches the movie and I find watching him to be more entertaining than the film. He looks over and catches me watching him. I turn my face back to the television but am not completely successful at hiding my smile. Even out of the corner of my eye, I can see him smirking.

"You finished eating?" he asks.

"Yes."

He starts to gather up the remains of our meal, so I get up to help him. "Sit back; you're a guest."

I ignore him and continue to help clean up. He picks up the remote and pauses the movie. When everything is put away, I excuse myself to go to the bathroom.

I'd forgotten that beer runs right through me without the courtesy of a decent buzz unless I drink a lot of it. The unfortunate thing about drinking a lot of it, besides all that peeing, of course, is that it usually leaves me with a headache.

When I get back to the living room, Carlos is sitting in the middle of the sofa instead of one end and eating a brownie. There is also a brownie on a small plate sitting on the coffee table beside a glass of milk. I plop down on the sofa next to him.

"Decided to move, huh?"

"If you tell me to move back, I will."

"Nah. We've already wasted a lot of quality snuggling time."

He chokes on his milk and coughs. I pound him on the back a few times until he gets his breath, then sit down to eat my brownie and drink my milk, smiling to myself.

We're sitting close, but there's still a space between us. Once I finish eating, I take our empty glasses and plates to the kitchen and run water over them.

I come back and grab a throw blanket off one of the side chairs and resume my seat next to him, arranging the blanket over my legs.

"Cold?" he asks.

"A little."

He lifts his arm and puts it around my shoulders, pulling me to his side. I lean into him and all his warmth.

"Better?"

"Much," I answer with a sigh, then pull my legs up and tuck them under the blanket next to me. This pushes me even deeper into his side.

He smells good, but it's not like any cologne I've ever smelled. I close my eyes and inhale, his scent filling my senses. For several minutes, I sit there, letting him surround me.

I'll bet if he kissed me right now, he'd taste like chocolate. Just the thought of it makes my blood warm and my core heat. He has such nice lips that look like they'd be really soft.

His hand reaches up and tucks my head against his chest. He kisses the top of my head.

"Hey, baby, you need to wake up," Carlos says quietly.

Bleary-eyed, I try to sit up. "What?"

I'm no longer just sitting next to Carlos. He has leaned over, and I'm draped on top of him for the most part, with my hand resting over his heart. Understanding dawns, and I try to scramble off him.

Holy crap! What am I doing? I'm so embarrassed.

"Sorry," I say. I wipe my mouth, wondering if I drooled on him. "How long have I been asleep?"

He pulls me back into his arms. "Hush. You were tired."

"Yeah, but that kind of makes me a lousy date."

"Nah. I enjoyed having you all snuggled up against me. Plus, you talk in your sleep, so I found out all kinds of juicy things about you."

"No, I don't!"

"No, you don't," he confirms with a grin. "I kept hoping, though."

I swat him with my hand without strength or heat and leave my hand on his hard stomach.

"Although I wish I could just stay here like this, I'd better go home. I have an early surgery tomorrow."

"I know, that's why I woke you," he says, "but I'm looking forward to being able to hold you all night."

A thrill zings through me at his words. I don't want to move, but he saves me from having to try to find the strength to pull away from him. He moves and shifts me off him, then stands, pulling me up with him.

"Are you going to be okay to drive?" he asks.

I stifle a yawn and nod. "Yeah. As you know, it's not that far. I'll be fine."

Once I'm shod and have my coat, he walks me to my car and opens the door for me. He pulls me into a hug, and I wrap my arms around his waist. The strong beat of his heart pulses in my ear as I press my cheek against his chest.

God, he feels good.

"Thanks for inviting me over and sorry again for being such lousy company."

He kisses the top of my head.

"Hush. You're welcome to come over here and lay all over me anytime you want. Text me when you get home, so I know you made it safe."

I smile. "I will."

Chapter 19

Carlos

The photo Ford showed me of Alicia all dolled up didn't come close to doing her justice. When she opens the door wearing a sapphire blue form fitting dress, I have to pick my jaw up off the floor. I'm so tongue tied that she speaks first.

"You look handsome."

I know she's being completely sincere, but look down at my suit, knowing it doesn't compare to her. She is stunning. Like stepped out of the pages of a magazine stunning.

"Baby, you look gorgeous."

She looks away, smiling shyly. "Thank you."

How can she not realize how beautiful she is?

I offer her my hand and lead her to the car. I'm not sure what to make of where we're going tonight, but I'll roll with it to spend time with Alicia. It's some kind of fundraiser where Masters Construction purchased a table.

The pregnant friend, Ella, has been put on bedrest for the remainder of her pregnancy, so Demi and Kellen offered Alicia the tickets that wouldn't be used otherwise. When she asked me if I wanted to go, I said yes without hesitation, just because it would allow me to be with her for a few hours. I never thought I'd find someone who worked more than I did.

She's told me she is interested in learning more about the world of philanthropy, so this will be an excellent opportunity for her. The Masters family is well off. From what Ford says, Cait is richer than God. This is definitely a new class of people for me, but if Ford can hang, I can, too.

I know that there's no way I could ever match up to the amount of money she will make as a surgeon, but I also know that the money isn't the motivating factor for her. She even seemed put off by Dang's overt extravagance. Although she may not need someone to take care of her financially, she definitely needs someone to take care of her.

The event is smaller than I thought it would be, but there are still plenty of people. We make a circuit of the room and I know she's looking for her friend, so I help. When I see them, I maneuver her that way.

I'm surprised at how nervous she seems. She has a death-grip on my hand as I lead her through the crowd. As soon as she sees Demi and Kellen, she relaxes.

I enjoy seeing these facets of her personality. When she's in familiar surroundings with familiar people, she's very confident and gregarious. But put her in an unfamiliar situation where she doesn't know someone, and she becomes quite shy and reserved. Me, I can bullshit my way through just about any type of situation.

We sit through a program by a comedian followed by a presentation by the organization putting on the event. None of us eat the food, but we do take advantage of the bar. Once the program is over, a band takes the stage and I see there is a dance floor up front.

Kellen and Demi don't hesitate to head for the floor.

"Do you want to dance?" I ask Alicia.

"Sure. I'm not very good, though."

I grin at her. "That's okay. I am; just follow my lead."

She turns out to be a better dancer than I expected based on her comment, and I'm enjoying leading her around the dance floor. At first, she was a little stiff, but was able to follow my steps really well and after a few songs, she's relaxed and moving more loosely.

That's another tidbit to tuck away. She's cautious at first, but learns and adapts quickly. A slow song comes on and I pull her close.

I lean down and whisper in her ear. "I thought you said you weren't very good."

"I know my limitations," she replies.

"Well, moving your body isn't one of them."

She shivers and it makes me wonder what she's thinking.

The song ends and Alicia's friends come over. "We're going to go. I'm starving, so we're going to go get something to eat. Do you all want to come?"

Alicia looks up at me. "Up to you," I tell her.

She bites her lip. "I am hungry."

Fucking adorable. "Then let's go."

I completely expected them to want to go to some fancy steakhouse, so I'm pleasantly surprised when they give me directions to a Mexican restaurant in the Plaza. We talk over tacos and drinks. I drink more from my water glass than from my beer since I'm driving.

Demi talks Alicia into trying a margarita with an assurance of, "They're really good here."

The glass they bring her is almost as big as her head.

I like her friends. They seem like good people and I'm glad to know she has good people in her life. We part ways with a promise to go dancing with them sometime.

I learn another thing about Alicia. She's a total lightweight when it comes to liquor. A giggle escapes her when she stumbles on the way to the car. I put a hand on her elbow to steady her.

Like I said, fucking adorable.

I open her door, but instead of getting into the car, she turns to face me. She slides her hands up the front of my shirt, around my neck, and presses her body against mine.

"I'd really like for you to kiss me," she says as she looks up at me. Her soft brown eyes are full of heat.

I put my hand to her delicate jaw and stroke a thumb across her cheekbone. "Baby, I think you're intoxicated."

She giggles again and puts a hand to her mouth as if she's astonished the sound came from her. Those fiery eyes go round just as another giggle bubbles out of her. "I think you might be right."

"Let me get you home." I try to maneuver her into the car, but she resists.

She strokes her hands across my chest again. If she keeps this up, I'm going to have to pick her up bodily and put her in the car before it gets out of hand. The woman is a temptation from head to toe, but is in no position to know what she's doing.

"Not until you kiss me. Kissing is fine, even if I am intoxicated. I wanted you to kiss me when I was sober at your house the other day, but I wasn't brave enough to tell you before I fell asleep," she divulges, under the influence of 80 proof truth serum and lime juice.

"Okay, fine." I lean down and give her a kiss on the forehead.

Her brows furrow, and while she's distracted, I bend down and take her off her feet to put her into the car. We only make it a few blocks before she goes quiet. I look over to see her eyes drooping. This woman needs to get more rest.

Instead of waking her, I take her keys from her bag and let myself into her house before going back and lifting her out of the car. Thankfully, her grandmother is still up and comes to meet us when the door opens. I whisper to her so as not to wake Alicia.

She shows me to Alicia's bedroom, and I gently lay her on the bed. I smooth the hair out of her face, then press another kiss to her forehead. She stirs and smiles up at me, a smile so pure and beautiful that it makes my heart squeeze.

At that moment, it all coalesces in my chest, and I don't know how it's possible after just having met her a couple of weeks ago. I haven't even kissed her yet, but I know this woman is mine.

Mine to care for.

Mine to protect.

Chapter 20

Alicia

C arlos and I are supposed to spend the entire day together today, but I am exhausted and just want to be lazy all day. We had a great time Friday night, and I was hoping to get to sleep in yesterday, but I got called in to cover a shift for someone who was sick besides my own shift. What was supposed to be a short day ended up being a very long one.

I'm just about to text him when my phone dings with a text from him.

Carlos: *Good morning, beautiful. Have some things to wrap up this morning at work. Should be done by lunch. How about you come over for lunch with Mom and me, then we can take it easy and just hang out?*

Me: *Good morning. Are you psychic?*

Carlos: *Nah. Just figure you needed something low key after the week you've had.*

Me: *I do. Thank you. Be safe.*

Carlos: *Always. See you in a few hours. XO*

I stare at my phone. XO. Hugs and kisses. I'd really like to hug and kiss him. And a lot more.

I'm about to set my phone back onto my nightstand when another text comes in.

Carlos: *Wear those yoga pants.*

I laugh out loud into the silence of my room.

Me: *Pervert.*

I'm relieved that he's not bothered by my need to spend a day recharging. It's refreshing to have someone who understands. Tai didn't.

If I ever had time off, he either made plans for us, or we didn't see each other. There was no lazing around the house together, just hanging out. Anytime I told him I needed some downtime to recover from a stressful week, he'd get irritated with me and give me the silent treatment for a few days.

Hindsight truly is so much clearer. I didn't recognize that pattern when I was in the midst of our relationship, but now it's clear as day. Looking back, there are so many signs that Tai and I were a disaster waiting to happen.

Although I would have much rather discovered it without having to go through that blow up that had him choking me, I'm glad I did. I'm also very glad his true nature was revealed before I kept going along with what he wanted right up to the altar.

I haven't heard from Tai since the night he stopped me on my way into the hospital. A big part of me is hopeful that he's gotten the message that we're over and he's going about his life. However, there's a niggling suspicion that I haven't seen the last of him.

There were lots of times when he'd go radio silent and ignore me for a week or more, so I can't be completely sure that his recent absence means he's gone for good. Putting away thoughts and worries about Tai, I roll out of bed and go in search of breakfast.

I arrive at Carlos' house with chocolate and some quality Vietnamese coffee courtesy of a few stops on the way over. This is the first time I will be officially meeting his mother, so I want to make a good impression. I've never met a man's parents before.

Well, technically, I'd met Tai's parents, but it's not the same thing. We were kids, and they were our neighbors. Other guys I dated never got that far.

I take a deep breath and ring the bell. Carlos answers the door but sadly I don't get a peepshow this time. However, the broad smile that has his dimples winking at me is almost as good. Almost.

"Hey," he says and leans in to kiss me on the cheek.

"Hi."

He looks down at the items in my hands and nods. In Vietnamese culture, it is considered rude to show up empty-handed when invited to someone's home, particularly when meeting the elders in the home. He might not expect me to bring anything when it's just him and me, but this is an important part of making a good first impression on his mom.

I toe off my shoes, leaving them by the door, and follow Carlos toward the kitchen. The house smells wonderful, like phở but with some different spices. There's the earthiness of phở but some tangy smells blended in that I can't identify. His mom is in the kitchen stirring a large pot on the stove and it causes my stomach to rumble.

Carlos speaks in Vietnamese. "Mom, I have someone I'd like you to meet."

Turning away from the stove, she wipes her hands on her apron. Although there has to be at least thirty years between them, I'm immediately reminded of my grandmother and approach this woman with the respect and care I'd expect someone to use with Bà.

"Mom, this is my friend Dr. Alicia Pham. Alicia, this is my mother, Linh Gutierrez.

I nod and hold out the gifts I brought and also speak in Vietnamese. "Mrs. Gutierrez, these are for you. It is wonderful to meet you. Thank you for inviting me into your home."

She smiles shyly and nods back, taking the gifts. I take care to keep my eyes on hers and not scrutinize the scar on her cheek. It's an old wound, but whomever treated it at the time did a less than spectacular job of stitching.

The delicious smell is from a pot of phở, one of my absolute favorite dishes, but it's not a typical phở. We sit down at the table together and I stir my bowl. The broth is red instead of clear and there is what looks to be hominy in it.

"It's Mom's invention; a blend of phở and Mexican pozole," Carlos says.

"If it tastes even half as good as it smells, it's going to be heavenly."

Carlos holds out his hand for mine on one side and his mother's on the other. He says a quick quiet grace over the food. This must be something he does for his mother because when it was just the two of us, he didn't pause for grace.

I wait for his mother to take the first bite, as is customary, but she waves at my bowl and says in Vietnamese, "Please, eat."

I take a bite and groan. "This is incredible."

We talk over the meal and his mom asks questions about my family, which I happily answer. She actually takes it pretty easy on me. As much as I love Bà, I know she's going to be a bear when she officially meets Carlos.

However, even though she's taking it easy on me, also like Bà, she doesn't give much away. I have no idea if I'm passing this test or not. I've never had a test I wasn't sure if I was passing and this one means so much.

What will I do if she doesn't like me? Would Carlos break things off with me, whatever this thing is we have going on? I really, really like him, but I have no idea how he feels about me. Meeting his mom has to mean something, right?

By the end of the meal, I still have no idea if I'm passing or failing. Carlos and I clean up and his mother excuses herself, saying she wants to go take a nap before going back to church. We move around each other in the kitchen, putting things away, rinsing dishes and putting them into the dishwasher.

I finish the dishes and lean against the counter as he puts the last of the leftovers into the refrigerator. He bends down, stretching his jeans tight across his butt. His very nice butt.

I wonder what it would feel like in my hand. Maybe it's hard muscle like his arms and I'd be able to feel the muscles flexing as he...

He steps in front of me, moving close. "What are you looking at?"

Looking up at him, he has a wicked grin on his face.

Oh my.

Getting caught ogling sets my face on fire.

He puts his hands on the counter on each side of me and leans in, his nose inches from mine. "Do you see something you like?" Humor dances in his dark eyes.

I put my palms on his chest and slide them up along the hard planes of muscles. "Yes, I do."

God, I love the feel of him. I love the way he likes to play even more.

Leaning in, I nuzzle his neck.

I love the way he smells.

I kiss him there, right above the collar of his t-shirt at the juncture of neck and shoulder. He puts his hands on my butt and boosts me up to sit on the counter, putting us face to face.

With gentle hands, he cups my jaw and gives me a little smile. "I'd like to kiss you, Alicia."

I bite my lip and nod, suddenly feeling shy.

He leans in slowly, as if giving me a chance to stop him. Little does he know that the last thing I want to do is stop him. I'm ready to hit the gas, not the brakes.

His lips are just as soft as I imagined them to be. He moves closer, wedging his hips between my spread legs. I put my arms around his neck and press my chest to his.

My nipples tighten at the contact. His tongue swipes between my lips and touches mine, sending a thrill through me. With hands on my hips, he pulls me against him, his body pressing against my core.

Everything inside of me turns to liquid heat. I hear a door open down the hall and another one open and close. Mrs. Gutierrez must be going to the bathroom. The thought of her walking in on us and ruining her opinion of me has me pulling away from Carlos.

If she's already having doubts about me, I don't want to give her a reason to go ahead and stamp me with a big red fail. That's if she hasn't already. I put a hand on his chest and apply a little pressure.

"I think we'd better cool it down until we're alone," I say.

He puts his forehead to mine. "Yeah, you're probably right."

One more quick kiss and he helps me down from my perch. We go to the living room, and he pulls the pillows off the back of the sofa, placing them on the floor.

"Wait here," he says, and disappears down the hall.

He returns with a couple of pillows and tosses them on one end of the sofa. Then he grabs the throw blanket I used last time and stretches out on the sofa, his back against the back of the sofa.

He unfurls the blanket and holds it up, inviting me in. "Come'ere."

I lay down in front of him, my back to his front, and rest my head on the pillows. He uses the remote to select something on the television, then lays it down in front of me. I relax back against him, feeling his warmth and scent surround me.

He strokes a hand up my thigh to my hip.

"I really like these pants," he says, his mouth near my ear.

I giggle and wiggle my hips against him. His hand grips my hip.

"Stop that. We're supposed to be good for the moment, and if you keep that up, I won't be able to keep my halo in place."

I sigh dramatically. "Okay."

His arm goes around me, and we settle in to watch the boob tube. My eyes start to feel heavy, as they always do whenever I lose inertia. After a few minutes, he slips his hand under the blanket and snakes it under my shirt to rest his palm on the bare skin of my stomach. A few minutes more and I hear him start to snore lightly as I doze off.

Fingers are stroking lazy circles on my abdomen, sending tendrils of tingles over my skin as I wake. The television is still on, and it seems like it might be the same program that was on as I was dozing off, so maybe I wasn't asleep that long. It's embarrassing to be perpetually falling asleep anytime I'm still for more than a few minutes.

"That feels fantastic," I say, my voice full of sleep and dreams.

"Hmmm..."

"How long did I sleep?"

"We both slept about an hour." He stops his stroking to pull my hair back and kisses my neck.

"Good, if you were asleep, too, I know I didn't divulge any secrets."

He chuckles as his fingers return to their work and lengthen their strokes, brushing up across one side of my rib cage, then circling just an inch or so below my bra to stroke down the other side. My eyes drift to the television. It's showing some sporting event.

Football, maybe. I'm completely hopeless when it comes to sports. Not that I could pay attention, anyway. Those fingers of his are distracting.

Carlos drags the tips of his fingers across my skin, scratching lightly with his short, manicured nails. Gooseflesh springs up in their wake and my pulse kicks up. When he circles around this time, he grazes the band of my bra. My nipples perk up at the promise of possible contact.

He circles down, extending his stroke to brush against the top of my pants. The upstroke circles over my bra to graze the bottoms of my breasts. Down he goes again, tucking his fingers beneath the waistband of my pants.

The tension in my body is ratcheting up as parts of me long to feel his touch. My nipples are achingly hard, and I can feel myself growing wet between my thighs. I wonder if he knows what he's doing to me.

He kisses my neck as his hand tracks down, dipping farther into the waist of my pants. My clit throbs with expectation, only to be denied as his stroke swings back up. His fingers trail across the swell of my breasts as he kisses below my ear.

I gasp and mewl, "Carlos, please."

"Please what, mi alma?"

He nuzzles my neck, making me shiver and my voice goes breathless. "Please touch me. You're driving me mad."

Another sweep down, tucking far enough into my pants to graze the top of my pubic bone and he sweeps out again, drawing a whimper out of me. Fingers brush up my rib cage, then, finally, his hand cups my breast and strokes a thumb over the hard peak straining against the thin fabric of my bra.

"Are you sure this is what you want?"

I know we kissed, really kissed, for the first time a few hours ago, but this attraction between us is like a black hole, the gravity of it irresistible. Every time I'm near him, I almost instantly become aroused. Heck, even just talking on the phone with him conjures up all kinds of lustful thoughts.

"Yes," I gasp as he tweaks the nipple gently. I turn my head and he leans over and kisses me as he molds and reshapes my breast. Then his hand pulls away and strokes down again.

I growl in frustration until his hand dips into my pants, cupping my sex. "Or is this what you want, mi alma?"

I roll onto my back and move my legs to give him better access. "Yes, touch me, please."

He grins down at me before lowering his head to mine and kissing me deep, licking his tongue into my mouth. His finger strokes circles around my opening as my hips keep time.

One long finger slides into me, pressing deep. It's soon joined by another. He buries them as far as he can and curls his fingertips. I gasp against his mouth as he finds the sensitive spot and teases it.

I feel the pressure building in my core, a slow boil picking up speed. My hips grind in time with those talented fingers. I'm getting close.

A door down the hallway opens and closes, then another opens and closes.

Holy crap. His mom is up. We need to stop!

I don't know if he didn't hear or just doesn't care, but Carlos isn't stopping. If anything, he's working harder. I push on his chest. All he does is smile against my mouth.

The Orgasm Express is hurtling down the tracks and if he doesn't stop, I'm going to scare the shit out of his mom when I scream as it enters the metaphorical station. I pull my mouth from his.

"Carlos," I hiss, "your mom."

A door opens and just as the click of its closure reaches my ears, the orgasm rips through me. Biting into his shoulder to keep from crying out, I let the waves pass over me. As soon as I am able, I roll so that I am facing front again so that by the time she makes the short walk down the hall, it looks like we're just lying there watching the game on television.

Nothing to see here. Continue on your way. Nothing to see.

Carlos moves his fingers still inside me. I flex my muscles to grip them and grit my teeth to keep from making any noise. My face is so hot it must be tomato red. I just hope she doesn't notice in the low light, but for all I know, my cheeks are glowing like embers.

"I'm going to church now. You two have a nice evening," she says as she passes through the room. Whether she realizes what we've been doing or not, she doesn't let on.

"You, too, Mom. I'll see you when you get home."

"Good night, Mrs. Gutierrez. It was nice to meet you." I say, trying to infuse some chipper into my voice.

She doesn't reply, just goes out the door and closes it behind her.

Fuck, she must know what we were doing.

I turn my face into the pillow and groan.

She probably thinks I'm a gigantic ho, but then I kind of am, aren't I? Making out with her son in the middle of the living room while she's in the house.

Chapter 21

Carlos

As soon as Mom's out the door, I'm kissing Alicia's neck again. She groans, but not in the breathy turned on way she has before.

"What's that for?"

"Oh nothing, only that your mom probably thinks I'm some skank who just orgasmed all over her couch with her only son. Definitely not a good first impression. I might as well have reject stamped on my forehead."

That makes me chuckle. "More like she's jumping for joy because there's a hope for grandbabies in her future."

She goes quiet for several long minutes, lost in thought. It must be something important whirring around in that big brain of hers because my kisses seem to be having no effect on her. I pull my hand away from her crotch, but leave it in her pants. Now that it's there, I can't fathom a reason to remove it.

"Do you want children?" she finally asks.

I stop and pay attention, getting the feeling that the answer is important to her. The memory surfaces of her saying that she broke it off with Tai Dang because they didn't really know each other. I definitely want her to know me.

Kids have always been a part of my future equation. However, some might call me selfish because I've never envisioned a huge brood of children. I loved the intimacy our family had with just the three of us. If I ever wanted company, I had dozens of cousins.

"Yeah, someday, maybe one or two, but not like tomorrow or anything. However, a lot of that will depend upon my partner."

She's quiet again.

"I don't think I'd be a very good mom."

I frown. She said it so quietly that I hope I heard her wrong.

"Why do you think that?"

"I've been Kimmy's guardian since she was three. Recently things have been good, but for most of the past ten years it seems like all we've done is fight with her regularly telling me how much she hates me. That doesn't give me much hope for any future children I might have."

"I don't think you can go by your relationship with Kimmy. She was in the midst of trauma when her parents walked away. Even though she was an infant, it had to affect her. Then, a second set of parents was removed from her life when she was three, with one of them still around physically, but absent in virtually every other way. That's a lot to deal with, but I know she loves you because you only act out to the degree she has with the people you love most. She's pushing you away so hard to make sure you won't leave, too."

She doesn't respond.

"Also, you've been completely overworked and overwhelmed for the past ten years. You had a tough choice at the time, but you made it and have done the best you could. When you finish your residency and your schedule smooths out, I think you're going to see a big change in things at home."

"Maybe. I fear it will be too little, too late, though."

"All kids claim to hate their parents at one time or another. It's a part of growing up and exploring boundaries. You're doing a good job."

After a few minutes of silence, she rolls in my arms to face me. I slide my hand around under her clothes to cup her ass, which fits nicely into the curve of my hand. God, I love these pants.

She grins at me. "Pervert."

I grin back. "It's these yoga pants. They're very conducive to a variety of things."

She rubs the tip of her nose with mine. "So, what do you want to do now?"

"I want to take you into my room and get you out of these pants and everything else, too."

She sucks in a breath, then kisses me. When she pulls away, her eyes are dark and heated. "I'd like that."

I like that she's not shy about her sexuality and having sexual desires. Not in a casual way, though. Nothing about her is casual. I don't want to be casual where she's concerned, so I have to be sure.

"Would you really?"

Her eyes lock with mine, and she speaks with certainty. "Yes."

I roll over her on elbows and knees without letting her feel my weight up onto my feet, then pull her up. She looks up at me with a smirk. "Wow. I'm not sure how you did that, but I'm impressed."

"You ain't seen nothin' yet," I reply, all cocky and teasing.

She laughs. I throw her over my shoulder like a caveman, and she laughs some more. The sound is beautiful.

As I take her to my cave, she reaches down and slides her hand into the back of my jeans, cupping my ass, and that makes me laugh. I push the door to my room open with a foot and the laughing stops.

She gives my butt a squeeze just before I toss her onto the bed. I crawl over her, hook my fingers in the waistband of her pants and pull them off along with her panties. Backing off the bed, I go lay her things over the back of a chair I like to sit in when I read.

When I turn around, she's crawling toward me on all fours, but stops when I undo my jeans and let them fall to the floor. Then she sits back on her haunches and just watches the show. I pull off my shirt, and she pulls hers off. Next, I push off my briefs and stand naked for her perusal.

A wicked smile quirks her lips as she reaches around to undo her bra, flinging it to the side when she pulls it off. God, she's beautiful. Her tits are small, but perfect and tipped with dusky pink peaks, her hard nipples begging to be sucked. When she leans forward to resume crawling toward me, I hold up a finger.

"Stop right there."

An eyebrow quirks, but she obeys. I put a knee onto the bed and crawl toward her. After a quick kiss to her lips, I flop onto my back, then shimmy up until my head is between her thighs. She giggles when I kiss the inside of one thigh, then the other.

When my fingers spread her pussy lips and lick the length of her slit from the rosebud of her ass to her hard pink clit. Her laughter turns to a moan. My intention had been only to put myself into a position to taste her, so I'm surprised when her small, strong hand wraps around the base of my dick.

I'm doubly surprised when a shockwave of sensation surges through me with the contact of her hot, wet tongue swirling around the head. Ay Dios mío, this woman might be perfect. My attention is turned back to the dripping wet cunt above me and I focus on licking, sucking, nipping and teasing every moan out of her I can.

She's moving her hips so much that I keep losing contact, so I wrap my hands around her to keep her still. When I hold her butt still, her mouth and hands take over the motion, stroking and sucking me faster.

I need to get to work because at the rate she's going, I'll be blowing my load in about two point five seconds. My lips wrap around her clit to give little pulsing sucks. She stops what she's doing.

I lave her with my tongue then give her that sucking move again.

"Carlos," she gasps.

I slide my thumb into her wet heat and slip the tip of a finger into her ass as I suck her again. All three connections moving in time seem to be doing it for her. She's still not moving and her thighs begin to shake.

Her free hand plants itself on my abs, her weight pressing down. I work my finger into her ass up to the first digit.

"Carlos," she gasps again and her hand on my stomach clenches into a fist.

I nip her clit gently, but firmly with my teeth and she breaks, her entire body going rigid for a moment before she begins to shake. She squeezes my dick so tight that it feels like she might break it off.

While I keep my grip on her hips, I kiss the insides of her thighs. As soon as her shaking subsides, she moves. "Condom," she demands as she swings around, going from straddling my face to straddling my hips.

When I reach toward the nightstand and can't quite reach, she impatiently climbs over me and grabs one from inside the drawer. A beautiful expanse of skin is stretched out above me, so I wrap my arms around her and start kissing and nipping at it.

Her weight shifts and I let her go, even though I don't want to. Her skin is so enticing I want to touch and taste her everywhere. She's back in position where she tears open the foil packet and rolls the condom over my shaft with nimble fingers.

I'm completely absorbed by the scene playing out before me as my body disappears into hers. When she starts to move, my attention is torn between watching where our bodies are connected and the expressions boiling across her face as her hips undulate.

The rhythm tells me again that when she says she can't dance, it's a lie. She's got more sensual moves than she realizes. In her gentle, unassuming manner lurks a goddess.

A tingling teases at the base of my spine so I lick the pad of my thumb and slip it between us, positioning it to worry her clit. Her eyes pop open and the grin she gives me is pure, unadulterated lasciviousness.

I grin back and hold her gaze as her eyes darken and turn molten. The skin around her lips tightens and her brow furrows. White teeth bite into her bottom lip before her mouth flies open. Her hands fall to my chest, and she digs her short nails into my skin.

One gasp, then two, and her entire body goes rigid. Her pussy squeezes me so tight I can't hold back any longer. I come so hard that I feel paralyzed for a moment.

When I can move again, I discover her limp form draped over me. My arms go around her, cradling her slight form against me.

The day she was put in my path was the luckiest day of my life.

Chapter 22

Alicia

Carlos and I stay in bed snuggling for a while, and I can't stop touching him. Tai liked for me to touch him while we were having sex, but once the act was done, he was done. He could touch me, but seemed indifferent when I showed him affection outside of a sex act.

Or in public, I realize now. He liked it when I fawned over him while others were watching, as if it would make him seem more desirable to others if I found him desirable. I don't know, and I really don't care anymore. Tai is in the past and that's where he needs to stay.

When I get out of bed to go to the restroom, I check my watch. It's getting late and Carlos' mom will probably be coming home soon. Instead of crawling back into bed with him like I want to, I set about finding my clothes.

"You ditching me?" he asks from where he's watching me propped on pillows with his hands locked behind his head. The crooked grin and teasing tone let me know he's not bothered, though.

"It's getting late and I'm sure your mom will be home soon. Plus, I know you have work in the morning."

He rolls out of bed to find his own pants and pulls them on. "I know, baby."

Still shirtless, he pulls me against him and kisses me, his hands snaking up under my shirt to caress my bare skin. When it seems he's not going to stop, I push against his chest, then laugh when it does nothing to move him.

"Stop that! We need to go straighten up before your mom gets home."

"She won't care."

"I do!" I exclaim, still a little embarrassed that she's probably going to know we were here boinking our brains out while she was at church, of all places. She was probably there praying for our souls.

"All right, all right," he grumbles as we leave the sweet cocoon of his bedroom and go to straighten up the living room.

It takes a while because we keep stopping to kiss and play, like when he side swiped me with one of the couch cushions. That devolved into a pillow fight when I hit him back. I was laughing so hard I kept missing my shots, but we finally settled down when we heard his mom's car pull into the driveway.

Carlos walked me to my car and kissed me thoroughly before opening my car door for me. All the way home, I keep thinking about making love with him and laughing with him. God, I love how he makes me laugh.

When I get home, Bà is in the kitchen, as usual. She's steeping bones to make stock for something and the house smells wonderful. Chicken, I think, from the aroma.

"How was your day?" she asks when I kiss her on the cheek.

"Good. Amazingly good. How were things here?"

She nods. "Kimmy spent the night with a friend last night."

"Oh?" This is unusual because Kimmy doesn't have any friends that I know of.

"Says it's someone new at school. I didn't tell you because I knew you'd probably stay here under my feet all day worrying. Must be going well, because she's not home yet."

I check my watch again. Although we've never needed to set a curfew with Kimmy because she's never been gone in the evenings. It's not her normal bedtime yet, so I don't reply, but begin an internal debate about whether I should stay up or take the opportunity to get a full night's sleep.

"Go to bed," says Bà, apparently becoming psychic in her old age. "I'll be up a while, and if she isn't home by bedtime, I'll wake you."

For a moment, I hesitate and pull out my phone, thinking I should call to check on her.

"Go, she's probably having fun."

Although I'm still conflicted, the idea of her being with an actual friend sways me. I don't want to be the nervous Nellie that interrupts her fun. Bà will wake me if Kimmy doesn't show up in the next hour or so.

After a quick shower, I collapse onto my bed and sleep overtakes me almost immediately. Bà wakes me up, but it's the next morning, a couple of hours before my alarm was set to go off.

"I'm so sorry. I dozed off in the chair and just woke up. Kimmy has not returned home."

Like a bucket of ice water has been dumped over my head, I go from groggy to wide awake. "Did you try to call her?"

"Her voicemail came on right away."

"Okay, that probably means her phone is off." I unplug my phone from the charger and call Kimmy's number. Her voicemail kicks in immediately. "Kimmy, where are you? We're worried about you because you haven't bothered to check in. Call me back immediately when you get this message."

I disconnect the call, unsure what to do. It's only six in the morning. I'm sure she's asleep, but what if she's not? What if she's been kidnapped or run away?

"What exactly did she say when she was leaving?"

Bà lifts a shoulder. "She didn't talk to me. She told your mother."

Mom. It might have been innocent, but I doubt it. Mom is the only one of the three of us that wouldn't have asked questions.

If Kimmy was looking to get away with something, she'd want to avoid telling me or Bà she was going somewhere. Anger and fear are vying for the top spot. I thought she was doing better, but maybe I was wrong.

This could all be perfectly innocent, too. She's not used to having friends and needing to check in to let someone know she's all right. Because of that, she could be completely unaware that we'd be here wondering if she's alive or dead.

I throw on some clothes and follow Bà into the kitchen where Mom is sitting drinking coffee. Gentle and calm aren't things I'm feeling right now, but I try to stir them up, otherwise, I'll get nowhere.

"Mom," I say. "Can you remember exactly what Kimmy said when she was leaving?"

I can tell I'm agitating her, but I need her to remember. Taking it slowly, I question her again. A tremor runs through her as I bear down, insisting she answer me.

After what seems an eternity, she finally responds. "She said she was going to spend the night at a friend's. That's all I know." Mom pops up out of her chair and skitters away.

Bà put a hand on my arm when I tense to go after her.

"You'll get nothing more."

I don't know what to do, but I know someone who does.

"Gutierrez," Carlos answers.

"Hey, it's Alicia. I'm so sorry to bother you."

His voice softer, he says, "You're never a bother. Did you miss me already?"

My face goes hot and a shiver trickles down my spine.

"Yes, but that's not why I'm calling. Kimmy hasn't been home since Saturday evening and we don't know where she is."

"I'll be right over."

Before I can say anything else, the call disconnects. I don't know whether to cry or laugh. There's someone out there I can lean on and the relief of it is overwhelming. I don't do either, though.

I need to call into the hospital and give them notice that someone will need to cover my rounds this morning. Thank goodness I don't have any surgeries this morning. However, I do have one this afternoon, but I'm only assisting, so they should be able to find someone to replace me, if needed.

Thirty minutes after my call, the doorbell rings and I open the door to Carlos. He pulls me into his arms and gives me a squeeze. Just as I'm about to lead him into the house, Mom comes to us.

In one hand, she's holding a stack of missing flyers she must have gone to create and print. Her cell phone is in her other hand, extended toward me.

"Hello?" I say once I put it on speaker.

"For fuck's sake," Kimmy says. "Chill out. I'm at school, so you can quit freaking."

"You're at school," I echo, seeing on the phone that it's a little after seven, so it's about the right time for her to be there.

"Yes. Here."

"Hello?" a voice says on her phone.

"This is Alicia Pham, Kimmy's guardian. To whom am I speaking?"

The voice on the other end sounded vaguely familiar, but once I hear her name, I know she is who she says she is. "Dr. Pham, this is the school's principal, Mrs. Winters, and I can verify that Kimmy has arrived for school."

"Thank you, Principal Winters."

Kimmy comes back on the line. "See, you can chill."

"You and I are going to have a serious talk this evening."

"Yay," she says deadpan. "Another talk."

The line disconnects. When I look up, Carlos is scowling at his phone.

"You need to go," I observe.

"I'm glad she's safe, but yes, something has happened."

"Go," I say.

He leans in to kiss me quickly before he turns and hurries back to his car.

Mom comes up beside me. "He seems nice."

"He is."

I dress and go into work, picking up the last half of my rounds. Furious doesn't even begin to describe what I'm feeling. Kimmy should be counting her blessings that there are a few hours between now and when she has to face me.

Maybe I'll cool off by the time I get home from work. However, when one surgery turns into two, Kimmy is given more of a reprieve because I don't get home until well after she's asleep. The next morning, I'm up and out of the house before even Bà stirs.

Chapter 23

Alicia

A giant of a man and his wife sit across the conference table from me. The big Russian looks like he just stepped off the cover of GQ in a bespoke suit that fits him perfectly. It is a beautiful suit except for the right leg of his trousers that has been hacked off to accommodate the bionic looking brace stabilizing his knee.

His wife looks like Barbie if the doll was born and bred in New Jersey. I know she's from Jersey because she told me when she introduced herself. However, I might have guessed it anyway because as soon as she opened her mouth, her accent reminded me of a television show that Kimmy used to watch all the time.

When Kimmy finally told me what GTL meant and about some of the escapades of the reality stars, I wondered if I needed to put some kind of parental lock on the television. Because we battle about so many things I decided not to pick that one. Soon she had moved on to some new program, so I let it go.

From Mrs. Belov's hair to her clothes to her jewelry, everything is over the top, but perfectly styled and put together. She's vibrant and boisterous, but sweet at the same time. Her love for her husband is transparent, too.

I try to exude confidence and competence as the Director of my residency program addresses the pair. Sasha Belov had to end his second season with the Thunder basketball team early because of an injury. He has had chronic problems with his knee and is experiencing yet another ligament tear that needs surgery.

He is slated for surgery in two days, but we've run into a problem. Dr. Fitzpatrick, the surgeon slated to do the surgery, took his wife on a long weekend of skiing before Valentine's Day, where he took a tumble and broke his leg in two places. Therefore, he will be unable to do the surgery.

Dr. Collins has just told the couple of Dr. Fitz's injury. "So, you have three options," he says. "The first is that we can postpone the surgery and wait for Dr. Fitzpatrick to return and recover enough from his own injuries to perform the surgery. The second is that we can wait until one of the other partners in Dr. Fitzpatrick's surgical group is available to do the surgery."

He pauses. I'm not sure if he's letting the information soak in or if he really doesn't want to tell them option three.

"So what's awptchun tree?" Mrs. Belov asks, holding tight to her husband's hand.

"Option three is that we move forward with the surgery in two days and Dr. Pham will be the primary with one of Dr. Fitzpatrick's partners on call and ready to scrub in should there be a case of extreme need. Dr. Pham is a surgical resident in our orthopedics program. She has less than a year to finish program and is one of the most talented surgeons we have on staff. She was set to assist Dr. Fitzpatrick with the surgery, so she is familiar with your case."

They both stare at me.

"This little girl right heyah is Dr. Fam?"

The Director nods in confirmation.

"Are you sure she's even old nuff ta be cuttin on my man's knee?"

I smile reassuringly as I reply. "I can assure you I am old enough."

She suddenly flings her hands out across the table to me, the giant rock on her left hand catching the sunlight. "Gimme yeh hands."

I look at her hands and at the Director. He gives me a little shrug, so I stand, because my arms aren't long enough to reach, and put my hands in hers. She closes her eyes, and we stay like that for several minutes.

I'm just about to pull away when she looks me straight in the eyes and says, "My grandmutha was Roma," she says by way of explanation. "You got a good vibe." She turns to her husband. "She's got a good vibe, baby. I think you should go wit the little girl."

I start to rankle at being called a little girl, but tamp it down. The goal is to do the surgery, not guaranty that I won't.

"You sure?" he asks, his Russian accent thick.

She nods vehemently.

He points a finger at me. "We go with her," Sasha Belov says.

I feel like jumping up and down even though it was my supposed vibe that sealed the deal instead of my years of training and skill. Although I've taken the lead on many surgeries, the attending was always present to observe. This will be my first surgery where I am the primary running the entire surgical team on my own, with no one looking over my shoulder.

We discuss the details of the surgery and instead of sending them downstairs to do a usual pre-op appointment; they get the VIP treatment, and a service clerk comes up to the conference room to do the pre-check in and provide them with instructions. When the clerk arrives, I bid them farewell and tell them I'll see them in two days.

Floating on clouds as I go downstairs, I find a quiet corner before I pull out my phone to call Carlos. He's the first person I thought to call, but when I read the text messages that had come in during the meeting, I have another reason to call him.

"Well, what did they decide?" he answers without preamble.

I chuckle. "Straight to business, huh?"

"I can't help it; I'm so excited for you. So, are they going to wait or go for it?"

I had told him all about today's meeting. Dr. Collins had called me yesterday morning after I arrived at the hospital when I was in the midst of stewing about Kimmy. His call had helped to bring me back to an even keel by pulling me into doctor mode.

"They're going to go for it." I tell him all about the meeting, including the weird hand-holding thing which makes him laugh.

"Congratulations, babe. That's fantastic news. I guess you've got the spirits on your side."

"I guess so." My laughter and excitement die down. "Kimmy came home after school yesterday and was still home this morning when I left. Mom took her to school this morning and will pick her up like usual."

"Thank goodness she's safe," he says. "How do you feel about it?"

How do I feel about it? I'm glad she's safe, too. I'm relieved she is back in contact. Happy she's home.

But most of all, I'm pissed. I am still so angry that she could just take off without a note without letting any of us know where she was or whether she was safe.

I was so scared for her; all of us were. She has a lot of explaining to do and I don't even know how to begin to punish her for this stunt. Part of me wants to hug her. Part of me wants to shake her until some sense sinks in, and part of me wants to spank her six ways to Sunday.

I sum it all up and just say, "Conflicted," in answer to his question.

"I can imagine."

"Anyway, I'll deal with Kimmy. How's your day going?"

I can't begin to express how thankful I was to have him there yesterday when I discovered Kimmy was gone. I don't know of anyone else who would have dropped everything and rushed over to be there for me.

I don't know what's happening, but ever since that night at Cait's and the day we spent at his house, Carlos seems to be at the top of my list for...well, everything. How can that possibly be? He slid in past my cool veneer before I even realized what was happening.

If he had tried to talk to me that day in the grocery store, he would have gotten the cautious, cold fish. Instead, his first conversation with me was when I was with friends, relaxed and open. Then all my shields dropped when I had the realization about Tai.

He saw me completely vulnerable and instead of running, he stayed right there and let me lean on him. Who does that in this world? No one but family, in my experience, and considering Kimmy's parents, even family can be iffy.

I don't know how exactly it happened, but just a few weeks ago, we were complete strangers and now I find myself thinking about him way too much.

When I get home from work, Kimmy is in her room as if she wasn't missing for thirty-six hours, and that pisses me off even more. I ask her to come into the living room where Mom and Bà wait. As soon as she sees the other women, Kimmy drags her feet, rolls her eyes, and lets out a whole-body sigh, as only a teenager can do.

She slouches into an armchair. "Let's get this over with," she says.

On the way home, I promised myself that I would be calm and logical. I told myself I would not lose my temper. Yet, here we are, two seconds into the conversation, and I'm ready to flip my lid.

I'm surprised when my voice comes out even because I don't feel very even on the inside. "Do you not think you owe us some kind of explanation?"

She shrugs, looking at the floor.

"Where did you go?"

"Nowhere; just around."

"Weren't you with someone? Mom said you told her you were spending the night with a friend, someone new from school."

She shrugs again.

"You either were or you weren't."

"Yeah, okay? I was with a lot of people and no one at all. I was just around, nowhere specific with nobody specific!" She isn't shouting, but her voice is raised, which makes Mom get up and go to her room.

Kimmy rolls her eyes.

"Why did you feel the need to take off like that?" I'm still managing to keep my voice steady, but all of this disinformation and attitude from Kimmy isn't making it easy.

"I just needed a break."

"A break from what?" My voice ratchets up now. "What could you possibly need a break from? Your only responsibility is to go to school, and you skip out on that often enough. What is so terrible or stressful in your life that you need a break?"

She shrugs yet again.

"Oh my God, Kimmy! You can't just shrug this off! You disappeared without a word. We were frantic. We called someone with the police and were on the verge of reporting you missing. All we knew was that you were gone, apparently of your own free will. Mom printed enough flyers to plaster them all over town. I had to get someone to cover my shift at the hospital so I would be able to go out looking for you."

"Oh. Yeah. Work. That's the important thing."

Her words hit me like a slap in the face. My voice isn't raised anymore. It's low and devoid of emotion.

"What? Who do you think I'm doing all of this for? If I don't work, none of us will have a roof over our heads. If I don't work, there's no food on the table, no cell phone in your pocket, none of those new shoes on your feet. I am working myself like crazy, trying to make a better life for all of us."

She doesn't answer for a long time and that pushes all my buttons. I should have stopped right there. I should have walked away and cooled off. But I didn't.

"I know you have a great deal of anger about your parents, but what I don't get is why you feel the need to take that anger out on me. Nineteen. That's how old I was when I became your guardian. I didn't ask for what happened to you to happen. God knows I didn't ask for my dad to die and leave me in charge of everything. But it all happened and I'm doing the best I can. I have been working my ass off to maintain a decent standard of living for our family and move us toward something better."

I'm not sure when I popped up off the couch and started pacing, but I stop. Rubbing my forehead, trying to ease the dull ache between my eyebrows. I wonder why I keep beating my head against this wall. Maybe it's time for a change.

"I thought you'd be better off staying with the family when Dad died and since Mom wasn't able to handle it, I agreed to become your guardian, but maybe that was the wrong choice. If you hate me and hate living here so much that you feel the need to run away, if you don't want to be here anymore, we can investigate alternatives. It is not what I want, but if it's what you want, we can talk about it."

I'm no longer angry, just empty and deflated. I just feel so exhausted.

"What do you mean?"

"I mean what I said. Fighting with you is exhausting and we never seem to get anywhere. I love you, but you obviously hate living here and hate me. This is your home and I want you here, but if you want to leave, perhaps we can find someone to take you in that you will be happier with."

She doesn't answer. She's quiet so long that I turn to look at her, but she's not there. A door closes down the hall and I realize that she's gone to her bedroom.

How is it possible to go from the highest of highs and lowest of lows all in one day?

I go to my own room. While I'm thinking about it, I send a message to Kimmy's therapist to tell her everything that has gone on over the past couple of days. Kimmy's appointment is tomorrow afternoon, so maybe she'll talk to her therapist about what motivated her to run away, even if it was temporary. At least I hope she will, but history tells me it's unlikely.

I check my phone and see a message from Carlos wishing me luck with regard to talking to Kimmy. Then I see another message in the notifications. A message from Tai.

Hey Monkey! Sorry for the radio silence, been wicked busy. How was your weekend?

How was my weekend? The last time I saw Tai, he was accosting me outside the hospital and calling me a whore and now he sends me a text asking me how my weekend was? Is he really acting as if nothing happened?

My thumbs are poised to text back, to tell him yet again that we're done, but instead I decide to call him. I think that right now, when I am not likely to be swayed into being nice by niceties and pretty words, is the best time to reinforce the fact that our relationship is over.

He answers the phone on the first ring. "Hey Monkey!"

"Hi Tai." I say, and I dive right in. "I'm not sure why you're texting me. I felt as if I made it perfectly clear that we're done. We want different things in our lives. Also, I think we just live in two very different worlds…" You're a gang leader and I hope to be a law-abiding, upstanding citizen. "…and have different priorities."

"Different priorities," he echoes. "What makes you say that?"

"There are things in your life that I'm not comfortable with."

I can almost hear his teeth grinding through the phone.

After a long time, he finally grits out, "You don't know shit about my life, so what exactly are you not comfortable with?"

I sigh. "That right there is exactly what I'm not comfortable with. You're secretive about even the most basic information. Whenever I have asked you anything, trying to get to know the man you are now as opposed to the boy I used to know, you evade and redirect. You're hiding everything from me while expecting me to hide nothing, and I don't want to have that kind of relationship. I've said it before, but I want to be crystal clear. I have no intention of resuming a relationship with you. We're never getting back together, Tai. I'm done. Was done when I first said it weeks ago."

"You're making a mistake, Monkey."

I frown. His voice is bitter, almost menacing.

"Are you threatening me?"

"No, I'm promising you. I knew when we were kids that we were meant to be together. Then I got older and learned about the promise your grandfather made."

"No, Tai, we're not. Please get that out of your head. I have to go. Best of luck to you, Tai. Have a nice life."

I disconnect the call. My phone starts buzzing a few seconds later, but I ignore it and go to the bathroom to shower. I'm so ready to wash away the dregs of this day. When I'm clean and refreshed, I'll call Carlos and end the day on a high note.

Chapter 24

Alicia

I shake off my nerves before I pull back the curtain where Sasha Belov and his wife wait. He has been prepped for surgery and I go over the procedure with them again. With a marker, I write on his knee to specify which one will receive the surgery and the approximate extent of the scarring.

I am hoping we'll just have the one tear to deal with. However, when I was reviewing his scans, I saw some things that didn't make me happy, so I pulled his previous scans. Reviewing those didn't make me any happier.

I would never presume to talk out of turn about another surgeon, especially one as seasoned as Dr. Fitz, but based upon what I'm seeing in the scans, Sasha's current injury could have been prevented. Because I wasn't there for the surgery, I don't know what Dr. Fitz found when he opened the knee up. Therefore, I could be wrong, but my gut is telling me I'm not.

Sasha deserves the best chance possible of resuming his career, so I will do the best that I can to repair the damage I find once I open him up.

The surgery goes as well as it could have. I was right about what I thought I'd find in there, but his knee is now cleaned up, the problems with his ligaments addressed, and he's stitched up. We'll keep Sasha here overnight just to be sure he comes out of the anesthesia without incident and has no post-op problems.

Tomorrow he will go to one of those fancy recovery hospitals that will take over his care and he will also go to them for physical therapy when the time comes. I stop in to do a recap of the surgery and see how he's feeling.

Although I'm technically off until I'm supposed to be back for rounds this evening, I hang out anyway. You know, just in case Sasha needs me. Yes, I'm that overachieving kid that wants everything to go perfectly, so I stay at work even though I don't have to. Happy Valentine's Day to me.

My phone buzzes. It's Carlos, which brings a smile to my face.

Carlos: *When's your dinner break?*

Me: *Night rounds start at four thirty. I'm still at the hospital, but technically off the clock for a couple of hours.*

Carlos: *Hungry?*

Me: *Starving.*

Carlos: *Meet me downstairs in thirty?*

Me: *Yes!!!!*

Thirty minutes later, Carlos is walking in carrying a brown paper bag and sporting a huge smile. He looks good dressed for work in a suit and tie. I thought he looked good in jeans and a sweater, but damn. His suits might be off the rack instead of custom made or tailored, but I don't care, suited up Carlos has my heart going pitty pat almost as much as Carlos in well-worn jeans and a tee.

"Hi," I say.

"Hey there," he says, putting one hand on my arm and leaning in to give me a chaste kiss.

We go to a table in the food court area situated toward the back, away from everyone else. He takes his coat off and drapes it over one of the spare chairs. When he puts his bag on the chair, like a magician with a bag of holding, he starts pulling things out.

He first produces a single red rose and holds it out to me where I sit across the table. "Happy Valentine's Day, baby."

My eyes go wide. I suddenly feel very shy, but I take the rose. "Thank you."

The next thing he pulls out is a heart-shaped aluminum pan with a colorful lid on top. He places it in front of me.

"What's this?" I ask.

He grins. "Open it and see."

I do as he says. As soon as I lift one corner, a delicious aroma seeps out, a mélange of chilis, onions, roasted meat, and cilantro. My stomach growls in response. I pull the lid the rest of the way off to find the tin filled with...

"Tacos! Oh, my goodness! You are the best!"

"I know," he says with a shrug and sits down across from me, which makes me laugh.

We tuck into the tacos with him telling me about his day and me telling him about mine. This thing with him, whatever it is, it's so easy. I look up to see him staring at me, at my mouth.

He reaches across the table and uses his thumb to wipe something off the corner of my mouth. "Salsa," he says, his voice gone husky.

I look down and use my napkin to wipe my mouth, my skin tingling where he touched me. "Oh, sorry."

"Don't be," he says.

I look up at him and his eyes are hot. Never in my life has a man looked at me like that. Like he wants to devour me whole. I feel heat bloom in my belly down low. Do I really need to work for the next four hours?

As if reading my mind, the alarm on my phone dings to let me know I have fifteen minutes before my shift starts. Carlos looks at his watch.

"It's about that time, isn't it?"

"Yes," I grumble.

"One last thing," he says and reaches into his bag again. When he takes his hand out, it's fisted around something. He places a single candy kiss on the table in front of me. "It's not Valentine's Day without a kiss."

I grin at him. "You're good at this romantic stuff."

He grins back. "I'm Latin; it's in our DNA."

I stand and take our trash to the bin and return to the table where he's putting on his coat. When I stand in front of him, I look up into his eyes. "Thank you, Carlos; this was wonderful."

"You are very welcome."

He looks down at me with a tender smile. I'm just about to turn away when he cups my jaw in his hands and leans down to me. My heart begins to stutter-step in my chest. My eyelids lower as he draws near, going shut as his lips brush against mine.

He pulls me closer as I kiss him back, his arms going around me as mine slide around his waist. His tongue gently slips into my mouth, our tongues dancing. He tastes like salsa and the savory spices from the tacos, and I never, ever thought of tacos as sexy until now.

He smells so good, a blend of something musky and citrusy. The sensory overload has my body going liquid as I'm pressed against all the hard muscle under his suit. I want to drag him into a closet somewhere and do naughty things with all that hard flesh.

An hour or maybe just a few minutes later, he breaks the kiss and pulls back. I open my eyes and look at him, wondering if I look as dazed as I feel.

"It isn't Valentine's Day without a kiss," I manage to say.

That makes him smile, his dimples teasing me. He drags his thumb across my burning lips, and I want to kiss him more. My phone dings with my next alarm, letting me know I have five minutes to get upstairs.

I sigh. "Sorry."

"Don't be. I totally understand it when work calls. Have a good night, gorgeous."

Now he's the one making me smile. Does he really think I'm gorgeous? Maybe he needs his eyes checked.

"Thanks, you, too, and thank you again for the tacos." I pull away and he catches my hand in his. "And the kiss."

He winks and lets go of my hand. I snag my chocolate and rose and go toward the stairs, turning back for one last look before I race back up to my floor.

Happy Valentine's Day to me!

Chapter 25

Carlos

Alicia dashes up the stairs. She seemed so touched by tacos and a little piece of chocolate. I wonder when is the last time someone did something for her or gave her something just to take care of her. Well, besides that asshole Dang.

He gave her stuff, but it was to manipulate and buy her rather than any kind of genuine affection for her. A guy like that is so narcissistic that he's probably incapable of truly caring for someone else. Never in my life have I wanted to take care of someone like I want to take care of her.

If it gets me more of those kisses and more days like the one we spent in my bed, I am all in. I have to admit, she surprised me when she kissed me like that here at her place of work. She looked surprised that she'd done it, too, but boy am I glad she did.

When she was talking about the surgery she did this morning, she was all confidence and in charge. As soon as that was done, though, she went a little innocent and unsure on me.

That's okay, I love that she seems so unjaded by the curveballs life has thrown at her. In that moment, I decide she can be the big-time fancy pants surgeon when she needs to be.

However, when it's just her and me, I like that vulnerability and I'm going to do everything I can to protect it. I understand now what my dad meant when he said Mom was his to take care of because that's how I feel about Alicia and the sensation is only growing.

I glance around the room as I fold up the bag I brought everything in. The back of my neck has been burning practically since I arrived, but I forced myself to stay focused on Alicia instead of scoping out the room. There are a few medical types in scrubs strewn around the room at tables. Some are in small groups and a couple are solo, either eating or reading.

There's one woman who definitely doesn't look like she's from Oklahoma with her big blond hair and flashy clothes. There's also a kid at the vending machines, but none of them puts up a red flag for me. However, someone has been watching. I know that for sure.

My first transition from being a patrol officer was into narcotics, where I spent a lot of time going undercover. When you're playing a role, you get excellent at situational awareness and knowing when someone has a bead on you. You have to develop those kinds of skills and grow eyes in the back of your head because if you don't, it could get you dead.

The blond comes my way. I expect her to pass by, but she stops in front of me.

"You Dr. Pham's boyfriend?" she asks. Her voice sounds like some Jersey Mafia Princess you'd see on television. Definitely not from Oklahoma.

"I'm working on it," I tell her. I hold out my hand. "I'm Carlos Gutierrez."

She shakes my hand. "Darlene Belov. Dr. Pham operated on my husband's knee this morning."

"She's an excellent surgeon, and she said the surgery she did this morning went particularly well."

"What you do?"

"Me? I'm a police officer."

She looks me up and down for a moment and then seems to make up her mind.

"Good. Cuz if you was anything else, I probably wouldn't tell you but since you know how to handle yourself, I wanna let you know that there was two guys awfully interested in you and the Doc. Specially the Doc."

I don't look away from her. "Did they leave when she went back to work?"

"One did, the other went over to the vending machines first, then sauntered toward the front exit." She points with a long red lacquered nail to show me the direction in case I wasn't aware.

"Thank you, Mrs. Belov. I appreciate you letting me know."

"Sure. You take care of her, you hear? She seems like a real sweet girl and she's been loads better than the condescending prick we had last time."

"I plan to."

She starts to walk away but stops. She turns back to me and holds out her hands.

"Give me youwah hands."

I put my hands in hers and she closes her eyes just like Alicia said she had the other morning. We stand there for several minutes. I watch her face go through myriad expressions from smiling to frowning to looking incredibly sad, then finally landing on relieved.

She looks up at me when she opens her eyes. "Carlos, I don't have details, but you two got a tough road ahead. She, especially, will have some hard things to weather. Hold tight to her with your heart even when you can't with your arms and it will all work out in the end."

She pats my chest with the palm of one hand and moves away. I stand there a little thrown off kilter. Of all the things I thought she might say, that was not one of them. I decide to file it away instead of trying to figure out exactly what she meant. That's a short road to driving myself crazy.

I take my time leaving the hospital, strolling out to my car. Although I need to get back to the station to finish up some paperwork before I call it quits for the day, I have nothing pressing. I'd thought about stopping by to see one of my confidential informants, but if there is even a remote chance we could be seen, it's better to skip it. My eyes skim over reflective windows to see if anyone is following as I make my way out to the parking lot, but still, I don't see anyone.

I keep an eye on my rearview mirror all the way back to the station, and I don't see anyone tailing me. However, I can't shake the feeling of being watched and knowing I was right in the hospital makes it even harder to keep it from lingering. Is Dang watching Alicia and could he be watching me, too?

Alicia said she has told him more than once to get lost, although I'm sure she was nicer about it than that knowing her. Somehow I'll need to figure out a way to ask her about any new contact she's had with him without freaking her out that she might be being watched.

I want to be with her and it's going to be a lot more work than I'm used to. Before her, I'd never met anyone I wanted to commit to, so I mostly just hooked up on a semi-regular basis. A hook-up isn't what I'm looking for with Alicia and I'm willing to put in the work. I know she'll be worth it.

Chapter 26

Alicia

Why can't I stop bouncing? I ran up three flights of stairs and once I got over feeling like I was going to cough up a lung, I started bouncing. As I'm making my rounds, my steps are all bouncy, like Tigger, on a diet of pop and chocolate.

I'm about halfway through the shift when my phone buzzes in my pocket. My heart starts bouncing, too, thinking I might have a message from Carlos, but I pull my phone out to see I have a text message from Tai. I frown and open it, irritated that he's still messaging me after I told him I wasn't interested in pursuing anything further with him.

Tai: *Monkey...stop misbehaving.*

I should just ignore it, but I don't. Tai needs to be gone from my life, so he needs to understand that I don't want anything to do with him. How could he possibly think any differently?

Me: *I told you, Tai, I am not interested in pursuing anything with you anymore. Please leave me alone.*

It buzzes again in my pocket, so I apologize to the patient and take a moment to turn the phone off.

I knock on the next door and am beckoned into Sasha Belov's room.

"How are you feeling?"

"Lazy," Sasha says with his thick Russian accent.

I laugh. "Not used to sitting still, huh?"

"No, not at all."

I do the usual checks of his heart and lungs and review his chart for the notations from the nurses. We talk about his transition to the recovery facility, and I make suggestions for him to be conscious of when discussing his recovery plan, since the surgery was more extensive than it was expected to be. They might not have gotten that information, so he needed to be sure they were aware.

"That boyfriend of yours is a sweetheart," Mrs. Belov says.

I feel the heat creep up my hairline. "Yes, he is, but he's not my boyfriend, not yet. It's still very new."

"Well, he wants to be your boyfriend. I can tell that by the way he looks at you. You need to hold on to that one. He's a keeper."

I thank her and we talk a while longer before I bid them farewell and move onto the next patient. After my shift, I turn my phone back on and find a picture of Carlos and me when he reached over and wiped away a drop of salsa from the corner of my mouth.

Is Tai having me watched? This is ridiculous. Everything he does makes me glad that I broke things off with him. I can't imagine what he would be like if we'd gotten married.

Maybe if I just ignore him, he'll give up and go away. That could work, couldn't it?

The next evening, I manage to make it to dinner with Cait, Demi, and Serena at the Society. Gabriella is at home enjoying her new baby.

After what happened at Cait's housewarming, I feel closer to these women than ever. I had forgotten how good it felt to have friends. The company of other women is something I want more of in my life.

I have focused my whole life on reaching one finish line after another and put so many things on hold. That may not have been the best way to go about things, and I might do some things differently if I had it to do over. However, right here, right now, I'm rather pleased at how my life seems to be coming together as I approach my next finish line.

I've done my first completely solo surgery, and a high profile one at that. I am excelling in my residency program. I have friends. And I have a budding romantic relationship.

The only dark cloud in my sky is Tai, but I'm sticking to the ignoring him plan, hoping it will work. If it doesn't, I'll have to investigate other options.

Kimmy isn't exactly a dark cloud, but she is still a concern. I need to figure out what I'm going to do with her soon. It's either move her out to some place she may like better or keep her at home and hope she settles down.

We've been talking about Demi's progress on her book and that led to discussing her upcoming wedding to Kellen. Demi makes a quick segue just as I'm taking a drink of water. "So, enough about my love life. How's Carlos, Alicia?"

I choke on the water and Serena pounds me on the back. "Demi!" I say when I regain my faculties.

She just looks at me with a smug smile on her face.

I roll my eyes at her. "Carlos is fine."

"Just fine?" Asks Cait with a knowing look.

"Who is Carlos?" Serena asks.

"Yeah, Alicia, who is Carlos?" Demi singsongs.

I can't help but laugh despite knowing my face is fifty shades of embarrassed.

"You met him, Serena. He's the man I met in the grocery store who then showed up at Cait's housewarming."

"And?" asks Serena with a grin. "I mean, there seems to be more to it than just him being a friend based on how you're acting all shy all of the sudden."

I can't stop the grin that spreads across my face. "He brought me tacos for Valentine's Day last night."

"He did what?" Demi asks with a laugh.

I tell them all about Carlos bringing me the tacos in a heart-shaped tin, the rose, the chocolate...and the kiss. They all react at the same time with "I knew it!" from Demi, "Oh my," from Serena, and "That's fantastic!" from Cait.

I don't tell them about our foray into his bedroom, Tai, or about Kimmy's disappearance. I like the happy, light feeling I have right now and don't want anything to bring it down. They want to know when we'll see each other again, and I have to be honest and tell them that with our schedules, I'm not sure.

"Boo!" says Demi.

"I totally understand how that goes," Cait chimes in.

We chat for a while longer, but soon I have to render my goodbyes because I have an early surgery the next morning. I go downstairs and am passing through the area we have come to call the lounge when I think of the mechanical box in one corner of the room.

The box is an old timey fortune teller like you'd see at a carnival or on the boardwalk of an amusement park. It is a beautiful representation, with a raven-haired beauty hovering a hand over a spread of tarot cards.

Ella swears that her wish came true. Demi says she didn't even make an official wish but made a comment about a male role model for Henry. Within a few days she had met Kellen, who turned out to be not only an excellent role model for her son, but a love match for her. Cait says her wish came true, too, but she doesn't talk about exactly what that wish was.

I look at the big yellow 'Make A Wish' button. I feel ridiculous, my logical brain mocking me for even entertaining the thought that the machine could actually work. If there is even a slight chance, what harm could it do?

I blurt out, "I wish Tai would go away and leave me and my family alone and never bother any of us again."

I snap my hand out and press the button. Nothing happens for several moments, but then the machine starts making whirring and clicking sounds. When it stops, a card pops out of a slot on the front of the machine. I take it and turn it over to read the message.

Sometimes the wrong paths are easier. Just take a step and pick a course. The best paths can be challenging, filled with twists and turns and even remorse.

Unsure of what to think about the message, I frown. I walk over to the nearest trash can, thinking I'll throw the card away, but I can't let it go. Instead, I tuck it into my purse, then continue toward the exit.

Chapter 27

Carlos

"Dr. Alicia Pham, P-H-A-M," Alicia says to the clerk at the will call counter.

The man flips through a file on the counter.

"Yes, here you are." He slides an envelope across the counter to her. "Enjoy the game."

I guide Alicia down the steps to our seats at courtside. The Belov's gifted her with courtside seats for any Thunder home game she wanted to go to. Amazingly, we were able to take them up on their offer the same week.

We had dinner before the game, then walked around Bricktown hand-in-hand, enjoying the unseasonably warm weather before we strolled over to the arena. She said she's never been to a basketball game, so this should be fun. I explain the basics to her during the pre-game show.

The Thunder score right off the bat and Alicia pops up on her feet and cheers. She watches the players intently as they race back and forth on the court. The ball goes up and through the net and she pops up and cheers again.

When she sits, I tell her, "Honey, that's the opposing team. We don't want to cheer for them."

She turns in her seat and faces me as her hand flies up to her mouth, her eyes go wide, and she laughs. "Oh, my gosh! I can't believe I did that!"

I laugh, too. She's so dang cute. The guy behind her leans forward and stage whispers good naturedly.

"You're supposed to be rooting for the guys in white."

She laughs again. "Sorry! I've never been to a basketball game before!"

"Never?"

She shakes her head at the man. "Never, ever."

"Well, you've got great seats for learning," he says with a wink and leans back in his seat.

The opposing team scores again and she starts to pop up again.

"Come'ere," I tell her and put my arm around her shoulders. "I'll hold you down."

I'm gratified when she leans into me instead of pulling away. She puts her hand on my knee, then looks up at me and grins. "Thanks!"

Several more times during the game, she gets caught up in the excitement and starts to pop up, but is stopped by my arm and we both laugh. At halftime, she relaxes back in her seat.

"I have no idea what's going on, but it sure is fun," she says, a big smile on her face. "The way they move is fascinating. I can see why Sasha has had trouble with his knee, but I think the repairs I did will help him a lot. Is he usually the guy in the middle? I would think with his height he'd be best in that position."

"Yes, that's usually his position; it's called the center."

The guy behind us taps me on the shoulder and motions at the big screen. We're on the kiss cam. I show her, and with no hesitation at all, she leans over and kisses me. Not a shy, tentative kiss, either.

The shyness comes afterward, so I pull her into my side again, and she snuggles into me. In the privacy of my bedroom, she wasn't shy at all, but in public, it's a different story. It makes me wonder if it's something Dang instilled in her.

He always did seem like a bit of a peacock, wanting everyone to believe the outer shell he presented to the public. I can see where he'd want Alicia to feed into that.

She only makes it through the third quarter before she's yawning, and her enthusiasm is waning. It's getting late and the Thunder have a tremendous lead so we're not likely to miss any surprises if we cut out early.

I lean over and put my mouth near her ear. "We can go, if you want. You look like you're ready for bed."

"No, really, I'm..." she yawns in the middle of her attempt to tell me she's fine.

"We'll go at the quarter," I say, pointing at the clock.

She nods and takes my hand, ready for me to lead her out when it's time to go. I lace our fingers together, pleased that she's becoming more relaxed and freer with her touches even when we're not alone. We have come a long way in a short time, and I want to keep that momentum going.

I take her home and walk her to the front door. We linger on the doorstep. Neither of us is eager to say good night.

"Thank you for taking me tonight," she says.

"Thank you for inviting me. It was fun."

She shivers. The temperature dropped with the setting of the sun and it's quickly dipping toward freezing.

"You're cold. I'll say good night and let you go in."

"Sometimes it stinks being a responsible child and having your parents living with you." She says it with a chuckle, but not really with any humor.

"I know. My mom lives with me, too, remember?"

"Yes. I remember. It would just be nice to be able to be alone occasionally."

"I agree. But for now, we're responsible children and that's a good thing." I put my hand under her chin and raise her face. "Good night, Alicia," I say and lean down and kiss her.

I know she's carrying a lot on her shoulders. It probably weighs her down sometimes and I want to be the person to help her with that burden, but we're not there yet. We're getting closer, though. Much closer.

Her arms go around my waist, and she leans into me, deepening the kiss. We're both breathing heavy when we pull apart. My dick is so hard that I would like nothing better than to drag her back out to the car and climb into the backseat and have my way with her. But I don't.

"Good night, Carlos," she says, and pulls away. "Call me tomorrow. I have morning rounds and some paperwork to catch up on, but I should be home sometime in the afternoon."

"If I'm not called out, do you want to do dinner?" I ask.

"I would like that," she says with a small smile, then a yawn takes her over.

I grin and kiss her forehead. "Sueños dulces, Alicia."

Chapter 28

Alicia

O ver the next two weeks, my schedule and Carlos' have magically aligned, and we've been able to spend more time together. We have had dinner or lunch several days and have even been able to have some fun dates. He gave me another first in my life when he took me out salsa dancing.

Even on the days we're not able to see each other, we talk on the phone or text. It hasn't been long since that day in the grocery store when he gave me his card, but he has become an ever-present part of my life. Is it weird that the significant men in my life have found me in grocery stores?

I don't know how he feels, but my heart flutters every time I even think of him. That's something I never had with Tai.

I've also made it to dinner at the Society a few weeks in a row. Everything is coming together better than I expected. I'm wondering if the fortune teller downstairs has granted my wish because I haven't heard from Tai at all. I still don't understand the part about remorse, but as long as he stays away, I don't care if I ever understand.

The only thing that isn't coming together is that Carlos and I still haven't managed any more alone time. If we don't find some soon, I'm going to jump his bones in the back seat of his car. Maybe we should rent a hotel room or something.

Bà has heard me talk about Carlos so much that she has issued a formal invitation to a family lunch on Sunday. I'm not sure what she has planned; our regular family meals are usually very casual. One thing I know for sure is that she will be grilling. Grilling him to see what his intentions are with me.

I've tried to tell her that we're just friends getting to know each other better, but she's not buying it. She doesn't interfere in my life, but when it comes to romantic relationships, she is extremely old-fashioned.

When I asked Carlos, he just shrugged and said, "Sure, okay."

Not much fazes him, but I'm concerned about him being stuck in a house with all this estrogen for a few hours. I'm most worried about Bà and Kimmy. Bà will be watching him like a hawk and Kimmy has no boundaries when it comes to asking inappropriate questions. I'll be surprised if Mom sits at the table with us.

Kimmy told me she didn't want to go live with someone else, so she's still here. Although she's not back to the brief spurt of being a happy-go-lucky girl she was a few weeks ago, we haven't had any major blow-ups either.

I'm helping Kimmy set the table when the doorbell rings. "I'll get it," she says.

"No, I will. You finish up here," I tell her.

She huffs and rolls her eyes.

I open the door and my heart does a stutter-step at the sight of him. It's been a few days since we've seen each other, and I've missed him.

"Hi."

He grins at me and steps inside. "Hi. You look beautiful."

I look down, knowing my cheeks are pink. "Thank you. Let me take your coat."

He sets down the dish he's carrying and takes off his coat, letting me take it and hang it up.

"You didn't have to bring anything," I tell him.

"Mom sent it. Honeycomb Cake." He pulls me into his arms and kisses me. "I've missed you."

My arms go around his waist, and I lean into him. When he breaks the kiss, I lean my head against his chest, enjoying the feel of him. "I've missed you, too."

Bà calls from the kitchen telling the world that lunch is ready. Carlos chuckles and kisses the top of my head.

"I'm sorry," I tell him.

"For what?"

"That's a preemptive apology on behalf of my family for anything they might say or do today."

He chuckles again. "Mi alma, everything is going to be fine. Trust me; moms and grandmas love me."

"What does that mean, mi alma?"

"You'll have to learn Spanish to find out."

Kimmy comes into the living room and sees us standing there, embracing. She stops and flinches back and stares for a moment. "Bà says get your rumps in gear."

I doubt she said that, but we make our way to the dining room. Carlos greets my mom and Bà, speaking flawless Vietnamese. He presents Bà with the cake, telling her his mother wouldn't allow him to arrive empty-handed.

Bà doesn't reply, just takes the dish with a nod, but I can tell she is pleased. We are about five minutes into the meal when she starts in with the questions. She wants to know what his major was in college - Criminal Justice. What his grades were like - good. Then she moves on to his job, asking him how long he has been on the police force - ten years - and what his aspirations are - for now, he likes where he's at.

She asks him about his personal life, whether he has been married before - no - and whether he has any children - none. He's never been married. She really likes that answer. She wants to know all about his father and his mother, so he tells her that story.

Carlos takes it all in stride and speaks in Vietnamese the entire time, which is great, or she would probably be asking him why he wasn't fluent. I keep one hand on his knee, patting it by way of apology for the grilling.

"What are your intentions with my granddaughter?" she finally asks. It is the question she has been wanting to ask most.

"Your granddaughter is smart, beautiful, and accomplished. We have become good friends over the past few weeks and are getting to know each other better."

"Are you her boyfriend, or what?" Kimmy blurts out.

"We have been out on some dates and like each other. I mean, I like her. She might not like me so much," he says, grinning over at me. "We haven't really talked about the whole official boyfriend/girlfriend thing."

"Maybe you should," Kimmy says.

"Yes, we probably should," he replies.

Bà must be satisfied because she doesn't ask any more questions, just gets up and goes into the kitchen to get the Honeycomb Cake.

"I'm sorry," I tell Carlos as I buckle myself into the passenger seat of his car after lunch is over.

He chuckles. "It really wasn't that bad. She loves you and is just looking out for you."

Carlos offered to help clean up after lunch, but Bà shooed us out of the kitchen and told us we should go for a drive or something and enjoy the day. We didn't argue and made our escape.

"We can go for a drive if you want," I say, "but really, I just want to spend some time with you."

"Roger that," he says as he backs out of the driveway.

"Is your mom home?" I ask when he pulls into his driveway.

"No, she's doing an overnight babysitting gig for a couple in her church. Over the past few weeks, she's been doing a lot more in her church and I'm glad to see it. For the longest time, she's just been sitting at home in the dark watching television."

"I'm glad for her," I say honestly.

Grief is a curious thing, and everyone has to go through it at their own pace. I keep hoping that someday Mom will regain at least some of the person she used to be, but it's been ten years, so I don't know if that will ever happen.

It feels strange being alone with him again behind closed doors. I've ached for this, but now that we're alone again, I find I'm a little nervous.

"Do you want something to drink? Water or tea? I have beer, too, but I have only seen you drink a beer at Cait and Ford's and that one time when you got drunk on margaritas and tried to have your way with me."

I swat at his arm because I know he's teasing me. "Tea, please."

He goes to the kitchen, and I see an array of photos on a bookshelf. The last time I was here, I didn't look around much so I go over to shelves. There are photos of him from toddlerhood to adulthood, some alone, most with others.

"Is this your father?" I ask, hearing him coming back into the room.

He sets two glasses on coasters on the coffee table. He comes to stand behind me and, with his hands on my hips, looks over my shoulder. I lean back against him.

"Yes, that's him."

I know Carlos' father has been gone for a little over four years and the photo looks like it could have been one of the last ones taken of them together.

"You look a lot like him," I say. "You played baseball?"

"Yeah, I played throughout school and even my first year of college. I enjoyed it, but I wasn't good enough to get much scholarship money or go pro, so I dropped it after my freshman year."

I ask him about another photo, and he leans down and nuzzles my neck, his breath tickling my shoulder as he answers. I start to ask about another one, but he kisses my neck right in the curve of my shoulder and I lose my train of thought as heat spreads low in my belly.

Chapter 29

Carlos

She turns in my arms. We're finally alone again, and I want to make the most of it. Her hands slide around my neck, and I pull her against me. The tight points of her nipples press into me as her breasts flatten against my chest, and my already hard cock is straining against her stomach.

My mouth crashes into hers, demanding, hungry. She kisses me back, just as hungry, her lips parting, allowing my tongue to sweep in. The taste of her is a blend of the spice from the tea and the lingering cake from dessert...so sweet. I tighten my grip on her when it feels like she sags.

I have never wanted someone like I want her. I've had a lot of decent sex, but nothing like this. There are all the good hormone feelings, but there are emotions melded with them and that's not something I've ever had before.

She wraps her arms around my waist, then breaks the kiss and pulls back. My voice is ragged when I ask, "Too much?"

With a small smile, she shakes her head. "Not enough. I need you naked and inside me."

She doesn't have to tell me twice. Hooking her under the thighs, I lift her up, her legs automatically going around my waist. Her arms go around my shoulders, holding on as I stride down the hall.

The fingers of one hand tangle in my hair while she leans in to kiss and nip at my neck. She's turning me on so much that if I don't get a grip, I'm going to come in my pants. It's been too long since the last time I had her.

"Baby, if you keep that up, we might not make it to the room."

With her mouth next to my ear, she purrs, "Would that be such a bad thing?"

A growl rattles up my throat and I put her back to the wall, pressing my body hard against hers. I kiss her again, grinding my erection into the heat settled against the bulge in my pants. She rolls her hips against me, dragging another growl out of me.

I either need to stand her up and strip her down so I can fuck her against the wall, or get her to the bedroom now. It's me pulling my mouth away this time. Gulping in air to see if I can get a grip, I rest my forehead against her shoulder.

"Stop that or this will be over way too soon. I haven't had you for weeks."

"I haven't had you either," she replies as she strokes her fingers through my hair. "Good thing we have all night."

"A Dios mio, mi alma, me estás matando."

"Sorry," she says, with a wicked gleam in her eye. "I don't speak Spanish."

"I said you're killing me."

Feeling more in control, I pull away from the wall. Eager to go somewhere we'll be able to get naked, I make haste to the bedroom with Alicia wrapped around me. She's behaving this time, clearly wanting a lot more than a dry hump against the wall.

I push open the door to my bedroom, making a beeline for the bed. Crawling onto the bed on my knees, I keep her wrapped around me. Gently, I lower my precious cargo to the mattress and cover my body with hers.

She pulls at the back of my shirt, wanting it off, so I sit up on my knees and remove it for her. Watching every move, once I'm naked from the waist up, she sits up and strokes her hands all over my torso.

I reach down and pull her shirt off. Fair is fair, after all. She reaches behind and undoes her bra, pushing the straps off her shoulders, then tossing it aside.

I cover her with my body again, kissing her lips, sweet and gentle, the frenetic need of before replaced with tenderness. The drive to simply have sex replaced with something else. Something deeper, more powerful.

I've had plenty of sex in my life, but never have I ever made love. That's what this feels like. It's not about a carnal need for release.

This is about connection and intimacy. At least that's how it feels to me. Her movements have also slowed, becoming purposeful, so maybe I'm not alone in these feelings.

I press my hips into her as her hips rise in response. Shifting onto one elbow, I move a hand to her breast, kneading and reshaping it. With forefinger and thumb, I tease the hard peak, drawing a moan from her.

Moving my mouth from hers, I plant a row of kisses along her jaw, along her neck, making her shiver when I reach the bend of her shoulder. I tweak her nipple, making her gasp before I whisper into her ear.

"You are so beautiful, mi alma. You are perfect in every way."

My mouth goes lower then, laving one nipple, drawing it into my mouth, sucking and teasing until she's writhing beneath me, grinding her crotch against me. I move to the other breast, giving it equal attention and extorting whimpers from her throat.

It seems she's on the verge of an orgasm, so I pull my mouth away and begin planting kisses on her skin. I want to savor this, build up the anticipation. My intention is to stoke a fire in her so heated that it's like a bomb when it goes off.

I cover her breasts with both hands, putting my mouth between them, kissing her sternum. Then I'm on the move. My lips move lower and lower, charting a slow course toward the center of her need.

Pausing my kisses, I unbutton her pants and draw the zipper down. I sit up and lift one leg, pulling off her shoe and sock, then pushing her pant leg up and kissing the inside of her ankle before pushing the leg back down. She giggles.

I repeat this ritual with her other leg, watching her intently the entire time. She's watching me, too, but still giggles when I kiss her ankle.

I hook my fingers in the waistband of her pants and panties and pull them down and off with her help as she lifts her hips and raises her legs. She's laid bare before me and it's the most beautiful thing I've ever seen.

Her skin is smooth and unblemished, creamy in the dim light. A sparse thatch of dark curls covers her sex, hiding the lush oasis underneath.

With gentle hands, I push her legs apart, exposing her body entirely to my scrutiny. The folds of her pussy are shiny with her juices, beckoning me to stroke a finger through them. When I discover the swamp of arousal we've created, I breathe, "Dios mío eres hermosa."

With one finger, I push deep into the heart of her, making her moan. English escapes me as I stroke it in and out before joining it with another. She's moving her hips, fucking my fingers while I watch. So fucking sexy.

My attention is drawn upward when she starts playing with her tits. Her back arches and her head is thrown back, and I can feel her pussy tightening around my fingers. She's close to coming, so I pull my fingers away because I'm not ready for her to come yet.

"Please," she whimpers.

I lean over until we're nose to nose. "Please what, mi alma?"

"Please, Carlos, I'm so close."

My fingers slide in again, pushing deep. Her head rolls back as her hips roll forward, pushing my fingers even deeper.

"No, I don't think so," I say.

I lower myself, wanting all that wetness on my tongue. Pushing her legs wide, I put my mouth on her. One long stroke of my tongue has her grinding her hips, trying to get closer. I hook my arms under her thighs, my hands gripping to hold her in place.

I lick her again, tasting, sucking, licking, teasing, slurping, and flicking. Her fingers tangle in my hair again, urging me on. I fuck her with my mouth until she's calling my name. She's close again, so I stop, blowing across her engorged clitoris. When she's calmed, I start all over again until she's shaking with the need for release.

I can tell she's on the edge again, so I don't stop. My baby needs to come, so I suck her clit between my lips and give it the little pulsing sucks that made her come so hard last time. Her entire body goes rigid, then begins to shake as she screams out my name. It's my favorite music.

She lays there shaking, riding the waves, completely oblivious to everything around her. When I lean over her to get a condom, she doesn't seem to notice. Once I'm sheathed, I kiss her, letting her taste herself on my lips.

"You're pretty great at that," she says against my mouth.

That draws a chuckle from me. "Thank you, baby."

I notch the head of my cock at the cleft of her opening and press myself into her. I kiss her until I'm fully seated, then kiss her some more. When I begin to move, that sense of taking my time fills me again. She follows my timing, letting me take the lead.

With lips and hands, she seems intent on touching and tasting every inch of my skin she can reach. I push up on my elbows, increasing my pace. She takes advantage of the proximity of my chest and leans up to flick her tongue over my nipple. When it draws a hiss from me, the minx does it again, then nips it with her teeth.

Turnabout is fair play, so I flip us so that she's on top, barely missing a beat, my hands going to her breasts. She undulates her hips, moving until she finds what she wants. Her breathing is accented by moans.

I lick the pad of my thumb and slide it between us, putting a match to her tinder. When she bites into her bottom lip, I know I have just the right spot.

She leans over and kisses me, our tongues dancing, then kisses her way down my throat and across my shoulder. The minx sinks her teeth into my shoulder, making me hiss and almost explode inside her.

As the bonfire inside her flashes into an inferno, she sits up straight, throwing her head back as the inferno turns into wildfire. When the orgasm takes her again, she collapses on top of me, her entire body going limp.

I roll us again and fuck her hard and fast, my own release tightening at the base of my spine. She lifts her knees, allowing me to go even deeper. Curses and prayers pour out of me in a tumble as I push up my arms straight and pound into her.

She reaches up and strokes her nails over my chest, then tweaks my nipples. I hiss and growl and just before I explode, she screams out my name and her pussy clenches around me again, taking me over the edge with her.

I'm breathing hard as I lower myself with shaking arms. Propping myself on my elbows so I don't crush her, I put my mouth near her ear. A man possessed by forces stronger than I, my heart takes over my mouth, "Te amo mucho, mi alma. Te amo mucho."

Kisses are placed in the bend between her neck and shoulder, making her shudder. She wraps her arms around me and strokes my back. We stay there like that for several long minutes before I stroke myself inside her a few more times, then pull away.

In the bathroom I dispose of the condom, returning to the bed and pulling back the covers. I hold them up until she scrambles underneath, then join her, pulling her close.

She snuggles into my side and rests her head on my chest as I keep an arm wrapped around her.

"Baby, you are amazing," I tell her

She turns until she's half laying on top of me and able to look at my face. "I think you did most of the work."

I shrug. "Nah, fifty-fifty, I'd say, so that means we're both amazing."

She laughs. "Okay, we'll go with that."

Turning her head to rest it over my heart, she wraps her arms around me. We lay there like that for a long time while I stroke her hair. The mood is disrupted when my stomach gurgles.

"I'm hungry," I say. "You hungry?"

"Sure, I could eat."

I roll out of bed and toss my discarded t-shirt to her and pull on a pair of shorts from my dresser. She puts the shirt on and pulls it up over her nose. "I'm keeping this shirt," she says. "It smells like you."

"Fine by me, baby."

We go to the kitchen, where I boost her up onto the counter. I put a skillet onto a burner to heat, then take several things out of the refrigerator and put them on the counter next to her. She watches while I work chopping vegetables, grating cheese and whipping eggs.

Once I drop a pat of butter into the skillet to sizzle and melt, I pour some of the eggs in then vegetables, cheese, and some crumbled sausage. Once I've flipped the omelet to let the cheese melt, I look up at her.

"I almost forgot about what Kimmy said. What do you think? Want to be my girlfriend?"

She laughs, dropping the cheese into her mouth that she snitched from my pile on the counter. "Oh, I think I could be persuaded," she replies demurely.

I swat her with the spatula. "Baby, I'm glad I'm making you my famous omelets, because if you need more convincing after all those orgasms, this will make you want to marry me."

She laughs again and leans toward me. "Is that so?"

I meet her halfway and peck her on the lips. "It's a fact."

Sliding her omelet onto a plate, I hand it to her with a fork. "Eat," I say and begin making one for myself.

She takes a bite. "Oh my, this is amazing."

"Told ya so."

She goes back to eating, feeding me small bites of hers until my omelet is done. About halfway through, she pats her stomach and declares herself full.

"Full?" I ask.

"Yeah, but I'll eat the rest for breakfast."

That makes me smile. "Planning on staying the night?"

She shrugs and gives me a coy tilt of her lips, but her eyes are heated. "Maybe. I have a surgery first thing tomorrow, so you'd have to take me home early enough for me to shower and get to work. I'd need to be home by sixish so it's up to you."

"No problem. I'm usually up by five."

I finish eating and put my plate in the sink, then find a container to put her leftovers in. When she starts to hop down from the counter, I stop her, moving to stand between her knees.

Some time and a couple of orgasms later, we finally get around to cleaning up the kitchen.

Chapter 30

Alicia

Although we didn't do a lot of sleeping, I feel more energetic than I have in a while after staying over at Carlos' house. I guess orgasm driven stress relief can do that. Who knew?

We're both tied up all day Monday and don't have the opportunity to see each other, but we talk on the phone during his dinner break. I make it home in time to have dinner with my family. My last meal here, Carlos was the one being interrogated. It seems that it's my turn during this meal.

"So, where were you all night?" Kimmy asks.

"That's none of your business," I tell her.

"Kind of a double standard, isn't it? I stay out all night and everyone loses their shit and calls the cops. You stay out all night and it's 'none of our business'," she says, making air quotes with her fingers.

I was feeling fantastic when this day started, but now it's going downhill fast. All day, the stress ball that usually lives between my shoulders has been gone, but it's back now.

"I am an adult and people knew where I was," I tell her, trying to maintain my calm.

"People? What people? I didn't know where you were. I only knew that you were with some strange guy."

"No, you didn't know his address, but I had my cell phone with me and didn't get a single message from anyone. If I had gotten a message from you, or Bà, or anyone, I would have responded because that's what responsible people do."

She has been better about staying in contact with Bà when she's out, which is more often since she disappeared for thirty-six hours. She used to come straight home after school and stay in all evening. Now, she comes home but goes back out. However, we gave her a curfew, and she's been abiding by it. She says she is with friends and even brought one girl home to meet us, but I can't shake the feeling that it's all a lie.

We eat in silence for several moments and just when I'm starting to think she's over whatever is bugging her, she asks, "Why do you like the cop instead of the rich guy?"

"Again, it's none of your business. My decisions about my relationships have nothing to do with you."

She huffs. "Well, I think you're nuts. Cops don't make any money, so he'll never be able to take care of you like the other guy could."

"In case you haven't noticed, I've been taking care of myself just fine, including taking care of Bà, and Mom, and you."

"Yeah, but if you were with the rich guy, he could take care of us, and you wouldn't have to."

"Kimmy, I appreciate your concern, but the rich guy, as you call him, was not who he purported himself to be. Carlos has been nothing but straightforward and up front with me."

"Purported, huh?"

I don't respond. She's goading me and I'm not sure why. However, I'm not sure I care why, either. Once I'm finished eating, I go to my room.

If I don't wind down so I can get plenty of sleep, I won't be in top form for a very important surgery tomorrow. They're all important, but this one is being supervised by a surgical autocrat who is also one of the best orthopedic surgeons in the state. I need to be in top form.

It's late evening when I'm cleaning up after the surgery the next day.

"Good work today, Dr. Pham," Dr. Shanbour says, coming into the room.

A compliment from him, even a small one, is high praise. He is notoriously difficult to work with and even more difficult to please.

"Thank you, Doctor," I reply with a nod, trying to keep my cool. I want to jump in the air and fist pump, but stay nonchalant until I get to the locker room. It has been a long, intense day, but my elation lingers, and I feel like I am floating on a cloud even after I'm showered and changed, ready to head home.

As I bounce through the exit, I lift a hand to Chester, the guard on duty. I can't wait to call Carlos and tell him all about it. Halfway to my car, someone takes me by the arm.

I had been so lost in thought that I hadn't heard anyone approach. When I try to pull away, someone takes my arm on the other side. Fear tickles down my spine on spider feet. I look between them. They're both big, beefy Asian men with steel grips.

"What are you doing? Let me go!" I raise my voice, my panic rising, but it's late and the parking lot is empty of people.

I plant my feet and try to pull away, screaming for help. They respond by picking me up off my feet and bodily hauling me across the lot. It's not difficult because I'm all of five feet two and don't weigh a quarter of what these two muscle bound meat heads weigh.

"Dr. Pham! Are you all right?" A voice calls from behind us.

"No!" I yell back. "Call the police!"

A big black car screeches up next to us and I'm pushed into the back seat as something goes over my head, blocking my vision. I try to fight, but I'm sandwiched between them in the back seat and can't move much.

My stomach turns to water and I'm so scared, I think I might pee myself. One man finally speaks, saying, "Stop, we don't want to hurt you."

He speaks in Vietnamese, and I immediately know who is responsible for this. Their ethnicity made me suspect, but now it is confirmed. The icy fear in my gut turns to white-hot rage. These are Tai's men.

I tamp down my fury and try to reason with them, telling them they have just been recorded kidnapping me and that if they would let me go, I would say it was all a misunderstanding. They are unmoved.

I threaten. I cajole. I plead. They are unmoved.

I haven't talked to Tai in weeks. He has been so quiet that I had hoped he'd moved on. Apparently, I was wrong.

I wonder what in the hell has brought on this flexing of power. Why on earth would he kidnap me like this? The utter lack of respect for me and my position at the hospital is astounding.

I can't tell how long we're in the car. It seems like hours because my adrenaline is making everything feel skewed, but I'm sure it's only minutes. Just about the time I'm going to go bat-shit crazy on them, we finally stop.

I poise myself to bolt. As if they can read my thoughts, one man gets a grip on me. Then I'm pushed across the seat where the other grabs me until they're both out of the car, flanking me again. Bastards.

A heavy metal door creaks as it is opened, and it's slammed closed behind us once we're through. I don't hear it lock, though, so that gives me hope. We continue on for several steps and through another door, or at least, I assume it's a door because of the way my man handlers have to shift and jockey to push me through. The familiar smell of antiseptic and blood assaults my nose.

The hood, or whatever it was, is pulled off my head. I squint and blink at the bright lights, my eyes adjusting. A man lies on the table, obviously wounded in several places. He's not conscious, but it's clear that he has been cleaned up and someone has started an IV drip. I grit my teeth.

"Where is Tai?" I bark out in Vietnamese, my tone drawn from training rather than any emotional strength I feel. Inside, I'm trying to keep from peeing myself from fear.

Not waiting for an answer, I turn on my heel and leave the room. One man stops me by holding out an arm and I repeat my question.

His eyes slide to a door in the back of the large room. The building appears to have been some sort of industrial space, all metal and brick with concrete floors. I duck under his arm and start toward the door before the man can stop me.

The young man whose side I stitched up bounces up off a couch where he was playing video games with another man and steps in front of me when I'm halfway across the room. "You don't want to go in there," he whispers.

"Yes, I do." I tell him.

He sighs. "You won't like what you find."

I look back at him, my eyes hard.

"Hit me where I was wounded. It's mostly healed, but still tender. You don't have to do it hard; I'll make it believable."

I understand that he's trying to help me by keeping me from seeing something I won't like, but he knows I won't back down. I growl and punch at his side as he howls.

While everyone is distracted by his act, I rush the rest of the way to the door. When I fling it open, I see Tai, naked, with some girl on her knees in front of him, her head bobbing at his crotch.

"What the fuck?" he yells at the interruption.

"I told you no more! I told you to stay away from me!" I yell back.

He moves, throwing the girl off balance and she falls back on her haunches. I can't believe what I'm seeing. The girl looks like Kimmy. Thirteen-year-old Kimmy.

I'm stunned, immobile, but only for a moment as it sinks in that it's not a girl who looks like Kimmy, but it is her. I fly at him.

"She is a child! You'll go to prison for this!"

I scream and claw at him, calling him every despicable name I can think of as he fends me off. He finally has enough and grabs me by the throat with one hand as he backhands me with the other, sending me sprawling onto my butt. He bears down on me, grabbing a fistful of hair to raise me to my feet before he slams my back against the wall.

Chapter 31

Alicia

Pain radiates across my spine as the air whooshes out of my lungs. My head swims from the impact. His hand grips my throat again, squeezing off my air. I claw at his arm, drawing blood, but he acts as if he feels nothing.

He tosses me like I'm a rag doll. I hit the ground on my shoulder and try to roll with it, but the angle is all wrong and the pain radiates across my entire body.

"You think you can tell me to stay away from what's mine?" He bellows.

He stalks over and grabs my hair again, pulling me up. After a punch in the stomach, I go down on one knee, unable to breathe.

"You think you can tell me when it's over?" Tai growls.

Another fistful of hair and I'm yanked to my feet. His hand goes back to my throat and I'm pressed back against the wall. I'm gasping for breath, black spots dancing before my eyes.

He leans into me, grinding his erection against my hip. I try to raise my leg to knee him in his groin, but he has me pinned. Immobile.

His face is inches from mine, and I can see his eyes are dilated, so I know he's high on something. Spittle splatters across my face, along with the stink of his breath, as he hisses at me.

"You'd better get with the program, and do as I say, because if you don't, you're not gonna like what happens."

He pours out all the vile things he'll do to Kimmy if I don't fall in line with his plans, culminating in selling her to a foreign brothel. His voice is low, so I know he doesn't want her to hear. She probably thinks he loves her or something.

Poor idiotic girl. I believe that most likely, Tai targeted her as leverage against me so that he could have his own personal doctor on call to patch up his men should they be wounded while committing crimes. All the while, standing on his arm, making him look like an upright citizen married to a doctor. I don't think it's just my ego speaking, either.

My vision starts to tunnel, and I feel my limbs going weak as I'm passing out. He pulls me away from the wall and throws me forward, bending me over a table, grinding my face, exactly where he hit me, into the surface. He has released my neck, so I drag in great heaving gulps of air.

He leans over my back, his mouth above my ear as he keeps yelling. "Don't you know who I am? I am the King of the VCB and this is my town!"

He slams a fist on the table. "I got so many cops in my pocket that I do what I want, when I want. I take what I want, when I want, and no one can stop me. You think you can spread your legs like some whore for that spic, that filthy pig, and I won't know about it? You need to be educated about who you belong to."

Then I realize what he's doing. His hands are pushing my clothes out of the way, rucking up my shirt and coat while he pushes down my pants.

"If you ever see that pig again, I'll kill him. I'll have him killed and leave his corpse on your front doorstep." He grabs my hair again and pulls my head up off the table. "Do you hear me? I'll kill him!"

He lets go of my hair and my head hits the table with a *thunk* as he does what rapists do. Either I'm dreaming or hallucinating because I hear peals of laughter. Maybe I'm dead.

But I'm not dead and I haven't passed out. The pain from what he's doing makes that clear. It's Kimmy who is laughing. Bent over with full belly, hysterical laughter, apparently unbothered by her lack of clothing.

"Fuck her harder!" She cries. "Maybe you'll dislodge that giant stick she has rammed up her ass."

Kimmy comes over and leans down, her mouth close to my ear. "I'm the one who told him all about you," she singsongs. "The big hot shot doctor who used to be his play pal. I was hanging out with one of his guys and he told me I reminded him of someone. When he told me, I laughed so hard and told him everything."

She pauses to laugh. I'm not sure why, though. Maybe she thinks she's being clever.

"He's the one I was with when I was gone. You should have listened when I tried to tell you that you'd be better off with him. But you didn't so I'm the one who told him about you spending the night with that cop. You act like you're so perfect, so smart, but now you'll see just how stupid you really are."

She starts laughing again and I realize that she's probably high, too. Knowing she's on something doesn't negate the knife of hurt and betrayal slicing through my heart. I scream and claw at the tabletop, trying somehow, someway, to get some leverage to break free.

I can't. He has me thoroughly pinned down, unable to move. Unable to get free. I lock eyes with the mask on the shelf, proudly displayed for anyone to see.

It's the same snarling devil kabuki mask the bank robber was wearing in the photo in the newspaper article Tai was so interested in two years ago. When I saw it at his house, I hadn't remembered the article or the bank robberies, still thinking the best of Tai.

It's clear now that he is evil and I think that devil is here to steal my soul.

That's the last thought I have before I block it all out. I go limp under Tai's assault and turn into myself. Staring at the wall behind the mask, I let my mind take it in. Time stands still as I study the pictures on the wall, getting lost in them, everything else, the noise, the pain, all of it fades away into the background like it does when I'm focused in surgery.

When Tai pulls away, I am so lost in studying the wall that I almost fall to the floor. But I don't. I manage to get my shaky legs under me just in time.

Still naked, he walks away, crossing to his desk to pick up a pipe and a lighter, firing up another hit of whatever he's smoking. I reach for my underwear and pants and pull them up.

A grimace takes over my face when I feel his spunk running down my inner thighs. My stomach roils with the urge to throw up, but I swallow hard to keep it down. I push my shirt and coat back down as I drunkenly weave toward the door. Although I stumble, I don't fall.

"Give me some more," Kimmy whines like a petulant toddler, and the flick of the lighter, followed by the hiss of the pipe, fills the room again.

I go out the door. More sure-footed now, I walk as purposefully as I can back toward the front of the building where the injured man is.

My vision is tunneled, not noticing anyone else in the room. The two kidnappers are waiting for me, but I surprise them when, instead of going into the makeshift operating room, I suddenly bolt out the front door. The two sentinels outside the door are surprised and their clumsy grabs miss.

I run. Although I have no idea where I am, I put my head down and run. Voices call out behind me, but I don't stop; don't look back. Just keep running.

I run and run and run some more, thankful that I didn't change from my scrubs and sneakers into street clothes since I was just heading home. When I was with Tai, I always changed if there was a chance of going to his house. He hated my scrubs.

My feet eat up the blocks and possibly miles of concrete. My lungs are burning from the cold air. Nevertheless, I keep running like a rabbit with a fox on its tail, too afraid to stop.

It has been a while since I have heard anyone behind me, so I duck behind a large commercial dumpster in a dirty alley and take out my phone, pulling up a mapping app. I'm glad I don't carry a purse because they likely would have kept it. When I'm working, I only have my phone, keys, and a small wallet on my person, zipped into an interior pocket of my coat.

I scroll through the streets. There is nothing close by and I have no idea which direction Tai's lair is in, but I move the map around until I find a twenty-four-hour convenience store a couple of miles away.

I need help. My thumb hovers over Carlos' contact, but I hesitate, Tai's words ringing in my ears. Instead, I call Mom and ask her to come get me at the store.

She gets nervous and starts to balk. Almost in tears, I plead and assure her I just need her to pick me up and that she won't have to interact with anyone. Finally, she agrees and says she's on her way.

Making my way toward the store, I keep to the shadows and listen for any noise that might mean someone is close by - footsteps, echoes of voices, tires on pavement, anything. I jump at every sound and my nerves are unraveled by the time I get to the station.

I watch from across the street for a few moments before I dash across the road and race to a dark corner at one end of the building. With my back against the wall, I finally take the time to catch my breath.

"Are you okay?" A deep voice asks from deeper in the shadows.

I don't even have the energy to jump. I shake my head. "No." My voice is a raspy whisper, my vocal cords raw from screaming.

A thin black man shuffles out of the dark corner, wrapped in a sleeping bag. "Someone chasing you?"

"I think so. Maybe. I'm not sure. I have someone coming to pick me up."

"You stay back. I'll watch for you. Nobody pay attention to me."

"Thank you," I reply, wanting to sob at his kindness, but I need to keep it together. If I start to cry, I might not be able to stop. "My mom will be in a white four-door Honda sedan."

He leans against the wall, blocking me from sight with the bulk of his bedding.

"What's your name?" I ask.

"Most folks call me Whiskey Joe on account of me having a love affair with the bottle in my younger days."

I want to ask a million questions. Does that mean he doesn't drink anymore? How did he end up on the streets? And why is he still on the streets if he isn't drinking any longer? I don't ask any of those, though. I know it's just my mind trying to latch onto something that feels normal.

Instead, I say, "It's nice to meet you, Joe. I'm Alicia."

"Nice to meet you, too, Miss Alicia. There's a little white car at the stoplight."

I take out my phone and dial. Mom answers, confirming it's her at the light. I direct her to come close to my hiding spot when she pulls into the parking lot. She stops just a few spaces down so that the car's bulk is between my hidey hole and the front of the store.

I'm just about to dash out when Joe puts his arm out. "Hold on, Miss Alicia. There's a big black car pulling in with a couple big bad lookin dudes in it."

"Are they Asian?"

"Yes'm. They're both getting out and going into the store." He pauses for a beat. "All right, they inside."

While he'd been watching, I pulled out every bit of money I had in my wallet. I know that money will never be enough to repay his kindness, but it is all I have at the moment. As I pass, I tuck the bills into his hand and say, "Thank you so much, Joe. Thank you."

I don't give him time to respond before I dart out to the car, diving into the backseat behind Mom and staying down, out of sight. Mom raises a hand to Joe in appreciation before she backs out and we leave the parking lot.

"What happened?" Mom asks when we're several blocks away.

"I'll tell you later," I say. "I need you to take me back to my hospital."

Chapter 32

Alicia

It took some doing to convince her, but I have Mom drop me off at the emergency entrance, assuring her that my car is still here, and I will be home soon. I go inside, checking to see who is on duty tonight. Careful to keep the collar of my coat turned up and pulled closed to cover my neck, I hope no one notices any redness that might be showing where Tai choked me.

I am relieved when I see Eleanor Berry's name. She's a seasoned physician who might be willing to do what I ask. Detouring to the doctor's locker room, I get one of my extra pairs of scrubs before I quietly sneak into the emergency treatment rooms.

It is as calm as an emergency room ever gets and I see Dr. Berry at the desk. I approach her, trying not to draw attention to myself. "Excuse me, Dr. Berry?"

"Mmmm?" she answers as she makes notes on a chart. When I don't go on, she looks up. "Dr. Pham! Someone said you were kidnapped from the parking lot!"

"Shhh, please," I say low, holding up a hand. When I notice my fingernails are ragged and bloody, I close my fist and lower my hand to my side. "I…"

I swallow. "I need..."

She tilts her head.

My breath comes in gasps as my heart starts to pound. I gulp in air and put a hand on the desk as spots begin to swim before my eyes. My words come rushing out in a tumble. "I need you to do a rape kit on me."

Her eyes go wide, and she puts a hand under my arm to steady me. "Of course! I'm afraid I'll have to call the police because of the kidnapping. Do you want that to happen before or after the exam?"

Now that I've made my declaration that I have just been raped, my body settles, and I am able to draw on the cool detachment we learn as doctors. I can break down later, but for now, I just need to get through this.

"After, if you don't mind. I'd like you to seal the evidence as if it were going to be turned over, but instead of giving it to the police, I want to take it with me."

She puts a hand on my arm. "Are you sure? If those men raped you..."

"It wasn't them. They took me somewhere, gave me to someone. I have my reasons for wanting the DNA and other evidence without filing a report. It's better if you don't know."

She studies me for a moment, then nods. "Come on, let's get you taken care of."

I focus on taking deep breaths as I'm poked and prodded, given a shot of ceftriaxone for STD prevention, and my injuries are photographed. Panic crawls under my skin as I strip down and put my clothes into a large plastic bag.

After more pictures of the bruises on my back and hips, Dr. Berry does a pelvic exam and takes samples from inside my vagina and from my inner thighs. I breathe deeper, focusing on a spot on the ceiling through that part.

Just when I'm about to lose my shit, she pats my leg and says, "All done. On the table, I've left the oral meds you'll need for further STD prevention to take over the next few days, along with some emergency contraceptive for you. I'm going to go call the police and once you're dressed, Mack will escort you to security. I'll tell them to meet you there instead of here, where they'll most likely get in the way."

With a nod of understanding, I say, "Thank you, Dr. Berry. I can't tell you how much I appreciate this."

By having them meet me in security, they won't need to know that I had an exam if I don't want them to. I don't care if they know, it's my choice to file a report or not. To press charges, or not.

I want to hold off on that so that I can use the evidence as leverage against Tai. Leverage for what, I'm not sure. Based upon what happened, I might be able to tell him to stay away from Kimmy, but I don't know that it will do any good if she's the one going to him.

Right now, I'm not sure I want to. The things she said with such vehemence in her voice. The way she watched as he raped me, laughing and urging him on. I am angry and hurt and ashamed, and, in this moment, with my hurt and anger at the fore, I don't care if I ever see her face again.

On the way to security, I draw on every bit of compartmentalization I've learned from my job. Every emotion related to what Tai did to me gets stuffed into a box in the back of my brain. I will feel the feelings later. For now, I just need to be able to convey the facts.

"Dr. Pham?"

I am perched on a chair in security when two officers arrive at the security office. When I look up to see two uniformed officers, a man and a woman, relief washes over me that neither of them is Carlos.

One officer introduces herself as Officer Padilla and the other officer as having the last name of Roe. We go to a small conference room attached to the security office and at first I'm shaky about it being completely walled with no way to see out. No way to see anyone coming.

I remind myself that I'm with the police now. They're both armed and would protect me should anyone come bursting in. At least, I hope so. They could be on Tai's payroll, but there's no way to know.

Once we're seated, Officer Padilla takes the lead while Officer Roe sits back and scrutinizes me. I tell them the basic overview of the story with a few slight fabrications—kidnapped, hooded, taken somewhere unknown, pushed into a room, raped, escaped, came to the hospital.

"Is that your rape kit?" Padilla asks, pointing to the large bag on my lap.

"Yes."

"We can take that into evidence," she says, reaching out a hand.

I tighten my arms around it. "No. I do not wish to file a report or file charges on the rape. The only reason I agreed to stay to talk to you is because of the kidnapping. I know a report was filed for that, so I wanted to assure you I am no longer kidnapped."

She quickly becomes frustrated with me and for a moment, I think she's going to tackle me and take the bag from me. She starts to argue, but seems to think better of it.

"Can you identify your attacker?" she asks.

I look down and away so she won't see the lie and shake my head. "No, he wore a kabuki mask. A red-faced devil. I can identify the two men who took me, but they're the only ones I got a good look at. You probably have their pictures from the security cameras, too."

"Do you know where they took you?"

I shake my head. "No, they put a hood over my head and didn't take it off until I was inside the building." I describe the interior of the building to them.

"And when you escaped? You didn't take note of where you were at then?"

"No. I was able to break away and surprise them when I ran out the front door. I just ran. I didn't pay attention to street signs or anything like that, just put my head down and ran and I kept running."

I tell them about taking a chance and checking my phone when I stopped hearing signs that anyone was behind me. And about calling my mother when I had a moment to breathe. The officers write down the location of the convenience store since it is the only solid point of reference in my flight from my captors.

The door bursts open. I scream and fall off my chair, crab walking into the corner and cowering there. There are shouts from the officers and the newcomer. Then I recognize his voice.

Carlos says, "Here's my badge. I'm Detective Gutierrez. Please, she's my girlfriend."

My panic and fear morph. I'm still afraid, but for an entirely different reason. I have no recall of standing, but I'm on my feet. I don't look at him, though; I can't. "No! You can't be here!"

They all look at me, confused. Carlos sounds confused and hurt when he asks, "What did they do to you?"

Remembering what Tai said about having police in his pocket, I switch to Vietnamese.

"Will they understand this?" I ask.

He looks between the officers and answers me in Vietnamese. "It doesn't look like they do."

"You can't be here. He'll kill you. He said if I ever saw you again, he'll have you killed and leave your corpse on my doorstep. You have to stay away from me, Carlos!"

His eyes go hard.

"What's she saying?" Officer Padilla asks.

"Can you guys just give me a minute with her?" Carlos asks. "Please, just a minute."

I look at the officers and say to them in English, "Yes, please let me talk to Carlos alone."

Officer Padilla looks like she's about to protest more when Officer Roe touches her arm and jerks his head to the door. Padilla's not happy, but she leaves the room, and they close the door behind them.

Carlos steps toward me, but I flinch away. "What did he do to you?" he asks, returning to Vietnamese.

I stare at the floor, still unable to bring myself to look at him, even though I know this is probably the last time I'll ever see him. "What happened to me doesn't matter. The only thing that matters is that you stay alive, and that means you need to stay away from me."

He reaches for me, but I move away, his hand catching the sleeve of my coat. He pulls, trying to pull me closer, but the coat slides off my arm instead. I gasp and try to pull it back, but it's too late.

With the coat gone, he can see the red marks on my upper arms where the goons held me, the sleeves of my scrub top not long enough to cover them. He captures my wrist and pulls me to face him and gets his first good look at me since he entered the room. He sees the damage to my face where Tai backhanded me and the red marks of fingers that surround my neck.

"I'm gonna kill him," he says low, his voice menacing.

I ignore his statement. The adrenaline that had been pumping through me when I was racing away in terror is gone and now, I just feel empty and exhausted. It will be better for both of us if I just get this over with and let him get on with his life.

"He says he has lots of police in his pocket and that he can do whatever he wants and no one can stop him. You have to stay away from him, Carlos, and you have to stay away from me. I wouldn't be able to handle it if anything happened to you because of me. I love you, but I'm not worth you dying."

"Don't I get a say in this?" he bites out.

"No. Not when I'm the one holding your life in my hands."

I pull my coat back on, turn away from him and pick up the bag of evidence I dropped when Carlos burst into the room.

"What's that?"

"Leverage," I say. "I think I can use it to keep him away from me, but it's not powerful enough to keep him from killing you. It would just mean he wouldn't do it himself, but would have someone else do it for him."

He drops his head and his shoulders slump. "How can you be so calm about this?"

"I am anything but calm."

"Can I have one last kiss?"

I start to shake all over as I whisper, "Please, Carlos. I don't know how much longer I can keep it together and I don't want to shatter into pieces here."

"I'm gonna fix this," he says quietly. "One way or another, I'm gonna fix this."

He yanks the door open and walks out, fury radiating off him.

The other officers return to the room, thankfully blocking my view of Carlos' retreating back. I tell them I've given them all the information I have and that I'm going home. They begrudgingly agree to escort me to my car when I ask.

I can feel the tears wanting to come, but I know as soon as I give into them, that I'll fall apart and that it won't be a good thing if I'm driving when I do. Amazingly, I manage to make it home. When I go inside, I don't talk to anyone, just walk stiff legged to my room and close the door.

In the dark, I strip out of my clothes, the first tears starting to fall. I go into the bathroom and take a shower in the hottest water I can stand, scrubbing my skin raw until the water turns cold. On the floor of the shower, letting the cold water run over me, I cry until I can't cry anymore.

When I'm utterly spent, I turn off the water, dry myself off, and crawl into bed.

Chapter 33

Carlos

I sit in my car and watch as Padilla and Roe escort her to her car. When they walk away, I see her drop her forehead to the steering wheel. Everything in me wants to go over there and take her in my arms and tell her everything is going to be okay.

That wouldn't be the truth. I can't make anything okay. After all, I'm the one who is responsible for what happened to her.

If I had been able to put Tai Dang behind bars, she would have been safe from him. I have been chasing him for years, but I didn't try hard enough because if I had, surely I would have shaken something loose by now.

I recognized the bag she had. Goodness knows I've seen enough of them to know exactly what it contains.

Rape kit. That son of a bitch kidnapped, beat, and raped her in a bid to subdue her.

Impotent fury surges through me to think of her being used like that by him. I wonder if he was the only one; gangs are notorious for passing women around. My fist pounds against the steering wheel, needing an outlet for the rage I'm feeling. The woman I love was kidnapped, abused, and threatened, and it's all my fault.

She said she loves me. I thought hearing those words would set me on top of the world instead of making me feel like a failure. I have to fix this. There must be something I can do, although I don't know what that might be. It can't end like this.

I go back into the hospital to the security office and ask for a copy of the footage showing Alicia's kidnapping. Padilla and Roe probably didn't think to ask for one since she'd showed back up in such a short period of time.

The guard on duty hands me a CD that he'd had ready, obviously surprised that no one had asked for it. The other officers might realize their mistake and come back for one, but I'm sure the hospital will give them whatever they want, considering it was one of their own that was taken.

I take the CD back to the office and pop it into my computer to view it. The hospital has excellent cameras. There's no sound, but the visuals are sharp, giving a clear view of the two men who took her.

I recognize them. Although I don't know all of Tai's lackeys, I know these two; the Nguyen brothers have been with Tai for a long time. They're a couple of meatheads, long on muscle and short on brainpower. It's no wonder Alicia could outwit them.

There's a third person driving the car, but the cameras are at the wrong angle to get a good view of them. There's also not a clear view of the license plate. However, the make and model of the car is unmistakable.

I run the video several times, making notes of everything I see. When I have it memorized, I put the CD back into its case and take it to evidence, then email Padilla and Roe to let them know we have it. They probably won't be happy that I'm the one who got it, but if they don't like it, tough, they should have known to ask for one.

Returning to my desk, I continue to work and pull the rap sheets for the Nguyen brothers. I check to see if either of them has a car like the kidnap car registered in their name. They don't so I start pulling registration records for that type of car and get thousands of hits. I wish there was an easy way to cross reference the list with a list of known VCB members, but there's not, so I start going through it manually.

Finally, when I can't see straight, I decide to call it a night. I sit back in my chair and pinch the bridge of my nose. Just as I'm about to shut down my computer, I get a message from Roe telling me their report for Alicia's kidnapping has been logged into the system.

Eager for the information they might have that I don't, I pull it up. Most of it, I either knew or surmised based upon what she'd told me, but to see it there in black and white that she was raped, cuts me to the core.

To know for a fact that she was out there, running for her life after just having been brutalized, sets my resolve. Tai Dang has to go down. The baser part of me wants him dead, but the cop in me would settle for putting him behind bars for life.

The one tidbit I didn't have is the location of the store her mom picked her up from. When I look at the clock, it says it's after two in the morning and I should go home, but I know I won't sleep, so once I'm in the car, I turn it toward the south side of town.

When I reach the store, I do a drive by and circle the block. It's located on the outskirts of a tiny neighborhood of rundown houses that edge an industrial area. For blocks, there are warehouses, most in decline.

Having rounded the block, I pull up in front of the store and go in, surprised that it's still open. Establishments in this area usually shutter their barred doors early. That they're open tells me they likely have protection from one of the local gangs. Possibly even Tai's gang.

After a few circuitous questions, I know he's going to be no help. The clerk is the sort that you usually find in this type of location, tight-lipped and blind-eyed. If you go blabbing about everything you see in this kind of neighborhood, you'll end up dead.

I buy a bottle of water and thank him for his time. As I'm getting into the car, a flicker of movement at the corner of the building catches my eye. Instead of making a production of going over, I pull out of the store's lot and park in the driveway of an abandoned house about ten yards down and walk back so I won't be seen.

The man in the shadows is a lean African American man wrapped in a ratty sleeping bag. He sees me coming. "Was wonderin when someone was gonna come lookin," he says.

"What do you mean?"

"That pretty little girl was here runnin from someone. When her mama came and got her, I thought sho she'd go to the police."

"She did. Will you tell me what you saw?"

"Only if'n you take me to the motel. I hanged out in case someone came by, but I need to be gone by the time whoever that weasel at the counter is calling right now gits here."

He's right. The clerk will want to do his job for his protectors and will be calling to let them know someone came asking about Alicia. I don't care if Dang knows it's me, but this guy doesn't need that kind of trouble. They'd probably kill him just for hanging around their store.

When he gets in the car, he gives me instructions to take him to a hotel that is well out of this area of town. I don't mind because the minute his butt hits the seat, he starts telling me everything about meeting Alicia, including about the money she gave him.

Shaking my head, I tell him, "That sounds just like her."

At the motel, I go in with him and instead of paying for one night, I set him up for a week. When I observe him eyeing the small toiletries that the place sells for an astronomical fee, I stock him up on those, too. Back outside, I give him all the cash in my wallet so he can get food for the week.

He protests, but when I tell him he probably saved Alicia's life and is due a reward, he grumbles, but accepts. I go to the door with him to make sure he gets inside, then tell him to get some sleep and go back to my car to head home.

I wonder if Alicia is sleeping. When I first saw her huddling in the corner, I wanted to wrap her up in my arms, but then she stood and her entire demeanor changed. She was cold and distant. I should have known it was an act.

There, at the end, when I looked beyond my ego to truly see her. She was holding on by a thread and I was only making it worse. As usual, my big-hearted girl decided it was her duty to take the weight of the world onto her shoulders.

I have no doubt that Dang would try to make good on his threat if we kept our relationship out in the open, but I'm not willing to let her go so easily.

Chapter 34

Alicia

I'm pressed to the table again, Tai violating me. Instead of being plunged into the pain and fear, the objects on the wall come to life, floating up in my consciousness and coming together. I see pictures of a building inside and out. Another page has dates marked on a calendar.

My alarm goes off and I want nothing more than to throw it across the room. I try to roll out of bed, but my entire body is seized by pain so acute that it takes my breath away. I sit on the side of the bed, waiting for the pain to pass. Hoping that it passes.

My phone pings with an incoming message. I pray it's not from Tai or Kimmy. I don't think I could handle that right now. I check the message to see that it's from the hospital's administrator.

Call me when you can, please.

After a recap of the night, she informs me of our EAP program that will allow me to talk to a counselor and tells me to take as much time off as I need, but nothing less than the remainder of the week. I was only going to be assisting with a few surgeries this week, so I thank her and tell her I will take the week, but should be ready to return after that, promising to keep her posted.

The relief of not having to go into the hospital today is enormous. However, not having a routine to adhere to leaves me shaking. How will I get through today without something to focus on?

I remember the dream and the bag of evidence. That allows me to take the worry, fear, and sadness and stuff them away into a box in the back of my brain. They'll push their way out eventually, but for now, the evidence and dream are things I can focus on. I can't keep the evidence here; Tai could simply come in and take it.

Someone needs to know about what I remembered in my dream, but my first choice would be Carlos. Kimmy might have only been a tool used by Tai to monitor me, but I have no idea if he has some way of seeing what I do on my phone or computer.

Although I'm unsure about using my personal electronics, I have an idea of what I can do with the evidence bag, so I latch onto that. One thing at a time. With a deep breath, I grit my teeth and manage to stand.

Shuffling into the bathroom, I take some pain relievers to help dull the pain that I feel everywhere. I don't look at myself in the mirror. If I do, I'm afraid it will send me spiraling into reliving how all that damage happened.

Painstakingly slow, I pull on a turtleneck to cover the marks on my throat. I also don comfortable yoga pants that won't bind me anywhere or put pressure on the broad expanse of tender flesh across my back. That makes me think of Carlos and his obsession with these pants and a sob wells up, but I stuff it back down before it can escape.

I start up my computer while I wait for the painkillers to start working. Choosing my words carefully, I type a note and print it, then take the note and the bag of evidence and shuffle toward the front door. I should have known better than to think I could escape without being caught by Bà.

She stops me, asking if I want breakfast and I tell her no. She tells me that Kimmy didn't come home last night, but I don't respond, moving toward the door again when she barks out a command for me to come into the kitchen.

She sees my face and asks, "That devil hurt you, didn't he?"

"Yes, it was Tai."

"Did you tell Carlos?"

"He knows." I feel the tears start to prickle and I can't let them come or I'll never complete my mission for the day. "Bà, I really can't talk about this right now."

She studies my face for a moment. "Get done what you must."

"Thank you. I love you," I tell her and leave the house.

With the evidence bag in hand, I go to one of those pack and ship places. I don't intend to ship it anywhere, but I pay them to put the bag into a box and then that box into a larger one along with the note I typed.

The clerk is eyeing my face the entire time. The sunglasses I'm wearing aren't enough to cover the damage to my cheek, so God only knows what he's thinking. When I have everything packed up, I go out to my car and call Gabriella.

"Hey, Alicia, what's up?"

She sounds so cheerful. I was going to tell her what happened, at least the broad strokes, but I decide to keep it very minimal.

"Hi Ella. I need to ask a favor of you."

"Anything. What do you need?"

Her willingness to come to my aid makes another wave of emotion flow over me, but I take a deep breath and choke it down. "I have something I need to keep safe, and I can't keep it at home. It's nothing illegal, but if something happens to me, I'd like you to give it to Cait and ask her to give it to Ford."

My first thought was to take it directly to Cait, but as soon as she got a look at me, she'd likely open it up and give it right to Ford. That can't happen, though. I need it to be held somewhere safe so I can use it as leverage against Tai.

"Are you okay?" she asks, clearly worried.

"I am, and I will stay that way if I can keep this information away from the person who'd like to have it. Would it be possible for me to drop it off at Masters Construction and have Morgan bring it home to you?"

"Why don't you just bring it by the house?"

I chuckle without mirth. "Because you'd get one look at me and want to talk about it, and I just can't do that yet."

She draws in a sharp breath. It was less than a year ago that she faced an attack of her own. "I understand," she says. "Take it by the company and I'll call Morgan and let him know to expect it."

"Thank you, Ella."

"You're welcome and when you're ready to talk, I'm here."

I disconnect and head toward Ella and Morgan's offices. Once it is safely at the front desk, I text Tai.

Me: *Stay away from me. If you bother me again or anything happens to me, the police will receive the rape kit I had done.*

On my way back toward home, I drive past a library and have another idea. I turn around and go back to the library. With a quick flash of my library card, I go to their computer area.

Once logged in, a new email address is easy enough to set up. There's no way for Tai to know about the address or to track me on the library's computers. I open a new message window and begin to type.

Chapter 35

Carlos

I feel like hammered shit today. After no sleep last night, the only reason I'm still vertical is because I've been sucking down coffee all morning. Everybody is pissing me off, so I figure I'd better get out of the office for lunch before I start to throw hands at someone over something trivial.

I'm putting on my jacket when Ford comes rushing over to my desk. "Did you see it?"

"See what?" I growl.

He raises an eyebrow at me. "Obviously, something happened last night. Between the way you look and what she says, I can read between the lines to understand that much."

"Ford, I'm not in the mood for games today. What the hell are you talking about?"

"Look at your email. She sent it to both of us."

I sit back down at my desk and push a button on my keyboard to wake my computer. I log in and pull up my email.

"She? She who?"

Then I see it. The account is on one of those generic services, but the username is DrMiAlma2CG. My breath hitches.

I click it open and start to read.

Hi. I'm sorry I didn't tell you this last night, but as you know, I wasn't at my best. When I woke up this morning, I remembered. I can't trust that my phone and home computer aren't being monitored, so I went to a library to set this email address up.

When what happened was happening, I tried to find something to focus on rather than, well...you know. It was in his office, and I saw the red devil mask the lead bank robber uses. Then I looked at the wall behind the mask and saw photographs of a bank inside and out. Based on the sign showing in the pictures and the map on the wall, it's the FirstBank branch at Sunnylane and SE 44th. There was also a calendar with three dates circled the 22nd and 29th of March and the 5th of April.

I can't say for certain if those are date options for the robbery, but that's what it looked like to me. They also had weather projections posted, so maybe that's a factor for when it happens.

Someone is probably following me so I'd better keep this short before they come in looking for me.

A

I read through it three times before I sit back in my chair.

"That's Alicia, right? What happened last night?" Ford asks.

I look around, remembering what she told me about Dang claiming he has a lot of police in his pocket. "Yes, it's her. I'll tell you, but not here. Want to go to lunch?"

Ford scowls. "Yeah, sure."

We go to a deli not too far from the office and take a booth in the back.

"So, what was Alicia talking about?" he asks without preamble.

"Tai Dang had her kidnapped from the hospital last night. It seems like he found out about her staying all night with me Sunday night and didn't like it. Two goons put her in a car and took her to him. She didn't tell me everything that happened, but I know he raped her, and she escaped. He also told her she had to stay away from me, or he'd have me killed."

"How do you know he raped her?"

"She had a rape kit."

"Did she file a report and turn it in?"

I shake my head. "No, she said it was leverage to keep him away from her. I guess she's going to threaten to hand it over to the police if he doesn't stay away from her. She says it's not strong enough to keep him from having me killed, though, so she said we can't see each other anymore."

He sits back in his seat, absorbing what I've told him.

"Oh, and he also told her he has several cops on his payroll, so that means he can get away with whatever he wants."

Ford raises an eyebrow. "If it's true, it could explain why he keeps slipping through our fingers."

"That was my thought, too. It's funny how he always seems to know what we're going to do before we do it."

"Did she give a location for where she was taken?"

"No. Padilla and Roe took her report about the kidnapping and only about the kidnapping. She claimed she didn't see the man who raped her and refused to turn over the rape kit to them. She said she was hooded as soon as they put her in the car and when she escaped, she just ran and focused on getting away rather than noting any street signs. When she finally stopped and checked a map on her phone, she was a couple of miles from that QStop off Meridian and southwest twenty-ninth."

Ford nods. "Lots of rough neighborhoods and industrial properties out that way."

"Yeah. Finding what she described the interior of would be like trying to find a needle in a needle stack."

I tell him about my fruitless visit to the store, meeting Joe, and his confirmation of her coming there, which doesn't help us much at all.

We eat our lunch, both of us thinking about what Alicia sent us. At least that's what I'm thinking about. I'm thinking about how, in the aftermath of being traumatized, she still sets herself aside to get information to Ford and me about what she saw. My great brave, beautiful girl; she just keeps amazing me.

I hope this information lets us finally put him in prison where he won't be able to hurt anyone else except his fellow inmates. It would be poetic justice if the information that Alicia gathered while he was trying to bring her to heel was what finally did him in.

"I know a couple of the folks in the local Fed office," Ford says. "We talked with them some when we chased that serial last year. Banks are their jurisdiction, but they might be willing to let us in on it in exchange for what we know, especially with the gang angle."

"Considering Dang's boast and not knowing who we can trust in our own house, I'd almost rather work with the Feds on it."

Ford nods. "That was my thought, too. Let me get in touch and put some feelers out there."

"Okay."

Last night I felt like my entire world was falling apart, but now I can see a path through to the other side. I know it in my bones that her information is solid and that we're on the verge of putting Dang behind bars. I hate that she had to go through what she did to get the information, but I won't let her sacrifice be in vain.

She just has to hold on a few weeks, and we'll be back together again.

Chapter 36

Alicia

Two things. I only had to accomplish two things today and as soon as I finished them, I knew that was all I could do. All the things I stuffed away in the box in the back of my brain have curled their oily fingers around the edges of the lid and are rattling it, trying to push it off.

The hopelessness and feeling of being out of control begin to creep under my skin. Tears pool behind my eyelids, brimming at the edge despite my attempts to hold them back.

Barely, I make it home before I lose control again and go to my room, closing myself into my dark room, crawling into bed, and letting the tears come. Pain overwhelms me, both emotional and physical and it's all I can do to keep from calling Carlos just to hear his voice and beg him to tell me that somehow everything will be all right. God, I miss him.

The blackness of my room is where I stay. I don't know how long I've been in here; my windows are covered with blackout curtains I installed when I started working so many crazy hours in the residency program so there's no rising and falling of the sun to measure time.

Sometimes I wake screaming from a nightmare and covered in sweat, my mind replaying the attack in my sleep. Sometimes I wake to find some food that Bà has left. I have no desire for food, though. The only thing, only person I have a desire for, I can't have, so I pull the covers over my head and close my eyes against fresh tears.

Someone knocks on my door. With a groan against the pain, I roll over in bed, hoping they'll get the message and go away. They knock again. And again. And again. I get out of bed, my healing muscles stiff.

I open the door to see Kimmy standing there and push to close it.

"Wait," she says. "I'm sorry. I didn't mean...I was high..."

I close the door in her face. I'm halfway back to the bed when she calls out through the door. "I said I'm sorry!"

The sharp flush of anger burns away the shame, humiliation, and sorrow, turning them to steam. Stalking back to the door, I throw it open.

"You're sorry? Sorry? You stood there laughing and egging him on while he beat the shit out of me and raped me!"

She backs up against the wall, but I don't back down. I crowd her personal space, standing nose-to-nose with her. And yelling.

"What? You think you can just say sorry, and everything is going to be okay? Oh, yeah, that's right, you think I'm stupid. I gave up having a life of my own and have worked my ass off since I was nineteen years old to keep you with family. Never have I wanted anything but the best for you and this is how you repay me. Just when I start to get a life of my own and find someone who I love and he loves me back, you repay me by telling Tai while he is raping me to fuck me harder to dislodge the stick up my ass."

My hands are fisted at my sides, and I feel like the top of my head is about to blow off when Bà steps in. She puts a hand on my shoulder, and I am one second from slapping it away when it dawns on me whose hand it is. I take a step back, breathing hard. In my head I say, *Fuck you, Kimmy, and fuck your sorry.*

Somehow, I keep the words in my head, which is probably a good thing. The rage burns off, and the sadness overtakes me again. Turning on my heel, I go back into the safety of the darkness in my room, closing the door behind me.

The next time I wake, I check my phone to see how much time has passed. I was taken from the hospital on Tuesday night. It's now a little after three in the morning on Saturday. I figure everyone is in bed, so it's safe for me to get up.

I have no desire for food, but I know I need to eat something to keep my body functioning and healing. Opening the refrigerator, I find a big bowl of phở. Bà's phở is one of my favorite foods, but I only get a few spoons down before my stomach starts to feel as if it's going to revolt. I stop eating and let it settle.

Carlos comes to mind and having his mom's version of my favorite dish. I miss him so much, but when memories of the time we spent together laughing and making love try to surface, I push them away.

I need to stop that. I need to figure out how to let go. To let *him* go.

With that cheerful thought, I put everything away and go back to my room. I need to return to work on Tuesday, so I set my alarm to help reestablish my sleeping schedule. Maybe going back to work will help me get through this.

Having something to focus on has always worked well for me. As much as I want to, I can't be like Mom and just completely check out; I have no choice but to keep moving forward.

This dance is a familiar one. When Dad died and Mom checked out, it was much the same. Mom and Kimmy needed me and Bà couldn't do everything on her own. So, I didn't break down; I stuffed it all away and kept going through the motions just like I need to now.

Tuesday comes, and I go to work. The box in the back of my brain where I stuff all my pain and sorrow is the size of a steamer trunk. The Administrator comes to check on me and I tell her I'm absolutely fine, smiling the entire time.

While I'm at the hospital, I'm able to put on my Dr. Pham costume and go through the motions. My performance in the surgical suite is meticulous. Patients chat with me and I respond to all their questions and concerns while I'm on rounds. I must be pretty good at pretending because no one seems to notice thanks to a turtleneck and a dump truck amount of concealer.

Once I leave the hospital, the weight returns. Dr. Pham, the professional, is replaced with Alicia, the walking wounded and heartbroken. The sadness settles around my shoulders again, and I can't keep the lid on the steamer trunk.

At home, I close myself in my dark room and crawl into bed.

Chapter 37

Carlos

F ord and I met with the Feds, and it took them an entire
week to decide whether they wanted to play ball with us.
We have a strategy meeting later today to go over how we want
to approach the situation. I'm eager to get a plan in place.

Maybe having a plan will help me stop obsessing over how
long this all seems to be taking. It is killing me to stay away from
Alicia. We had the most amazing night and then that asshole Tai
Dang not only kidnapped her, but assaulted her.

She wouldn't tell me what happened, but based on the evidence bag I saw, it was bad. I wonder how she's doing and if
anyone is there for her. The role she has in her family as the
breadwinner and de facto head of the household with an elderly
grandmother who seems to only speak when necessary, a mom
who's checked out, and a troubled niece doesn't leave a lot of
room for emotional support.

I would rather it be me, but I hope she's talking to someone.
For fuck's sake! I need to be there. She's going through this all
alone and that's the last thing I want for her.

That's just like her to shoulder the burden all by herself. She will always choose to sacrifice herself rather than inconvenience anyone else or put them at risk...hardheaded woman.

I've sent her an email every day to the account she used to mail us the information she saw on Dang's wall. So far, she hasn't replied. She's probably worried that he's monitoring her movements somehow.

God, I miss her. If I could just see her and see that she's doing okay, it would help. Maybe Dang really is still having her followed. It's better not to risk trying to see her. I'd never forgive myself if she was hurt again because of me.

Because I'm thinking of her, I spend the thirty minutes before the meeting with the Feds sending Alicia another email. I send her one first thing every morning just hoping that she'll respond. Hopefully, in just a few weeks, we can put this all behind us and start building our future.

I'm in the middle of the meeting with the Feds when my phone buzzes in my pocket. The number isn't one I recognize, so I silence it to go to voicemail. Our Captain is allowing Ford and me to work with the Feds. We're setting up plans for staking out the bank on the potential dates of the robbery along with two days before and two days after, if nothing happens on the day of.

We're arranging a schedule for monitoring both outside and inside the facility and coordinating with the bank's management team. In order to keep it as quiet as possible to prevent word getting back to Dang that we're on to him, we're playing our cards close to the vest.

He told Alicia that he has ears in the department, so we're operating from the viewpoint that it's true. Only the two of us on the OKCPD will know about the operation.

When we have a plan that everyone is happy with, the meeting breaks up. I completely forget about the phone call until I get back to the station. The caller left a voicemail, so I queue it up and press play.

It's Alicia's grandmother and her message makes my blood go cold.

Do not call me back. The house has ears. Alicia needs help. I know she cannot see you, but she says you're friends with the partner of one of her friends. Please contact them and tell them she needs them.

Do not call me back. The house has ears. What the fuck does that mean? Has Dang bugged their house? Alicia needs help. What is going on over there?

I don't think. I grab my jacket and throw it on as I head for the door. Thankfully, I run into Ford before I get downstairs.

"Where's the fire?" asks Ford.

I know she cannot see you, her grandmother had said. But she can see Cait. "Can I get Cait's number from you?"

Ford lifts a brow. "Why would you need her number?"

I look around the room. There are people everywhere and although none of them seem to be paying any attention to us, I can't shake the notion that I don't want anyone to overhear.

"Can we go somewhere private?"

"Sure," Ford says.

We go to a conference room and close the door. I relay the message from Alicia's grandmother and how someone needs to check on her.

Ford pulls out his phone and dials.

"Hey honey, what's up?" Cait answers.

Ford tells her she's on speaker and I'm listening. I tell her quickly what I know about Alicia's kidnapping and what I surmise about her attack, then relay the information from her grandmother.

"Oh, no!" Cait says. "I had no idea. I knew she missed dinner last week, but her schedule is so busy, she's not always able to be there. Ella told me about leaving a package at Masters Construction that should go to the police if anything happened to her. I have tried to call her, but haven't gotten an answer, but again, that's not unusual with her schedule. Sometimes it's weeks before she's able to call me back. I'll call Demi and see if she can go with me. Demi's professional skills might come in handy."

I rattle off my number to her and ask her to update me after she sees Alicia. She says she will, and we disconnect the call.

"Demi. Why Demi?" I ask.

Ford nods. "If she can go with Cait, it will be good because she's a psychologist. Trauma isn't her area of expertise, but she has some personal experience and she helped Gabriella a lot after she was almost a victim of that serial killer we had killing women last year."

"Okay, good. We went to a fundraiser with her and Kellen, but I didn't know what she did for a living."

That's what I say, but it's not good. Not good at all. I'm glad Alicia has friends, but I'm supposed to be the one taking care of her. That's my job!

I am boiling over with impotent energy. A need to hit something or someone is overwhelming.

Ford must see something in me because he says, "Since we've been pulled from everything except for the Fed case, our day is pretty much done. How about we go to my house and have a drink? That way, you can be there when Cait gets back."

I scrub a hand down my face. "Okay...okay...yeah, that sounds good."

Chapter 38

Alicia

I'm home earlier than usual today. The Administrator took one look at me on my first day back and put me on a very light schedule. Normally, I'd be excited to go to dinner at the Society with my friends, but I don't think I could handle that right now.

There would be too many people to fool into thinking everything is normal. The people who don't know me would be easy enough, but my friends wouldn't be so easily hoodwinked. I can imagine they have enough going on. They don't need me dumping my problems all over the table.

I go to my room and close the door. After a shower, I set my alarm, turn off the lights, and crawl back into bed. In the distance, the old wall phone in the kitchen rings. I pull the pillow over my head to block it out.

Sometime later, my door is opened. I know who it is and say in Vietnamese, "I'm not hungry Bà."

She has been leaving food on my nightstand every evening, but I have no desire to eat.

The curtains are thrown open. "I'm sorry. I have no idea what you just said," Cait says.

I put the pillow back over my head to block the glare.

The pillow is pulled away. "No pillows," Demi says. "This is an intervention."

I hear my drawers being opened and something soft lands in the middle of my back. "Put that on," Gabriella tells me. "We'd hate to drag you out of the house in what you have on now."

What I have on now is a t-shirt and my panties. Carlos' t-shirt, to be exact. It probably stinks because of how much I've been wearing it to sleep in, but I don't care because wearing it makes me feel close to him.

I don't want to be dragged out of the house in them either. Scowling, I sit up and grab the yoga pants Ella tossed at me.

"Why am I being dragged anywhere?" I grouse.

Cait looks down at me with a soft look on her face. "Because you've been in this room for almost two weeks and your grandmother is worried about you."

"I haven't been in here for two weeks. She should have told you I've been going to work all week."

"And coming home to close yourself into a dark room," Demi says. "You're depressed and probably suffering from PTSD."

Ella continues. "Based upon what your grandmother says and that mysterious package you left me, something happened. I'm thinking it's most likely an assault, but for some reason, you're intent on keeping it all inside where it can fester."

"So," Cait says, "we're taking you to dinner. You need to get out of this room, and you need to talk."

"No!" I say, holding up my hands. "I don't want to be around anyone."

"We're going to my house." Cait clarifies. "We'll send Ford into the den to watch football or basketball or something and it will just be the four of us, completely private."

I sigh. "You don't have to do this. I'm fine."

Demi just looks at me and raises an eyebrow.

Huffing, I pull on the pants and a sweater, then put on shoes. I grab my jacket and follow them out of the room. Bà is hovering in the living room.

Cait stops and takes Bà's hands in hers. "Thank you so much for calling. We're going to take her to my house and force feed her. She will be back at a decent hour."

Bà smiles at Cait and gives her a small bow of her head.

I stomp out of the house with them, knowing I'm acting like a petulant child, but unable to stop. Why was it that I wanted some friends?

We get into Ella's big SUV, that has Masters Construction emblazoned on the side. "Where's Liam?" I ask.

"He is with his Mimi Masters being spoiled rotten," Ella replies with a grin.

They chatter around me all the way to Cait's house, not pushing me to participate. However, I know my leeway to be silent will end soon enough.

We park in Cait's garage and go into the kitchen, the other women still chattering up a storm. Cait puts her things away then goes to the refrigerator to pull out items to cook. Demi perches on a stool at the island.

"I'd help," Demi says. "But you want something edible, so it's better if I stay out of it."

Everyone laughs. Everyone but me.

Ella starts helping Cait. "That's okay, I totally understand," she says. "Kellen has told me that if it weren't for your mom, you would have starved to death long ago."

"No, I wouldn't have," she retorts with a grin. "I'm great at ordering take out."

I am about to sit on a stool next to Demi when I hear Ford speak as he comes down the hall. "I thought I heard you come in. You're back early. How was A...leesh...uh?"

Turning to see why he did the slo-mo version of my name, I look over his shoulder and see Carlos. I push away from the island and the stool tilts over to clatter on the floor. "How could you do this?" I hiss at Cait.

Carlos starts toward me. Backing away toward the door to the garage with my hands up, I shriek, "Nonononono! You can't be here! Stay away from me or he'll kill you, Carlos. He will KILL you!"

My back hits the door and I fumble with the doorknob. I manage to twist it open, and turn to run, but powerful hands grab me. "Honey, relax. It's okay. No one knows I'm here."

He turns me and pulls me close, wrapping his arms around me. All the pain, loneliness, and stress of the past two weeks comes flooding out of my eyes and I break down in sobs, my legs losing their strength. "Nooooo...I can't let you die because of me."

Everything after that is unintelligible. He holds me tight, keeping me from falling to the floor. Whispering quiet words, he strokes my hair and tries to console me.

"Shhh...mi alma. It's okay. Everything is going to be okay."

I'm not sure if I pass out or if I lose track because I'm so overtaken by the crying, but when I become aware of my surroundings again, we're no longer in the kitchen. Carlos is sitting in an armchair with me bundled up on his lap.

"You idiot," I say. "You're going to get yourself killed."

He kisses the top of my head. "Don't put me six feet under just yet. Me being here when Cait and your friends arrived with you is a total coincidence. They didn't know I was here and no one else does either. I'm glad I was, though, because I've missed you."

I finger the front of his shirt, which is still damp from my tears. "I've missed you, too, but this can't happen again."

"Let's not borrow worry against tomorrow. How about we enjoy tonight and deal with the future when it comes?"

Demi comes in and squats in front of me. "Eat first or talk first?"

"I don't want to do either," I reply flatly.

"That's not an option. You've been holding it all in and you need to get it out so you can start healing. However, it looks like you haven't eaten a bite since the last time I saw you over two weeks ago. You were near underweight to begin with and now your body weight is dangerously low. You need to give it some fuel or you are going to start losing other functionality. As a doctor, you know this."

I sigh. She's right. I do know that.

"Talk first. If I eat first, I'll probably throw it up when I try to talk."

She nods. "All right. Stay put, we'll come to you."

I try to push off Carlos' lap, but he tightens his arms around me. "Nope. You're staying right here." He kisses the top of my head again. "Did I tell you I missed you?"

I keep my eyes glued on the front of Carlos' shirt, but in my peripheral vision I can see the others come in and sit around the room. When they're all seated, I begin to pour out my story. With stutters and stops, it takes me a while, but I get it all out.

Cait and Ford know about Tai and my discovery of who he really is from the night of the open house, but Demi and Ella don't so I start there and catch them up. When it comes time to start with the new information, the words catch in my throat.

"Take your time," Cait says. "We aren't in any hurry."

I curl my hand in the front of Carlos' shirt to keep it from shaking, take a deep breath and dive in. The kidnapping is first. The men, the car, the hoods, and trying to bargain with them.

I describe the building with the men all around, including the wounded man who I assumed Tai wanted me to treat.

"Anger was my first reaction. I had told him I'd never do that kind of thing again, so I went to the only closed door in the back of the room, assuming it was his office. I burst in, mad as a hornet."

I turn into Carlos. He puts his mouth to my ear and says low, "It's okay, mi alma. You're safe."

I'm talking to his shoulder when I continue and tell them about finding Tai and Kimmy. Carlos' arms tighten around me when he hears about how Tai beat me. I can feel his fists clench when I describe the rape, including Kimmy being Tai's cheerleader.

"That little bitch," Ella breathes.

"If she's still in the house, that may be what your grandmother meant when she said the house has ears," Cait says.

"You're probably right," Demi agrees.

"How did you get away?" I hear Carlos' tight voice rumble against my forehead.

"The men in the building must have heard me screaming and expected me to be cowed by the abuse. They expected me to go do what I was supposed to for the wounded man, but as soon as I was near the door, I bolted. I was lucky enough to catch them off-guard and ran, not stopping until I couldn't hear anyone behind me anymore."

"So, what's in the box?" Ella asks.

"When Mom picked me up, I had her take me back to the hospital, where I asked one of the emergency room physicians to do a rape kit. That's what's in the box, the rape kit sealed in an evidence bag, along with an accounting of what happened. I messaged Tai and told him that if he didn't stay away from me or if anything happened to me, it would go to the police. It might be strong enough leverage to accomplish that, but it won't keep Tai from killing Carlos if he finds out I've seen him."

"He threatened to kill Carlos?" Ford asks.

I nod. "Yes. Tai told me I belong to him and if I ever saw Carlos again, he would have Carlos killed."

Ford makes a *Hmmm* sound in his throat.

I feel exhausted, but less burdened. If I could go to sleep right here in Carlos' arms, I think I could make it through the night without a nightmare. My stomach has other ideas, though. It lets out a loud growl to let me know that it's ready for my fast to be broken.

"Okay," Cait says cheerfully. "That's enough talking for the time being. Let's get some food into you."

Carlos lets me go long enough for me to get onto my feet, but as soon as he's up, too, his hands are back on me. The stool I knocked over has been righted, and he helps boost me up on it before taking the seat next to me. Cait sets a plate full of food in front of me as the others serve themselves.

"Eat." Cait commands. "Don't even think about waiting for everyone else."

I push the food around my plate, taking a few bites. It is delicious, but once I have three or four bites in me, I'm disinclined to continue. I take another bite and chew it slowly, the noise in the kitchen fading into the background.

When I was a teenager and would get stressed, I would often...well...not really forget to eat, but I just wouldn't be in the mood to eat. It wasn't a conscious decision. I didn't have the typical symptoms of anorexia; there was no calorie counting, exercise obsession, or pickiness about types of foods, just no desire to eat.

Mom and Dad simply took an assertive approach to ensuring that I ate at least something at every meal. Ten bites were their requirement and once the stressful situation eased, I would simply go back to eating normally. I know that over the past four plus years of my chaotic schedule, there have been times when I would recognize that I was sliding back into that pattern and would institute the ten-bite rule on myself again.

I take another bite and chew it. Demi is right. I'm naturally pretty small, but I've been hovering at a lower than normal weight for the past year. With everything that has gone on the past few weeks, I've lost even more weight and am too thin. Demi is also right about me being depressed and having PTSD and I need to talk to someone.

Carlos sets a plate on the counter next to mine, then leans over and kisses my temple, drawing me out of my thoughts. I smile over at him.

"You okay?" he asks as he slides onto a stool.

I nod and lift a shoulder in a shrug, taking another bite. Having lost count, I'm not sure if it's number four or five, but figuring I'm in dire straits, I decide ten bites might not be enough and start the count at one.

When I start to feel nauseated, I push the plate away.

"Are you already finished?" Carlos asks.

I nod. "I'm sorry, Cait, it really is delicious, but I can't eat anymore."

Cait just gives me a small smile and takes the plate.

"After two weeks of not eating, your stomach will need some time to recover," Demi says. "And it can only do that if you start eating regularly again."

There's no censor in it; she's just stating the facts. Facts that I know, too. She was right when she said I needed to start eating because it would help my body recover. Without fuel, my body can't do its job.

"So," Gabriella says, "what's the plan?"

"What's what plan?" Carlos asks.

"I think we let the police do their jobs," I say. "There are things Carlos and Ford know that can put an end to this and to me, it's the best way forward."

"She's right," Ford adds before anyone else can say anything.

"I promise there will be no more hiding in the bedroom when I'm not at work. Although I probably won't be much more social than I was before, but I'll do better. Demi, if you'll give me a recommendation, I'll start seeing a therapist."

"Certainly," Demi replies.

"The woman I've been seeing is wonderful," Gabriella says. "She might have an opening."

I nod. "Thank you."

"We do need one plan, though."

Surprised, I turn and look at Carlos. I would think he'd be in Ford's camp of maintaining the status quo while he and Ford catch Tai robbing a bank. But then again, I could be wrong.

He smiles at me. "I can't handle the radio silence between us. You set up the email at the library and I've been sending you messages, but you haven't replied."

My eyes go wide. "I never thought of you replying."

He pulls my hand to his lips and kisses the back of it. "Well, I did, and it would be very helpful if I had some way to keep in touch with you." He pushes a lock of hair behind my ear. "I think it might be helpful for you, too."

"Yeah," I breathe. "It would."

"All right, now that we've got that taken care of, it's getting late," Cait says. "We should get Alicia home while there's still enough daylight for anyone who might be watching to see her leave with us girls. Ford can take Carlos back to the station once we've been gone a while."

"Yes, ma'am," Ford says with a smirk.

Carlos rises, still holding my hand. "I'd like to spend a minute alone with you, if you don't mind."

I nod and let him lead me away. He takes me to the den where we'd been before. As soon as we're out of sight of everyone, he pulls me into his arms and holds me.

When he tucks my head against his chest, I can hear his heart racing. My arms go around him and I press my body against his. The smell of his cologne wraps around me, and I wish I could stay here forever.

"I love you," I say to his pecs.

He kisses the top of my head. "I love you, too, mi alma. We're going to get through this and come out the other side."

With everything in me, I hope he's right.

Chapter 39

Carlos

Seeing Alicia last night was a miracle. I had no idea Cait would be bringing her home when I let Ford take me to their house. Thank God I did, though, or I wouldn't have gotten to see her and hold her. Having her in my arms was heaven for the few minutes we were allowed.

I hated seeing the toll it's all taking on her, but she ate some food last night and her friend is going to get her hooked up with a therapist. That's all well and good, but she needs someone to lean on while she heals, and that should be me.

As much as I want that, she was also right when she said Ford and me catching Dang in the midst of robbing a bank was the best way to make sure this was over for good. Until he's out of the picture, she'll be afraid and looking over her shoulder.

The first date on the calendar Alicia saw is next week. I'm keeping my fingers crossed that Dang will make his move that day. Otherwise, it will be another week or two before we have a chance to catch him. That's if we're interpreting the information Alicia saw correctly.

It could possibly be appointments with his hairdresser marked on the calendar.

"You ready?"

I look up to see Ford. "Is it that time already?" I'd been so lost in thought about Alicia that I lost track of time.

"Yep."

Unlocking and opening my desk drawer, I take out my service weapon and stand, hooking it on my belt. I lift my jacket off the back of my chair and follow him out of the station to go meet with the Feds.

While Ford and I are working with the Feds, our partners are working on other projects. The stakeouts begin next week. We'll have eyes on the bank for the two days preceding and the actual date that was marked on the calendar. If nothing happens that day, we'll have people on site the two days after.

"Here's the schedule we've arranged," Agent Jarreau says, handing me a piece of paper. "We'll rotate teams in the area so no one stands out as obviously watching the bank. An agent has also been inserted into the bank as a new employee, but only the bank manager knows who they really are in case the suspect has a mole on staff."

"I wouldn't put it past him," Ford says. "You'll be sending the schedule to us electronically? I'd hate to have a piece of paper floating around."

"Of course," Jarreau answers.

"I'm not on the schedule on the day of," I observe, a little teed off at that.

"We think it will be unlikely they'll strike on this first date because the weather is forecasting thunderstorms for the better part of the week. You know how spring is. All their other robberies took place on clear days."

I'm slightly mollified by that, but only slightly. When Dang goes down, I want to be there and I want him to know I'm there. As much as I'd love to see the look on his face, I won't tell him it was Alicia that clued us into his plans.

Even if he goes to prison, he'll still have friends in low places with greedy hands who'd be more than happy to carry out his wishes. No, that little tidbit will have to stay hidden.

The meeting doesn't last long. They have the lead and are letting us tag along because we gave them the information. Just as easily, they could have said thanks and kicked us out the door, so I'm thankful for whatever they'll give.

When we get back to the office, I log back into my computer, surprised to see I've received an email from Alicia's generic account. She said she'd reply, but I didn't expect it to be so soon. I guess with both of us on light duty, there's more time for corresponding.

Hi. Haven't read through all your emails yet, but I will. Noticed a car following me, but I'm still acting like zombie me. Can't spend too much time here or they'll become suspicious. Mostly, I want to say I love you and I miss you.

Schooling my face so it doesn't appear like I'm reading anything but one of my usual emails, I send a quick reply.

Love and miss you, too, mi alma. We'll be together soon, one way or another. Things are coming together, but the meteorologist seems to think the first round is unlikely. We'll play it by ear, but every day that passes brings us closer.

Have you eaten today? I need you to take care of yourself.

I love you, baby.

Although I'd love to write more and pour my heart out to her so she knows how much I miss her and need her in my life, I keep it short. As she said, she can't be hanging around in the library too long or they'll figure out she's doing more than just looking for books.

If Dang figures out she's communicating with me, he might make good on his promise, or he might go after her again. That's the last thing I want. She's been hurt enough.

I've already decided that if things don't work out the way I hope they do, I'll approach her about moving away from the City once her residency is complete. The entire family, lock, stock, and barrel, can be moved to anywhere we want as long as it's far away from Dang.

I wonder how things are going with Kimmy. Alicia's big heart probably won't be able to send her away, but the girl needs some help. If Dang's got her hooked on drugs, she will probably need rehab.

After that, who knows? It will be up to Alicia and her family, but I don't see how the girl could ever be trusted again without some major changes on her part. Whatever happens, we'll work it out.

Whatever it takes, I'll do it.

Chapter 40

Alicia

After I email Carlos and read through two of the messages he sent previously, I hurry to the library's stacks and find the book I looked up ahead of time. I want to read all of his messages, but the car that was continually in my rearview mirror after leaving the house let me know I was being followed.

Fine, let him follow me. Now that I've seen Carlos and we've developed a plan, the fog of depression has lifted enough to let me breathe. Getting some food into me probably helped with the energy I feel today, too. Next week I'll step back into the regular swing of things and I'll be glad for something to focus on.

I wonder if Mom would have faded away like she has if she'd had friends like mine to drag her out into the sunlight, stuff food down her throat, and engage her in conversation. Maybe I could have done more for her instead of leaving her in her dark room to become permanently gripped by grief and fear.

After another uneventful day of rounds and paperwork, I see the same car in my rearview on the way home. I'm tempted to play games with them by making multiple stops, but I don't. If I deviate from going to work and home, Tai might be tempted to grab me again. A tremor of fear rolls through me at the thought.

When I walk into the house, I can hear Bà and Mom in the kitchen, so I go that way. Their conversation sounds cheerful and I'm looking forward to joining in. The promise of light-hearted conversation dies in my throat when I see Kimmy sitting on the small table in the kitchen. The same table where I stitched up Tai's minion.

She's been going to school every day. Well, Mom's been dropping her off and picking her up from there every day, but who knows if she's actually staying there. Kimmy has also been home most evenings and making a show of doing her homework. Otherwise, I probably would have already called someone, DHS, treatment facility, someone, to come get her.

All conversation stops when I enter. Without speaking, I put my things on the counter and go to the cabinet for a mug. My actions are purposeful as I make myself a cup of chai.

"You're looking better today," Bà says. "It must have been a pleasant visit last night."

"It was," I answer.

"Who did you visit?" Kimmy asks, but I don't answer.

Once I get a container of yogurt from the refrigerator, I take my mug of steeping tea toward the door, intent on going to my room.

"So, are you just not going to talk to me anymore?" Kimmy asks in her whiny voice.

My back goes ramrod straight. After carefully putting my things on the counter, mostly so I don't throw them at her head, I turn and face her. She has the good sense to flinch when she sees the barely controlled rage on my face.

Does she seriously think things are just going to go back to normal? I know that the good behavior we had was only because of Tai's instruction so I'd feel comfortable being open with her. Now I see her for what she is, Tai's mole and tattletale. I'm not about to tell her about the women I was with last night lest they be put in danger.

"Why do you want to talk to me, Kimmy? So you can run back to him and tell him everything I say? After the vile things you did and said that night, why would I *want* to talk to you? If you need something, Bà and mom will let me know." I turn to gather my things.

"Fine, if you don't want me here, I'll leave."

I spin around, twinging my still healing back, and point a finger at her. "Don't you dare try to play the victim in this. I've bent over backwards to give you a decent life and you repay me by helping a gangster hurt me. Do you think you can just say you're sorry and everything will be wiped away?"

"Like I said, I'll just leave if you don't want me here. In fact, I'll leave whether you want me here or not and go where people care about me."

"Ha!" I bark out before I can stop it. "I'm not sure what you think has been going on for the past ten years if it wasn't caring about you, but if you think Tai gives two shits about you, you're sorely mistaken."

She lifts her chin in defiance. "He loves me and I love him."

Bitter laughter pours out of me. "You want to know how much Tai loves you? When he was whispering to me with his hand around my throat, choking the life out of me, he was telling me what would happen if I didn't do what he said. He told me what he would do to you. I believe his exact words were, 'just so you know, I haven't fucked her yet, she'll be worth more to a brothel in Mexico if she still has her cherry'."

Kimmy sucks in a breath and looks as if I've slapped her. I draw in a deep breath, too, and let it out. My voice is calm when I speak again because I want her to hear it.

"Tai is a narcissistic sociopath and is incapable of loving anyone, Kim. You are smart and clever and beautiful. You could have any kind of life you want and I hope you see that before he drags you down any further."

I turn back to the counter and gather my things, and go to my room. Maybe I was too harsh, but she needed to be told. Tai has nothing but the worst intentions for her and I just hope she opens her eyes in time.

She told me that she'd been the one to tell him about me before he got in touch with me again. In my gut, I have no doubt that he staged our encounter in the store that night. But that was over two years ago and Kimmy would have only been eleven years old.

That's about the time she started acting out. Tai and his gang have had their hooks in her for so long I'm not sure we'll ever be able to help her see beyond the pipe dream he's selling her, whatever that is, to see what's right in front of her.

When I take my mug and empty yogurt carton back to the kitchen, Bà and Mom are still in the kitchen, putting things away after supper. Kimmy is nowhere to be seen.

"She went out," Mom says.

"Of course she did." She has to go tell Tai everything I said.

I wish I could sequester her to her room until she's eighteen, but that's implausible. Nothing we've tried has been successful because she just waits it out, then returns to her previous behavior. Maybe I should send her to one of those ranches for troubled teens.

With that thought in mind, I go back to my room loaded down with the plate of food Bà shoved into my hand.

Chapter 41

Alicia

This week holds the first of the three dates marked on Tai's calendar. It's spring break for Kimmy and surprisingly, she's been home all day, every day. That gives me hope that Tai will make his move.

Him commanding her to stay home because his attention is needed elsewhere is the only thing I can think of that would make her stay put without complaining. Although I haven't seen it for myself, Bà and Mom are keeping me updated.

I'm back on my regular schedule so my days are exhausting as I try to reacclimate to the demanding program. However, I'm also back in the surgical rotation. My fingers have been itching to get back to work, so this makes me extremely happy.

Every day I check the news on my phone, but when the weekend arrives with no reports of a new bank robbery, my spirits deflate. Maybe I got it all wrong and the dates on the calendar are meaningless. If nothing happens over the next two weeks, we'll have to come up with a new plan.

Although part of me is happy to be back in my normal routine, my heart is not. My communication with Carlos has dwindled because most days I'm at work before the library opens and coming home well after it's closed, which means no more daily emails. I wonder if he is as frustrated as I am.

On Thursday, I go to dinner at the Belladonna Society. Before the attack, if I had an evening free, I'd spend it at home to spend as much time as I could with Kimmy. The way things are between us right now, it's probably better that I let her have a peaceful evening without me there to antagonize her. Not that I'm trying to do that; my mere presence does it all on its own.

Still not sure what all Tai has done to track me, I leave my phone in the car. Perhaps I've watched too many thrillers on television. They make it look like a simple thing to turn a cell phone into a listening device. It might be pure fiction, but I'm not taking any chances.

"You look like you're in better spirits," Cait says when I sit at the table. It appears to be just Cait, Gabriella, and me for the meal tonight.

"I am. The first few days back on a regular schedule were exhausting, but I'm back in the groove again."

"How are things at home?" Gabriella asks.

"Challenging. I just don't know what to do with Kimmy. This week she's behaving and staying home, but I thought it might be because of that event we're waiting for. Looks like this week is not the week, though."

"Challenging is probably a massive understatement," Ella replies. "I can't say that I'd be able to stay in the same house with her."

"She's doing okay with my grandmother and mother this week and thankfully, my schedule is keeping me away from the house. I'm exploring options, though. Maybe one of those ranches for troubled teens. They'd be better equipped to deal with her because goodness knows nothing I've tried has helped."

Cait reaches out and puts a hand over mine. "You should know, the guys are just as frustrated about the lack of activity this week as you are. In the hope that I might see you tonight, Carlos gave me this."

She slides an envelope across the table to me. With wide eyes and shaking hands, I take it from her. Afraid I'll break down and cry if I read it now, I slide it into my purse.

"You're not going to read it?" Gabriella asks.

I swallow and shake my head. Thankfully, a server comes to the table to take our orders. The rest of the conversation is kept light. Ella gives us all the updates on how baby Liam is doing. Cait tells us the news that her daughter is getting married.

For the rest of the evening, we talk about babies and weddings and all manner of joyous things. Ella tells us that the house she and Morgan are building will be finished before summer. He added more crews to it because he wants his son to grow up in a house with a yard where they can play ball together.

"I have told him a million times that it's going to be a year before Liam is even walking and more years before the boy will know the difference between a city street and a backyard and more time still before he'll be able to play catch."

"Once a man like him gets something into his head, he's going to move mountains to make it happen," Cait replies with a grin.

"That's for sure," says Ella.

By the end of dinner, my spirits are lighter than they've been in ages. The only times I've felt better were the times I was with Carlos. God, I miss him.

Before I go outside to go home, I take a seat in the lounge and open the envelope Cait gave me. My hands shake as I unfold the page and a smile is pulled from me when I see the firm hand evident in the bold lettering. Like his emails, it's not a long missive, but the words are profound.

Mi Alma,

I love you and miss you with every beat of my heart. We'll get through this and even if things don't go like we hope, we'll be together. Even if we have to steal moments like this until your residency is complete, we'll be together. When that happens, we can go anywhere you want, the whole family, just so you're out of his reach. I can be a cop anywhere, but I can't imagine a life without you. You are my heart and soul wherever you are is home. Te amo, mucho.

-C

Tears slide down my face. This man. He has stolen my heart away and, like him, I can't imagine a future without us together. I glance over at the machine squatting in the room's corner.

Cait and Ford. Ella and Morgan. Demi and Kellen. All so perfect for each other. Is it fate that brought them together or that infernal machine? Perhaps a bit of both?

Is Carlos my future? If I'm honest with myself, I hope so. He seems to be perfectly okay with just letting me be who I am. That's something I never had with Tai. I just didn't realize it at the time.

However, I didn't ask the machine for love like Ella did or a mentor for my child like Demi did. I wished for Tai to leave me alone. That makes me more akin to Cait, who asked for the death of her husband. Although she really just wanted him gone from her life, he ended up dead anyway.

Ford came to her side and was with her the entire way and now they've found their happily ever after. Can I dare to dream such a life for myself?

Maybe. I want so badly to. I want to dream of the future and everything that might be possible.

However, those kinds of dreams are too lofty for me to consider while I'm in the midst of all this turmoil. If I dared to have those dreams and they were taken away, it might just break me. When we're through this trouble and Tai is behind bars, then I'll be more daring.

At home, I leave Carlos' letter in my car. Because there's not a lock on my bedroom door, I can't be sure Kimmy isn't going through my things while I'm away from home for the better part of every day. I tuck the letter into the glove box and close it tight before I get out.

We never go anywhere together anymore. If she needs something, I take care of it. But our carefree days of shopping alone together are long gone and I don't know that our relationship will ever recover unless, like Carlos suggested, we go somewhere far out of Tai's reach.

When I go inside, Mom isn't in the kitchen with Bà, so I can only assume she's already gone to bed, even though it's not that late.

"Did you have a good dinner with your friends?" Bà asks.

As much as I'd love a cup of strong chai tea, I don't need the caffeine, so I fix some chamomile instead. "I did."

"What friends?" Kimmy asks, coming into the room.

I don't respond.

"I never knew you had any friends at all," she goads.

"Kimmy," I reply flatly, without looking at her. "I'm not going to tell you anything about anyone because I don't want them put in danger when you go telling Tai about them."

She huffs and stalks out of the room, probably lingering just beyond the doorway, hoping to overhear some tidbit she can carry back to Tai. Yeah, we've got a long way to go her and I and until we can take Tai out of the equation, I don't know how we'll ever find our way.

Chapter 42

Carlos

I thought for sure today would be the day. D-day or maybe it should be B-day for bank robbery day. The weather is clear today, albeit overcast, and next week has a cold front coming through with a chance for winter storms.

It's the last hour of the day, though, and all the other robberies have been in the morning. "Looks like today's a bust," Ford says, echoing my thoughts.

He shifts behind the steering wheel. We've been sitting here for several hours and in that time, even the most comfortable of cars starts feeling disagreeable.

"Looks like," I agree. "I was just thinking that maybe we're all wrong about what Alicia saw, since next week is supposed to have bad weather."

"I have thought the same thing, but it was worth a shot."

"Better to follow leads than to let them slide by, though," he replies with a nod. "Cait says she gave Alicia your letter."

"Yeah, she emailed me and said she'd gotten it."

Her reply had been the longest I'd received since we started this covert communication game. It was also the sweetest because she confirmed she could be on board with my thoughts of moving out of Dang's reach if that was needed.

She didn't start dreaming with me, though, because she said she needed to stay focused on the here and now. I understand that if something happens and our dreams get snatched away, it would be difficult for her to come back from. She's dealing with a lot in the aftermath of Dang's attack, and I don't want to drag her down further.

I was so hoping today would be the beginning of the end for Dang. Getting caught red-handed, or red-masked, as it were, is something he wouldn't easily find a way out of, even with the best attorneys. However, even if he's caught, it will take time for him to go through the court system and the court system does not move quickly, regardless of what people see on television.

A man across the street catches my eye just as I'm about to check my watch for the millionth time. "Hey," I breathe, unable to believe what I'm seeing. "On the corner in the jeans and gray t-shirt, I recognize that guy. He's a confirmed VCB member."

Ford sits up. "I see him."

Firing up the comms system, I quietly inform the others on the team of the man's presence and bring them to alert status. Besides Ford and me in a car parked across the street at a church, there are Federal agents planted in strategic locations around the area as well as the fake new bank employees.

The location isn't ideal for a stakeout, but we've managed to make it work. The people on the inside won't know that something could be about to happen, though. It would be too easy for their actions to signal a potential inside person to call off the robbery attempt. That's something we don't want to happen.

So far, the robbery crew hasn't hurt anyone. They've just gone in, grabbed what money they could and left without firing a shot. I hope that's the case today, too. The plan is to get them on their way out instead of trying to grab them while they're inside.

Ford and I watch the man as he goes inside the bank and comes out about ten minutes later. He stops outside the door, appearing to put something into his wallet, then walks away in the direction he came from. He takes off the ball cap he has on and turns it backward.

We are tensed and ready for anything, but when another ten minutes goes by with no activity, we begin relaxing by degrees. "Maybe it was a feint," Ford observes.

"Could be," I agree.

It's only fifteen minutes before closing and there are few customers remaining in the bank, which is a good thing. But not if it means they're not coming. I'm on the edge of uttering a curse word at another lost opportunity when an old car pulls into the parking lot of the bank.

It's the same make and model as the car that kidnapped Alicia. "This is it."

"You sure?" Ford asks.

"Pretty positive. That's the same type of car that took Alicia," I inform him.

Four people pour out of the car and race into the bank wearing baggy jeans, black hoodies, and a variety of kabuki masks. Ford starts the car and we race across the street to screeches of tires and honks from traffic. Agents swarm in from everywhere, surrounding the building so that all entrances are covered.

The theft happens so quickly that by the time the agents are in place, the masked gang is coming out of the building. Too late, they see they're trapped and the bank employees have already locked the reinforced bullet resistant doors of the entrance behind them. Law enforcement agents are shouting for the masked individuals to drop their weapons and get on the ground.

My heart is racing, pumping adrenaline through my system as I get out of the car, using it as a shield between me and the gang. Ford slides across the seat and gets out to take up a position next to me, aiming over the roof of the car. Our weapons are pointed at the suspects, but neither one of us joins in the cacophony. There's enough shouting going on.

The four in masks are trying to stay behind their getaway vehicle, but it's parked in a way that makes it difficult. Also, their driver is exposed and can't move without being easily shot. It was drilled into our heads that we want to take them alive, so everyone is acting to that end.

None of us will shoot unless they shoot first and so far, their weapons are pointed at the ground. But their bodies are not hitting the ground, either, as they're being commanded to do.

This is a powder keg and all it will take is a tiny spark to make the whole thing explode.

The man in the devil mask, who is the right size and build to be Dang, looks around at the gathered officers. When his gaze lands on me, he stops. He shouts something, but there's too much noise to understand what he said.

I'm not sure if it was my lack of reaction to what he said or just my being there. Quick as a lightning strike, innumerable things happen at once. His gun raises and the automatic weapon starts spitting bullets. The gang member next to him jumps in front of him just as the gathered agents return fire.

Something bites me on the shoulder as Ford knocks me to the ground. As I'm falling, I see the protective gang member fall as the devil mask wearer blooms several spots of blood across the chest and falls to the ground.

Chapter 43

Alicia

My phone buzzes when I'm on my way out of the hospital after my shift. I'm surprised to see Cait's number on the screen.

"Hello?"

"Are you at the hospital?" she asks.

"Yes," I reply cautiously. "I was just about to leave for the day. Why?"

"Go down to the emergency room. The bank robbery happened today and Carlos was shot..."

She continues speaking, but I don't hear it because I'm racing toward the stairs. I come to a screeching halt when I see Ford in the waiting area. My hands are shaking so hard I think I might drop my phone, so I put it in a pocket.

Ford holds up his hands in a conciliatory manner. "He got hit in the shoulder. They just took him back a few minutes ago."

"Thank you. Has his mother been contacted?"

"Yes. I requested a unit to go notify her and offer her a ride here."

With a nod, I point over my shoulder, "I'm just going to..."

"Go. I'll be here if she comes."

My feet want to run, but that's the surest way to create problems in the emergency treatment area. The staff are all moving quickly with purpose and don't need me getting in the way. After a glance at the board, I find Carlos' assigned space.

All eyes turn to me when I peek around the curtain. He's shirtless while they're working on his shoulder and despite them having cleaned him up, there's still blood everywhere. Blood is part of my everyday work life, but it's very different when it's the blood of someone you care about.

Carlos smiles and reaches out his free hand to me. "Hey, baby."

Dr. Jessup looks up at me as I take Carlos' hand in mine and move to the side opposite where the doctor is working.

"Hey Dr. Pham. Thankfully, it doesn't appear there's any major vascular damage. We're just getting the bleeding stopped and getting ready to send him up to x-ray to start getting a look at what's going on in there."

Carlos' mother comes into the room. I release his hand and move aside. She's flustered and crying and speaking in rapid-fire Vietnamese.

Carlos tries to calm her. "Mom, I'm okay. Just a little bite on the shoulder. Nothing major was hit, but they want to do an x-ray to see if there's any damage to my bones."

Just then, an orderly arrives to take him to x-ray. I take Linh's hand and lead her out to the waiting area, doing my best to comfort her. While we're waiting, two men dressed in trousers and dark windbreakers come into the waiting room.

"Dr. Pham?" one of them asks. I don't even notice their faces, my eyes are locked on the letters on the breast of their jackets – FBI.

"Yes?"

"We're agents Murphy and Johnson. We were informed that you might be able to help us with an identification."

"Identification? As in a body?"

"Yes, ma'am. It's our understanding that you might be acquainted with one or more of the perpetrators of today's robbery."

Tai. They must want me to see if I can identify Tai's body. I speak to Linh and tell her I'll return, but that x-rays don't take long so he may get back before I do. She nods and puts her hands in her lap, gripping them tightly.

"Normally, it takes a few days to do this sort of thing, but Detective Pickering said you were already here in the hospital."

I'm not sure who is speaking, whether it's Murray or Johnson. My limbs feel mechanical as I walk between them down to the hospital's morgue. Whomever is talking just keeps talking, explaining that the bodies were brought here but will be transported to the medical examiner's office soon.

When we step inside the frigid room with its lingering scents of the indignities of death, there are three bodies on tables covered with sheets. The sheet is pulled back from the first body to reveal the head and neck. Although I wanted Tai out of my life, I didn't want him dead; I just wanted him to leave us alone. My heart holds no love for the man he became, but the boy that he was still brings tears to my eyes.

I nod. "That is Tai Dang."

"You're sure?"

"Yes. We grew up together until I was twelve and we recently dated for over a year before we broke up at the beginning of this year."

They move around to the next body and pull back the sheet. I shake my head. "I don't know this man."

When they move to the next body, I say, "I only saw a handful of his crew, or gang, or whatever they are, and I didn't know any of their names."

They are pulling away the sheet and I turn to go, sure I won't know the person they're revealing when I catch sight of long black silky tresses falling over the edge of the table. I can't remember ever seeing Kimmy look so peaceful. The absurd thought swims through my mind as my knees buckle.

One agent catches me by the arm and prevents me from falling. I get my feet under me and I go to her side. My hand covers my mouth to keep the sobs from escaping, but nothing can stop the tears.

"Do you know her?" an agent asks.

All I can do is nod. This is all my fault. If only I'd done something, anything, to get her away from him, but no, I was too wrapped up in my own bullshit to take care of her.

They stand there awkwardly for long moments as I grieve. After eons, I take a deep breath and choke out, "Her name is

Kimberly Pham. She is thirteen years old. She is my cousin, and I am her guardian. Please let me know when I can collect her body so that we can mourn her properly."

Before I lose it again, I turn on my heel and depart the morgue. Once I'm through the doors and out of the overarching smell of decay that seems ever-present in that room, I lean against the wall and take in gulping breaths, trying to collect myself.

The low voices of the agents carry through the doors, so I make my way down the hall. Although I wan to, I can't just leave; I need to let Carlos know what I've discovered first. Otherwise, he'll think I've just abandoned him when he's hurt.

As I suspected, he's back from x-ray, his mother by his side in the ER treatment bay. The results must have been good because they're stitching him up. I must have been gone longer than I thought.

He's smiling again when he sees me come in, but as soon as he gets a look at my face, the smile disappears. "What happened? Mom said two men in FBI jackets took you to do an identification."

I nod, swallowing the knot in my throat. "Yes," I say, but it comes out week, so I swallow again. "Yes. Tai was one of the dead." His mouth opens to speak, but before he can, I tell him, "Kimmy was another."

His face falls. "What?" Understanding dawns and his voice goes quiet. "When Tai raised his gun to shoot at me, one of his crew jumped in front of him when law enforcement fired back.

I thought the person was awfully small to be one of his men. I'm so sorry, Alicia."

"I have to go home and tell Mom and Bà," I say, my burning, weepy eyes on the floor.

"Of course you do. Go, I'll follow as soon as I can."

I lean in and kiss him quickly, whisper a quick, "I love you," then hurry out to my car.

Chapter 44

Carlos

In the robbery's aftermath, many things have changed in the past three weeks. I'm riding a desk hoping the doctor soon gives me an all clear to return to my regular duties.

I was ready to go back last week, but the professionals didn't agree. It's been good though, because I've been able to be home more and I've been needed there.

The hospital gave Alicia a leave of absence considering everything that's happened to her and her family but will allow her to return to the residency program when she's ready. Apparently, a surgeon of her caliber doesn't come along often.

She's having a hard time with the grief and guilt for Kimmy. Her therapist and I tell her over and over that she has no reason to feel guilty, but she has to be able to tell herself. That's going to take some time, but I have a feeling she'll never be able to fully reconcile herself to it.

Mom's been going over to Alicia's every day. At first she went to help with the housework and meals as the family grieved Kimmy's loss, but it seems she and Alicia's grandmother have struck up a friendship. It's done more to bring Mom out of her shell than anything since Dad died.

I come into Alicia's house after work and find Mom and Bà, because she insists I call her grandmother, too, in the kitchen concocting something for supper. We're here so much it's becoming like a second home.

"Something smells good," I say as I kiss Mom on the cheek. She takes the small bag of groceries from me and shoos me out of the kitchen.

Spring is springing. Today the weather is beautiful, and the sun is shining, so I know where my girl will be. Going out the back door, I see her there, curled up in a chair in the shade of the tree as she stares off into the distance, pretending to read.

She's so lost in thought she doesn't even notice me coming up behind her.

"Hey beautiful," I say as I lean over to kiss her on the temple and hold a rose in front of her. Every day I bring her a fresh flower. Today, it's a rose. Yesterday it was a daisy. One of these days I'll find her favorite.

She leans into my kiss and reaches up to put her palm on my jaw. "Hi. Is it already that late?"

"Later," I reply as I come around and sit in the chair next to hers and take her small hand in mine. "I went by the grocery store on the way home."

"Oh."

"Looks like it's going to be a nice sunset tonight," I say, pulling the back of her hand to my lips.

She surprises me tonight when she gets out of her chair and climbs onto my lap, being careful of my shoulder. Once she's settled, she puts a palm against my chest.

"Thank you." She whispers it so quietly, I almost didn't hear it.

I kiss the top of her head. "Not sure what I did, but you're welcome."

"For putting up with me."

"Well, you know," I say with exaggerated patience, "you're such a hardship. I think I should get an award or something."

I can tell she's smiling when she replies. "What kind of reward do you think you deserve?"

"Oh, I don't know. Maybe your heart when you're ready to give it to me."

She lightly smacks her hand against my chest. "You already have that."

"Well then, I have everything I need. Everything else is just gravy." My stomach growls. "Speaking of gravy, Mom and Bà were cooking up something that smelled mighty good when I came through a while ago. The two of them are dangerous to my girlish figure. By the time I'm cleared to work out again, I'm probably going to gain ten pounds."

When she chuckles, my heart soars. A smile and a chuckle; we're definitely making progress. As long as that's the case, I know we're going in the right direction.

She climbs off my lap and holds out a hand to me. I let her pull me up and we go into the house to eat. Her mom is at the table waiting when we go in. She's more vacant than ever, which makes me think maybe Alicia isn't the only one feeling unwarranted guilt.

Maybe we need to see if a therapist has a family plan. Mom, Bà, and I carry most of the conversation, but Alicia joins in now and again. More progress that makes my heart happy.

I've still been thinking that perhaps once she's finished with her residency we might move somewhere else, away from all the sad memories the City holds. That's something to talk about some other day, though. The last thing she needs is to feel pressured.

Later that evening, Mom's gone home. Alicia's mom is in bed, and Bà is in the kitchen puttering around as always. We're snuggled up on the couch watching a comedy on television when she shocks me.

"You and your mom are here all the time; maybe you two should just move in here."

"How are you thinking that would work?"

"Well, your mom could have the fourth bedroom." She pauses, her hand over my heart, where she seems to always be putting it these days, toying with the buttons on my shirt. "And you could share my room with me."

Progress indeed. I'm about to reply when she goes on.

"For now, it's convenient because it's paid for, but once I finish my residency, maybe we could find something else that would fit all of us better, or maybe both sides of a duplex or something."

"Are you sure you want to stay in the City?"

"I think so. It's where Bà is most comfortable and it has all the grocery stores she loves. She's been here since she was a teenager. I think the City is fine, but I want to get us out of this house with all its ghosts."

"I'll talk to Mom and see what she thinks, but I don't think it will be a hard sell. She and Bà are two peas in a pod and it's been good for her to come here. I think she feels useful, and that's helped her a lot."

Unable to help myself, I tease, "I'll make a list of the materials I'll need to soundproof our room."

She giggles, and it is music to my ears.

Yeah, we're going to be just fine.

The End

Get a **FREE** copy of a bonus scene that gives a peek into the lives of Alicia and Carlos a year and a half later.

https://dl.bookfunnel.com/okdeoqptpp

If you enjoyed A Devil's Snare, do me a solid and leave a review! It's not a book report; it's okay to keep it short. Have fun! Be honest!

https://mybook.to/SnareKitMcKenna

Thank you loves!

XOXO

Kit

About the Author

Kit McKenna writes romance books that are dreamy, dirty, and sometimes have a splash of darkness and danger set against the backdrop of Oklahoma.

Kit is a born and raised Oklahoma gal who has lived here her whole life except for a brief detour to hang out in the mountains for four years. She is an artist and free spirit who loves roaming around in the woods and finds great joy in the unusually and sometimes darkly beautiful. Kit has worn a lot of hats in her life, a server, a factory worker, nightclub manager, office administrator, state drone, and business owner.

A bit of a dichotomy, she loves all things positivity and light, but still loves to play in the dark. Her favorite book offerings range from authors like Eckhart Tolle to Stephen King. Her favorite movies are horror and holiday is Samhain (Halloween) but she still loves a good romance. She's a huge sucker for a story where the underdog comes out on top.

If the bar doesn't have a good cider, she'll opt for a fine whisky.

She comes to writing later in life after tiring of reading books that seem to only focus on perfect, perky, barely legal heroines.

Her stories are about real people who have their own demons, drama, and challenges to overcome.

You can find her on online at:

Website – www.kitmckenna.com

Facebook – @authorkitmckenna

Instagram - @kitmckennaauthor

TikTok – @kitmckennaauthor